L.A. Breakdown

L.A. Breakdown

Lou Mathews

Our motto
– *In order that a good story may be told* –
reflects our belief that tomorrow's literary heritage depends on investment in today's writers.

To Order please call:
Tel: (805) 494-1918
Fax: (805) 495 7671
hillyzk@aol.com
PMB 178, 1014 S Westlake Blvd
Ste. 14 Westlake Village CA

}

USA Sales, Distribution and Rights

British Book Investors, LLC
PMB 178, 1014 S Westlake Blvd
Ste 14
Westlake Village, CA 91361

British Library Cataloguing in Publication Data
A catalogue record for this book is available
From the British Library

ISBN 0 947993 80 0

Printed in Malta by Interprint Limited

1.

The evening is fine. The air, even at this hour and even in Los Angeles, is warm and light, easily carrying the scent of the drive-in and bakery from across the street and from further south the singed grease smell of the railroad yards.

Traffic through Van de Kamp's has slowed and in the parking lot opposite, Fat Charlie lowers himself carefully to a squat, heels against hams, and pops the tab on another half-quart. "You guys should've seen Brody last night," says Charlie. "Druuunk! Lord he was drunk."

Fat Charlie tells stories regularly; you can see it in the tentative grins of the boys surrounding him.

"The cops pulled him over on Glendale Boulevard. Soon as he got out they could see he was smashed. He was just lucky they were locals and knew him.

"So the one, Martinez, shines his light on him and says, 'You been drinking Brody?' Brody says, 'No, just a few beers, not drunk or anything.' Martinez laughs and the other cop says, 'Maybe you're not but we'll have to give you a test to find out.' Brody tells him, 'Suuure. I can pass any fuckin' test you got.' So Martinez goes, 'Well, if you're sober you should be able to throw your keys as far as that billboard there.' He tells him it's a new coordination test.

"Brody was nodding the whole time, saying 'Sure, uh huh,' and he points to the billboard on top of this apartment building, says, ' That one? Yeah. You just watch me.' He pulls out the keys and throws them over the building. Martinez walks over when he's done and pats him on the back. 'Yeah.

11

You're not drunk,' he says, and they get in the squad car and leave. Brody must've stood around for half an hour just looking at his hand and at the billboard."

Charlie stops, sips, and looks around the grinning circle.

He's told them they should have seen it but none of them could have been there. They know it, Charlie knows it.

Charlie is a middleman. In the castes of L.A. Streetracing he's one of the few connections between the Legends and the Squirrels. Two groups, rigidly defined but democratic: there are Legends seventeen years old, known by their cars if not their names in the drive-ins racers frequent throughout L.A. There are thirty year old Squirrels - sad, wavering boys, beer buyers for the crowd.

The cars sort them out. There are only two admitted categories, fast and faster, and the fastest become Legends. Those with the slow cars or no cars, stay Squirrels.

Charlie's Chevy only borders on fast but the thing about Charlie is he's always around. He starts races, holds bets, runs errands and occasionally sells car parts that aren't too difficult to steal. He never forgets a car, and most of the time he can remember the face that goes with it. Watching him, it's easy to figure the pecking order at Van de Kamp's, his home drive-in. With the racers he is enthusiastic, convenient; with the hangers-on he's patronizingly wise and cynical.

Charlie, elaborating on his role, is interrupted by a roar coming around the corner. The car is a Ford, a year-old '66, but most car-dealers wouldn't recognize it. This Ford is squat, shortened by its posture - angled up, standing high, like a frog on a skate. The rear fenders are cut and flared for slicks, racing tires that stick out a foot on either side.

The sound it makes is pure jungle noise. A rolling bass as it idles at the light, and underway a racketing bellow that turns Charlie's circle of listeners into a line of envious faces along the curb.

The Ford stops for the drive-in entrance and travels up it in a series of lunges, the driver stutter-footing the stiff clutch. If he let it out all the way, the car would jump fifteen feet before he could put it in again.

Charlie watches the car coast down the lane and into an open slot. He crushes his beer can, a habit - the can is now aluminum and meaningless as a display of strength - and sucks up his belly to tuck in his tee shirt.

"I'm going to go talk to Brody," he says. "I'll see you dudes later."

Brody is the driver. The other man in the car is Vaca, the owner. Charlie doesn't know him well.

Charlie guns his Chevy across the street and wheels into the space next to the Ford. It's not far to go, the width of the street, but Charlie wouldn't walk it unless his car was broken.

As his front tires rebound from the curb, Charlie, in a practiced pattern flicks off the key and yanks the emergency brake. He scoots across the front seat and rolls down the passenger window. Resting his arms on the sill, he waits for Brody to shut the Ford off.

Brody is tall - over six feet when he pulls out of his characteristic slump - broad, pot-bellied, lazy-looking except for lively brown eyes and a neat goatee that offset his soft features. The little and ring fingers on his left hand are stumped, missing fingernails. The top joints were left in a boxcar coupling, tangible memories of a high school summer working for the railroad.

Brody's head is cocked out the half-open door, listening carefully to the rumbling idle of the exhaust. Satisfied, he pulls the door shut. With eyes closed and a smile, he listens to the resonance beneath his feet for a second more and then turns it off. He basks for a moment in the startling silence and looks across to Charlie, grinning. "Hey, Fats, how's it going?"

Vaca sits across from Brody. His head is even with the doorsill in the classic low-rider silhouette, but this profile isn't by choice; Vaca is a reversed dwarf, his arms and legs are normal length but his trunk is compressed. Two years ago his neck was broken, vertebrae were shattered useless and his spinal cord was nearly severed.

A surgeon saved his life but he had to fuse the spinal column into a series of crude switchbacks. His ribs now sit nearly on top of his hips. Above the ribs he is normal except that his shoulders bow slightly, making his head and chest look larger, and his arms are clumsy with muscle.

He is completely paralyzed from the waist down, or he is not completely paralyzed from the waist down. No one knows for sure. Cheryl, the only carhop who is not scared by him, swears she has seen him move but few people believe her. She occasionally lies to get attention and has started fights between friends.

There is a wheelchair in the Ford's trunk, seldom used. Vaca is vain and he doesn't get out of the car near the drive-in anymore. Brody sometimes drives a mile or more looking for a dark street so Vaca can urinate without getting out of the car. He hated being lifted into his chair and the long ride across the parking lot to the head. Vaca was convinced everyone there waited for him to come out, to see whether his shoes were wet.

Charlie and Brody have settled in to their talk. The carhop has picked up their window trays, brought their change and fresh coffee in go-cups.

Charlie was saying, "Brody, I swear to God that guy didn't beat me by more than a fender. I was creaming his ass, top end. Another ten yards I'd have had him. I'd have had him anyway if he hadn't jumped the start."

"Awww bullshit, Charlie," Brody says lazily. "You'd never've caught him. The dude beat you and took your money. That's all

you can say. Close don't count when there's money down."
Brody takes a last drag on his cigarillo and snaps it into the
air, watching the trail of sparks with satisfaction.

"Horseshoes and hand grenades," Brody says.

Charlie looks at him, "Say What?"

"The only time close counts," Brody tells him, "horseshoes
and hand grenades."

"Thanks, Coach."

Charlie and Brody have to stay in their cars, talking six feet
apart. The drive-in Rentacop is watching so they can't get out.

The Rentacops will tolerate just about anything inside the
cars, but on drive-in property they enforce one law: You cannot
leave except to walk to the head. Three violations and you are
thrown out. 86'ed. No appeals.

Vaca stares out the window at the Rentacop and then
raises a half-pint of bourbon to uncap it in his sight. He
swallows noisily and recaps the bottle. The cop looks away first.
Vaca stares over at Brody and Charlie. "Fuck it Brody, let's get
out of here." Brody glances to Charlie, shrugs, starts the
engine.

"O.K. Fats. I'll see you tomorrow."

"You need any help with the car?"

"Nah. It's all set." Brody backs out and heads for the
driveway. Charlie can see Vaca talking at him, and then the
Ford turns into the street.

2-

Vaca's accident was two years ago. He and three friends skipped school. It was sunny; they went to the beach. They tried hard to make the afternoon memorable, to justify detention the next day, and stayed later than they would have on their own time. None of them knew about tides, and in the sunset, as he had all afternoon, Vaca dove off the Santa Monica pier into two feet of water and snapped his neck. He was fortunate. One of his friends remembered something from a state-required health course and said Vaca shouldn't be moved. They supported him in the water, floating. If they'd dragged him up on the sand, they might have killed him.

When the ambulance came, the attendants drove onto the beach and backed close to the water. They rolled the gurney into the ocean and then floated Vaca over and gently eased him on. His head was wobbling dangerously when they put him in the ambulance, and the attendant improvised traction with a cloth sling he wound under the chin and tied to the back door.

When they reached the emergency entrance at Santa Monica General, an intern adrenalinized by the frantic radio call rushed out to meet them. Before the ambulance crew could warn him, he yanked open the back door. The gurney rolled back and crashed against the side. The slack body, tied to the sling, kept going, following the door. Vaca dropped loose of the sling and hit the concrete like a fish slapping down on a deck.

Eight months later he sued. The case was so good his family refused to give the lawyer more than 10%. The lawyer accepted eagerly and for the two-day hearing did little more than point to Vaca in his wheelchair and to an elaborate chart

17

that showed his client's potential lifetime earnings as an aircraft mechanic (based on a C- semester of auto shop and the lawyer's vision). The sympathetic jury awarded his client $850,000.

It was the first real victory in Vaca's lifetime. Others have followed, but he knows he would not have them if he had dived into ten feet of water and gone home. All of his life, until his feet left that piling, he was powerless, controlled.

He'd felt it first in school. A poor student, he'd fallen behind early and never caught up.

In overcrowded classrooms, his teachers maintained a strict alphabetical listing that governed every activity. He was nearly always the last checked off in gym classes, in homework received, the final desk in the end row. He knew the impatience of those who waited for his name so they could turn to something new, felt watched by all the A through U people who had already sweated the teacher's questions and could focus their bored irritation on him.

In junior high school, even when more enlightened teachers scrambled their roll charts, he chose the last seat in the end row and acted the same way, flinching when called on, until he was avoided and finally ignored.

By high school his counselor could sketch his future with sad accuracy. Gas station work ("loves cars but does not have the potential to be a full mechanic"), the service, then, at best, construction work, if he had a relative in a union. If not, perhaps a warehouse, factory, or with luck, an automobile assembly line. For his own enjoyment, the counselor wrote, "The possibilities are finite," and filed the folder.

But Vaca has broken out.

He hadn't gone back to school after the accident. It was the first decision he made and the first time that he'd ever thought of the future as his own. His only previous expectation after graduating, if he had graduated, was a vague desire to join the Navy before he could be drafted.

Of jobs, other than his compulsory attendance at a slide

lecture given by a cheerless representative of the telephone company on "Career Day," he had thought not at all. When the time came, he'd presumed that he would pick up a newspaper and look through the help-wanted offerings. It was the way his friends, everyone he knew, had found their jobs.

Later he'd realized the direction of his life could have been decided by reading the morning *Times* instead of the evening *Examiner*, and he considered himself lucky to be out of it.

In the year and a half since the settlement, he has owned three cars. The first was the Corvette he promised himself. An automatic with hand controls, nice-looking, but when he stopped cruising the high school and began racing, it was too slow. When he crunched the fiberglass front end against a freeway fence, they took away his license. So he bought a stick Chevy and let other people drive it. The Chevy blew up twice in six months and he bought the Ford, new. The salesman, who knew little about the car but understood his customer, promised 425 horsepower and added, "There ain't one of these mothers putting out less than 450 uncorked."

It was true. The Ford won more than its share of races, but it lost two that were important to Vaca and he sent it to an Armenian motor genius, Matthew Jamgochian, in Van Nuys. The engine work cost over two thousand dollars. Jamgochian hinted that secret parts were flown in, stolen from test stands by friends in Detroit. Wherever they came from, the engine now generated over five hundred horsepower. Jamgochian did the final tuning outdoors and swore that working inside he had lost an eardrum. He warned Vaca not to drive through long tunnels.

The car was trailered from Jamgochian's to Spence's alignment shop where the suspension was stiffened to match the engine's power. And from there, to Nada's Body Shop where the wheel wells were radiused to fit larger tires. The body shop sent the Ford along to a locally famous painter named Bert Homan. Homan, a classicist who expected to lose money on his serious jobs, worked lovingly for a month, applying 23 coats of hand-rubbed black lacquer.

The final stop was a backyard carport in the San Fernando Valley. The Ford was beautifully pinstriped, done and signed by Von Dutch. Von Dutch is the world's steadiest hand and in drive-in circles, he is considered too talented to survive. Rumors of his death, mostly overdoses, circulate almost continuously and people are always surprised to see new work by him.

In the next three months, Vaca regained some of his investment by racing for money, making the circuit: Bob's Toluca Lake, Henry's in Pasadena, the Witch Stand in North Hollywood, Stan's in Van Nuys. He went through three drivers before settling on Brody. Brody seems slow anywhere else, but he knows the car's limits so well he almost scares Vaca at times. He shifts so quickly the Ford nearly throws itself sideways. They haven't lost a race.

Van de Kamp's is packed. The Saturday night regulars are early. A line of cars is backed the length of the driveway and around the corner. The rounded tops of eighty cars, total capacity, feed around the kitchen island; the paints glare under neon overheads - pearls, metallics, candy-apples, metaflakes - exotic carnival colors.

Tonight is race night; racing goes on every night in L.A., but Saturday is special. Big-time racers and heavy bettors come out on a Saturday.

Charlie, a pale, painfully thin Okie named Lamont, and two of the Sanchez brothers, Barney and Gilbert, sit on the fenders of Charlie's Chevy across the street watching the parade. A rusty red and white Rambler pulls out of the line, chirping tires. The Rambler sounds like someone threw a handful of pennies down the exhaust pipes. The car blats by the Chevy, and the driver shifts his automatic transmission from low to drive. He lets up on the gas and then floors it, all the way down the block, trying to sound like a stick shift. Charlie spits at the curb and grumbles, "Cover your nuts, the squirrels are down from the hills."

Lamont boosts himself off the fender, runs to the curb and yells, "Mommie's wheels, mommie's wheels," at the vanishing Rambler. He spits and hits his shoe, "Goddamn squirrel."

Charlie and the others crack up as Lamont hangs the shoe out over the curb and tries to shake the spit off. When they've stopped laughing, Charlie stands and stretches. "Let's get something to eat," he says. Charlie and Lamont get in the Chevy. Barney and Gilbert head for their '49 Ford, a primer grey two-door with no door handles, insignia, or chrome.

The Chevy joins the line of cars. They are still backed up a block and the Rentacops are waving people through whether there is a space or not. Tonight, the manager makes them enforce the rule against what he calls vehicle loitering - parking without paying. A car without a tray has to leave.

Charlie drives around twice before he finds an open stall. A carhop hustles over and puts a number card on the back window as he parks. Charlie sees the nametag, "Donna," on a full white blouse and then she leans down, pad in hand.

"Hey, Babe, how's it goin'?"

"Oh, hi, Charlie. Busy. I probably won't get a break for another hour. That damn Cheryl went to the head a half-hour ago and I've been covering for her ever since. Do you need menus?" Charlie says no, and he and Lamont order. Donna reads it back. "That's coffee, cream, and two sugars, and apple pie for you. And fries, hold the salt, with a side of tartar, and a vanilla Coke for your friend." Charlie watches her blouse bob as she reads. Donna is divorced. She's big, almost his height, and Charlie likes her but her two kids get in his way. "It'll be about ten minutes," she finishes and leaves the car. Lamont turns and leers out the window as she runs across the lot.

"Oh yeah!" says Lamont. "The bigger the saddle the better the ride."

Charlie gives him a token, weary smile, adjusting the mirror.

Somebody pounds on Charlie's roof. "Reinhard's here."

He sees Reinhard's '58 Chevy roll up the driveway and heads turning to watch on both sides. The car is a faded powder blue with grey primer spots. Undistinguished, except for the racing slicks, huge treadless tires, and the unmistakeable noise it makes. Charlie swallows the last of his coffee. "Finish it up, Lamont." He leaves the trays on the curb with a dollar tip and drives around to the back.

Reinhard is surrounded, but he sees Charlie and waves him over. Reinhard is considered the main man at Van de Kamp's. In his late twenties, he is unbeaten on his home ground, and his car is known on sight in drive-ins across the 40-mile L.A. basin.

He is a skilled welder and machinist and can work whenever he wants, but most of his living is made on the street.

As Charlie walks over, Brody and Vaca drive in. Scattering people, they park next to Reinhard.

Brody and Reinhard climb out of the cars and Charlie joins them. Reinhard nods at each of them and shakes hands, "Brody. Charlie. Good to see you." A crowd of forty watches from behind the cars.

Brody is anxious to begin, before they attract more people. "O.K. We figured a hundred bucks a gear."

Reinhard shakes his head. "Winner takes all. Five hundred for the whole thing." Brody looks to Vaca and Vaca, almost imperceptibly, nods his head. Reinhard laughs and leans down to the Ford's window. "C'mon Vaca, lighten up. The third time's a charm." Vaca looks ahead and Reinhard straightens up, still laughing.

"All right," says Brody, "are we ready?"

The string of cars turns left out of the drive-in, on to Fletcher Street, moving slowly toward Riverside.

Reinhard leads. Vaca watches the back of his head, narrowing his vision so Reinhard seems smaller and farther away. His hands, hidden in his jacket pockets, curl and snap open repeatedly, pumping up his forearm muscles. A habit

22

ingrained in therapy when he'd carried rubber balls everywhere but to meals.

Earlier he'd tried drinking, but it had only chilled him. On the way over he'd thrown up, but he blamed it on nerves, not the liquor. At the drive-in, with something to do, it had been better. Now he was back to waiting, and his hands were beginning to ache.

Riverside Drive was once the city's longest street. In the fifties, before the freeways, it was the main artery from the San Fernando Valley to the Civic Center. The Golden State Freeway now runs parallel, ten feet above the street. Riverside Drive is six lanes wide and at this time of night, empty.

The course runs to Glendale Boulevard, over a half mile away. There is a bend at the Fletcher entry and the cars cannot be seen beyond it. Beyond the curve the quarter mile begins, marked by luminous paint on the curbs. To the east is the freeway, to the west a cliff the streetcars used to travel. There is usually enough room to come to a stop, but the races are always run with a green light on Glendale Boulevard.

Reinhard and Brody, with twenty cars behind them, pull around the curve and stop. The others park on both sides of the street and gather around the two cars. The talking is restrained. Reinhard slides under his Chevy and unbolts the collector flanges on both sides; with open pipes there is less back-pressure and a few miles an hour more in every gear. Brody and Charlie each take a side and uncork the Ford.

Brody pops the hood, and he and Charlie put in new spark plugs, battering and scorching their hands, while Reinhard and Vaca wait. Brody puts the hood down and climbs into the driver's seat. Most of the crowd has moved down to the finish.

Across Glendale Boulevard are two lines of flares to block cross traffic. Charlie collects the money from both cars and stuffs it in his back pocket. The engines crank around, straining, catch, and a crackling roar echoes off the west cliff. Charlie pulls a pink grease rag from his coat and walks to the center of the road.

He waves the cars up and stages them carefully, level with the curb markers and with each other. Blue and orange flames flicker underneath the cars and shoot down to the pavement in short bursts when the throttles get jabbed. Brody looks around, checking that all the windows are closed; Vaca braces himself against the dash. Reinhard watches Charlie.

When the traffic lights break green, Charlie raises the rag slowly and the engines rise with it. He stops for a beat when it is even with his shoulders and then waves it over his head. The engines build to a howl. A second. Two. The cloth flies from his fingers.

Before it touches the pavement both clutches are out, and the power is shuddering through the drivelines. At first the only motion is at the rear wheels. The tires wrinkle and smoke and then grab as they churn past Charlie, who is holding his ears.

Brody anticipated the start perfectly and breaks half a car in front. The cars rock sideways as they shift into second and Reinhard gains a yard. Vaca is going crazy, pounding the dash and screaming at Brody as he watches Reinhard creep up on them. With the shift into third, Reinhard is even. The exhaust notes keen higher and convulse as both cars' fourth gears slam home and the Chevy surges in front. It leads the Ford across the finish by five feet, and winding out, builds the edge to a car length.

Charlie sees the brakelights go on from the starting line. Both cars dip and then the Ford lunges to the left, barely missing Reinhard's rear bumper, and spins sideways, pinwheeling across three lanes. It slows, straightens into a skid, and finally drifts silently onto the dirt incline at the base of the cliff.

Charlie runs, puffing down the centerline. As he nears the Ford, he can hear yelling. He slows and sees Brody is out of the car, screaming through the window. Brody slams the door, opens it again and yanks out the keys, then slams it so hard this time something pops inside the door. He stumbles down the slope and walks stiffly across the street. His face is red and swollen, and his clutch foot shakes uncontrollably each time it leaves the ground. He yells at Charlie, "Don't tell me that little bastard can't move when he wants to."

"Jeezus, what happened?"

Brody sits down on the curb, takes off his shoe, and presses his foot until it stops shaking. He looks up. "He pulled the wheel. He tried to ram him."

Brody throws his shoe across the street. "Goddammit!" Charlie shifts his weight and looks at the curb.

Reinhard is coming back, driving slowly. He stops near the Ford. Charlie walks over and hands him the money. Reinhard points to the car, "Everybody all right?" Charlie nods. "What happened?"

"I'm not sure. You'd better ask Brody."

Reinhard laughs, "When he feels more like talking." He looks at Charlie shrewdly, and Charlie knows he knows there's more to it. Reinhard finally nods and lets his gaze slip away, letting Charlie off the hook. "Tell Vaca thanks, for the workout." Reinhard riffles the bills and slaps them down on the seat. "And tell him to come around again when he's ready." He looks past Charlie and waves to Brody, still sitting on the curb. "I'll see you back at Van de Kamp's."

Brody waves back halfheartedly and looks away. "See you later, Charlie."

"Yeah." The Chevy idles away and Charlie is looking across the space it left, at the Ford.

Charlie scrambles up the slope and around to the passenger side. He cups his hands around his forehead, against the reflection, and looks through the window. He sees some darker shadows moving on the floor of the car, hears fists hammering on the underside of the dash and dimly, what sound like growls.

Charlie holds his breath a little longer, then turns and skitters down the slope. More cars have pulled up across the street. Doors open; people climb out and run to meet him.

"Hey, Charlie. We missed it. What happened?" Charlie looks around the faces and brings a damp cigarette from behind his ear. Holds it, waiting for a match.

In the car, wedged under the dashboard, Vaca has become quiet. His hands and arms are wrapped and caught in the torn wiring. He is thinking, knowing this is one of the times he will divide his life by. "Two years building. And it came down to this. There should be more."

He concentrates, but no answers come. Gradually he gives up the unfamiliar strain; sure that he has met an obligation and can do no more to memorialize this time.

Relaxed now, no longer willing his thoughts, the images slip into him. Passing, with the clarity of dreams that wake you up: holes drilled into Reinhard's gas tank, gas pooling underneath the car, and the thrown flare skipping across the pavement. Shears clipping brake lines, the fluid spurting. Sand in the crankcase. Stabbed tires, air whistling out, as the car sinks to its wheel rims.

Vaca looked above him at the snarl of wiring. He picked absently at his wrists until one hand came loose and reached for the steering wheel to pull himself free.

3-

A blue International panel truck, bearing the faded advertising of a plumbing firm, was being pushed into the space next to Charlie and Lamont.

They had watched its progress for the last ten minutes. The truck had stalled, shortly after joining the line to enter the drive-in. After the driver had worn down the battery trying to restart it, the backdoors had been kicked open. Five teenaged boys had jumped down, yelling at the driver. They'd pushed it around the looping entry drive, waiting on the fenders and bumpers between advances.

The front tires of the panel truck hit the curb and rebounded. The boys at the rear struggled, trying to keep it from rolling backward. "Hit the Goddamn emergency," one of them yelled. Another, braced against an open door, said, "You asshole, Casey."

"Bob's is a weird place," Charlie said.

Van de Kamp's was closed. One of the busboys, delegated to carry a case of Cutty Sark scotch to the trunk of a visiting health inspector's sedan, had instead hidden the liquor in some bushes fronting the restrooms. The kitchen was shut down on the inspector's next visit and wouldn't reopen until the steam cleaning and exterminator crews were finished and the kitchen had been reinspected.

Local racers gathered in the parking lot across the street

the first few nights after Van de Kamp's closed, but the crowd was subdued. No one felt like racing or even, after a few hours, like hanging out. Non-locals did not stop. Without the lights across the street or the drift of engine noise, color, motion, or the tantalizing scent of deep-fried food, no one wanted to stay.

Charlie explained to Lamont that no heavy hitters were showing up. Reinhard's Chevy was apart; he was building new headers and changing the intake manifold and carburetors. The race with Vaca had been closer than expected; the modifications were to regain a clear edge. No one had seen Vaca, and Brody, at the behest of his probation officer, was working - a night shift at a crankshaft grinder's in Eagle Rock. He'd promised the P.O. at least a month. Brody thought Vaca might be working on the car.

When the weekend had arrived, Charlie and Lamont reluctantly decided to visit Glendale Bob's Big Boy, a choice mainly determined by a lack of gas money.

They had cruised the place twice, failing to spot anyone familiar, and were preparing to leave when someone in the parking lot yelled Charlie's name. Charlie recognized the car, a taxi yellow Chevy II belonging to Saint, a frequent visitor to Van de Kamp's. They parked and walked over to visit.

Saint was seated cross-legged on the hood, talking to an off-duty carhop. Saint was a tall, permanently tanned young man, with a smile that seemed practiced to Charlie. He worked days at a muffler shop and raced his Chevy II on weeknights. He was building up a Dodge van, designed for quarter-mile wheelstands, with the help of the shop's owner, but the muffler business was brisk and the project went slowly.

Saint was saying, "Is she going out with anyone special?"

The carhop pursed a small bitter mouth around her cigarette and blew the smoke at him.

"Come on," Saint said. "Who's she go with?"

"Who's that?" Charlie said, seating himself on a fender.

"Hey, Charlie. I thought that was you." Saint pointed to the carhop. "Charlie, this is Sharla. Sharla, Charlie."

Sharla stared at Saint. "She goes with half the cops in Glendale, if you want to know."

"This is Lamont," Charlie said. "Who are we talking about?"

"Joan," said Saint. "She works here days."

"The dairy queen," Sharla said. "She's so gross. You guys have got zero taste. You ought to see her when she's changing. She's got hair all over her stomach."

Saint looked interested. "Oh yeah? How far up?"

"What color?" Charlie asked.

"No, really," Saint said. "Can you see her belly button at all? Or is it like a rug?"

Sharla rummaged through her purse for another cigarette. "You guys are sick." She looked at Charlie, "Do you have any smokes?"

Charlie offered her a Camel. She turned the pack over to read the brand. "Never mind. I'll wait 'til I get to the liquor store."

Saint boosted himself down from the hood. "Come on. I'll give you a ride home."

"No thank you," Sharla said. "I wouldn't want to impose."

"I have to go by the liquor store myself. It's not that much further to your place."

"How would you know?"

"I don't, but I'll never find it on my own. Come on."

"I can walk."

"Yeah, but can you dance?"

"What's that supposed to mean?"

"If you have to ask, you'll never know. You can dance, or you can't dance. That's all."

"Oh God. You're so full of shit, Saint."

"I know it. That's why my eyes are this pretty brown. Come on, maybe you'll learn to dance." Saint got in his car, flashing her a smile.

"Why I put up with this, I don't know. I really don't." Sharla tucked her coat in around her, standing by the car door. Saint started the engine and leaned to tune in his radio.

Lamont realized she was waiting for him to open it and hurried over. He held the door open and closed it behind her.

They watched the yellow car drive off.

"You hungry?" Charlie asked.

"A little."

"Well as long as we're here," Charlie said, "we might as well eat."

The boys in the panel truck had begun a bantering discussion about leaving the van to pay for their Cokes. Someone's head thumped against the side.

"This place has always been weird," Charlie said.

"The food's good though." Lamont dipped a breaded deep-fried shrimp into a red cocktail sauce.

"Food's fine," Charlie said. "It's just not serious. It's just high school punks and cruisers wanting to race. Nobody really knows what they're doing here."

Lamont lifted his salad down from the window tray. "Did you know this is the original Bob's? It's a fact. The Main Offices are right across the street. I applied for work there once. I heard the owner still comes over here, and his kids. In disguises, you know? That's probably why the food's better."

"Did you get the job?"

"No," Lamont said, "I think you had to be out of high school." Reaching to snag some of Lamont's french fries, Charlie turned idly, drawn by a commotion in the driveway.

Down the lane, between the two ranks of cars, Charlie saw a thin girl walking towards them. She was dressed in a white button-front sweater and badly fitting black capris, tight at the calves, slack in the seat. She was walking in front of a Corvair convertible with the top down; the driver was half out of the car, yelling to her.

It looked like she was walking against a wind, head down, arms crossed on her chest, maintaining a stubborn pace. The Corvair's bumper crept up close to the backs of her knees, then dropped away, but she didn't seem to notice. Charlie finally realized who it was.

He opened his door and bellowed, "Ciccarelli. Hey. Connie." She raised her head and squinted in their direction.

"Over here," Charlie yelled. She squinted again, apparently recognized him, and started over. The Corvair followed along behind her. Connie stopped short and glared at the driver, slowing the car to a crawl, before walking on.

Charlie got out of the car. Her hair was chopped shorter than he remembered, but just as lank and dry-looking. Connie's features, except for the dark, deep-set eyes, seemed exaggerated: a long nose with a hump in the bridge, wide mouth, noticeable bones in her long jaw and chin. An intense face. Her eyebrows would have joined if she hadn't plucked them.

They had been close friends in high school, almost more than that, drawn together by mutual dislike for the school and teachers. They shared a caustic sense of humor. They hung out, at school and after, without thinking of themselves as a couple. They were well matched. Both of them bordered on good-looking. Charlie, without the weight that softened his features, would have been darkly handsome. Connie, at times, could overpower her gaunt frame and features by her liveliness. At that age, however, neither was ready to settle for the other.

They had drifted apart after graduation. They had seen each other since, usually in the company of others. They were no longer close, but a bond, some recognition of what might have been, remained.

Connie reached their car.

Charlie wasn't quite sure how to greet her. Connie shoved his hand aside and gave him a quick hug. "God am I glad to see you."

They climbed into the car; Connie got in the back seat and

smiled at Lamont while Charlie introduced them. The Corvair had stopped in back of them and then pulled out as one of the lot attendants started over.

"Is he gone?" Connie asked.

Charlie looked out the window, "Yeah. Was he with you?"

"He thought so."

"Where'd you find him?"

"Oh it was sort of a blind date. I mean, I'd seen him around before but I didn't know him. It was one of those friend of a friend deals. You know Freddy Madrid? He set it up. Is there such a thing as a lame date? That's what this was. I don't know what Freddy told him but I can guess. I'm gonna kill him, I really am. Creeps."

She lit a cigarette and began scattering ashes around the car. Lamont watched her nervous movements, fascinated. When she wasn't busy with the cigarette, she repeatedly snapped each fingernail against her thumbnail.

"Feature this," Connie was saying. "The guy picks me up and drives about three blocks. Over to Hillcrest? He parks and says something about really getting to know each other. I couldn't believe it. After about six elbows he's still moving in on me. He's one of these idiots that really, truly, believes that if he can just get his tongue in my ear I'm going to kick holes in the roof. After that doesn't work he gets very casual, you know, lots of shoulder rubs. 'I'm not going to do anything,' he says, 'I'm just trying to relax you. Your neck muscles are real tense.' Then he works down my shoulders and my back. Actually, that felt pretty good.

"He kept fumbling around, looking for the snaps, and I start cracking up. I was wearing a bra that hooks in front. So, anyway, I was sitting there laughing and he's going nuts. He says, 'How in hell do you put it on?' and I told him it's one of these you pull over your head." Lamont shifted uneasily and looked over at Charlie.

"It really bothered him when I started laughing," Connie continued, "so we left and start driving around. He wouldn't go by Vandy's."

"It's closed anyway," Charlie said.

Connie looked at him indignantly. "Well, he didn't know that! Anyway. We get over here, we're waiting in line, and he goes, 'Hey, you're not going to tell anybody about tonight, are you?' That really pissed me off. So I got out of the car and that's about when I saw you. Jeez, it seems like I never go out with anything but assholes anymore."

She lit another cigarette. "So what've you been doing with your life?"

"Nothing," Charlie said, "just working, making the big money, like it says on the matchbook cover. Where are you working now?"

"God, that's the only good thing that's happened to me all year. I was working for the phone company since May and they fired me last month, for giving out an address to some guy. He said it was his ex-wife and he just got back out of the service. I don't know, he sounded real. I think it was one of the snitches. They've got these old biddies that've been there about eighty years and all they do all day is listen in on the operators.

"Anyway, they canned me and I've been getting unemployment for a month. It's pretty good, the money's about the same when you figure what I was spending on gas and lunches. They call me up about once a week for job interviews. I take along my curlers and bubblegum and surprise! I don't get the job."

Their food arrived, second orders of fries, coffee, and dessert. Connie ordered a coke. She declined Charlie's offer of a hamburger and then ate most of his and Lamont's french fries, while they discussed former friends and high school.

Lamont interrupted politely and pointed out the window. The Corvair had returned. The driver pushed open the passenger door and honked. Connie rolled down her window and gave him the finger. The horn continued and Connie sloshed most of her Coke in its general direction. The lot attendant came and made him move. Lamont got out after a moment and cleaned the ice off his trunk lid.

Charlie was enjoying the reminiscing; he sensed Connie was also. Watching her face, the shining lively eyes, he wondered how he had ever thought she was anything but pretty.

The Corvair was back again, this time with the top up. The driver, a thin blonde, got out of his car and stood behind theirs, one hand dipped in his pocket, the other holding his sunglasses, the stems crossed between his fingers with the lenses covering his knuckles.

After a long stare between them, he told Connie, "You got about ten seconds to get in that car."

Connie leaned out. "My brother's going to kick your ass." Charlie saw the boy pale and his features twist as he tried to transform his scowl into an attitude of politeness. Charlie looked at Connie as she sat back in the seat; her expression was a mixture of petulance and fright. He knew it was not a casual threat. Richie Ciccarelli was a well-known madman. Connie had come to school wearing dark glasses several times and Charlie knew of occasions when she'd been excused from gym classes - not an easy sell given her well-known hatred of exercise - because of undeniable bruises and welts.

With a rush of placating words and gestures, Connie's date was backtracking. "Come on," he was saying, "I was only kidding. Let's get out of here. Anyplace you want to go."

"You want to come with us?" Charlie asked.

Her eyes dimmed in resignation. "I'd better go. Richie really would kick his ass if he heard about it." She climbed out of the car, leaned in to squeeze Charlie's hand and tell Lamont it had been nice to meet him. "Listen," she said, "you still have my number. Give me a call next week. O.K.?" Charlie nodded and watched her back away.

The blonde boy was waiting, holding open the door for her.

After Connie had gone, Lamont asked for refills on the coffee. Charlie smoked, his hand over the ashtray, poking at the jumble of butts and gum wrappers with the cigarette.

"Did you used to go with her?"

34

"No," Charlie said. "Not really. But we were tight, really tight. We sort of blew it."

On the way out, they stopped in the parking lot, attracted by a crowd in one corner. Lamont sat on the windowsill, craning to see, but couldn't determine the cause. They parked and got out.

A fight was beginning. Two fattish boys were being pushed together in the circle. The heavier one wore a Glendale High letterman's sweater. Affixed to the heavy white wool were three plaques: "Dynamiters" with an exploding firecracker, "J.V. Manager," and a small felt basketball. One of the boys holding him said, "Give me your glasses, Chet."

Chet handed his glasses over and faced his opponent; the oval dents on his nose were red against his pale face.

The other boy, wearing corduroy peggers, tee shirt, and an unbuttoned Pendleton shirt, was rolling up his sleeves. Someone shoved him forward.

After initial feints, they tried for headholds. Arms locked around each other's necks, they swung around, breathing hard, until Chet had his feet kicked out from under him and went down.

The other boy sat on his chest with a fist cocked. Chet glared up at him, eyes watering, and yelled, "Hit me, go on, hit me you lardass."

The boy on top said, "Why should I?" reflexively. He punched him in the mouth, twice, before Chet bucked him off. Chet kicked him in the shoulder while he was scrambling to his feet.

It ended with them circling each other. One of the cooks, on a break, had drifted over to watch. They'd both spotted the white uniform and checked neckerchief, and straightened up, panting.

"We'd better cool it," Chet said. The other boy agreed.

"Yeah, they've probably already called the cops."

The cook looked at them, openmouthed, and said, "Don't let me stop you," but they had already rejoined the circle.

The crowd broke into desultory groups. Further attempts to provoke them failed when neither would admit to winning.

The light was still on in front of Lamont's house. "Oh Lord," he said, "here we go again."

"You ought to move out."

"I can't even afford to live at home. I don't know, I've been thinking about the Army."

"Oh, man. Don't do that."

"You don't know my stepfather," Lamont said. "He makes the Army look good. They're going to get me anyway. What the hey."

"But don't enlist, man," Charlie said. "They've got you for three then, and they've got you by the balls. Don't do anything before you talk to me, alright? Maybe we can work something out. I'll talk to you tomorrow."

Lamont walked up the steps and went on in. The porch light winked off and another light came on deep in the house.

4.

Vaca decided that he needed to lose 600 pounds. The engine was perfect, there wasn't any way to substantially improve it. The only way to go faster was to go lighter. The Ford, at present, weighed 3900 pounds. If he could cut 600 pounds from that total, he would gain almost a second on his quarter-mile times. Enough to beat Reinhard, bad.

It was easy at first. The rear seat went; so did the spare tire, the jack, the radio, headrests, armrests and front bumper, a total of nearly 200 pounds. He kept records with a bathroom scale.

Soon, it required more thought. Nights, he searched through a current Ford parts book, seeking optional or newer parts that were lighter than the ones in his car. Days, he haunted the dealership, ordering and checking on previous orders.

He switched from drum to disc brakes on all four wheels, shaving 40 pounds, went to the smallest mufflers Ford made and then ripped the baffling and insulation out of them. He halved the weight of the gas tank with a model designed for newer compacts.

With an electric drill and a three-quarter inch bit, he began tapping holes everywhere in the frame and body that didn't mar the appearance or seem to weaken the structure. By then, he was weighing the day's savings in ounces on a kitchen scale.

The last item on his list was a fiberglass front end. By replacing the metal hood and fenders with fiberglass replicas, he planned to lose 300 pounds. The problem was that nobody made them.

Finally, he found a manufacturer in Gardena who agreed to make some up at an exorbitant price, using Vaca's hood and fenders for forms to draw the molds.

The parts were trucked to Gardena and Vaca settled in, waiting again. He kept busy, in and under the car, drilling, removing bolts and brackets he deemed unnecessary, scraping off the thick factory undercoating. He spent most of a day picking out insulating material from behind the door panels and under the dash, a tuft at a time.

The pile of parts taken from the car filled a corner of the garage, stacked up nearly four feet. He planned to leave it there. The scraps and shavings he tossed on at the end of the day would have seemed insignificant otherwise.

He started the engine up every night, to keep the oil circulating and the battery fresh, but mainly just to listen. The low rumble, a loping resonant bass, could be heard all the way around the block. A neighbor behind him complained that green fruit was being shaken loose from her apricot tree, but Vaca didn't care.

Some nights he sat across the street, absorbing the sound. He scarcely believed it was his. Watching the car, his eye was occasionally caught by the half-opened garage door shimmying on its frame rails. Shutting the engine off was hard, and it left him feeling hollow.

5-

Charlie tried phoning Connie on Monday night and again on Wednesday. Both nights, she was out.

On Thursday Connie was home, but she sounded vague, distant, and cut him off before he had a chance to ask her out, claiming her mother was expecting a long distance call from her father, who was away on a construction job.

Wounded, he did not call again. The following week he saw her in the parking lot at Van de Kamp's. She was with the same blonde haired boy, but definitely with him this time. She was backed up against him, with her elbows on his knees as he sat on the fender of his car. Her head was tilted against his chest.

When he left to make a beer run for two younger friends, Connie came over to the group Charlie was in.

"Hi," she said. "How you doing?" Charlie separated from the group.

"Good," Charlie said. "Really good. How about you?"

"Unreal," Connie said. "Charlie I'm so happy."

Charlie managed a smile, "Oh yeah?"

"I wanted to tell you when you called, but I couldn't explain right then. Mickey was waiting for me at the corner."

Charlie nodded toward where the blonde boy's car had been. "That guy?"

"Yeah. Same one. I don't know, it just happened. The last week's been crazy. It's gone so fast. That night, after we left you? We ended up at the beach and the next night we went and saw *Bonnie and Clyde*. He's a lot different than I thought. I don't know, he's exciting."

Staring moodily at her shoes, Charlie put his hands in his back pockets. Connie said, "I think I'm in love."

Charlie concentrated on the left shoe, the one with a scuffed toe. "So? Why tell me?"

"You're a friend. I thought you'd be interested in knowing." She lit another cigarette and fiddled with a blouse button. "I'd really like you to meet Mickey. I know he looks like sort of a punk, but he's not when you know him."

"He looks like a pimp, man."

"Thanks a lot, Charlie. So what does that make me? I just wanted to be straight with you. Thanks a heap."

"Well, what did you expect?"

"I don't know," Connie said. "I just wanted you to like him. I mean, I gave you a pretty bad impression of him that night." He felt her eyes on him.

Across the lot, Mickey had returned. He was out of the car and holding a grocery bag over his head, teasing the anxious beer purchasers. Charlie and Connie turned with the noise.

"Well," Charlie said, "I'll see you around."

Connie looked at him again. "Listen, you want to get together sometime and talk?"

"Sure. Why not?"

"No, I mean really. Next week maybe."

Charlie shrugged.

"I'll call you," Connie said.

"Sure."

Laughing, she pulled open his shirt pocket with a forefinger and tapped the dead ash of her cigarette inside. "You'll see," she said. He watched her walk away, intrigued and already chiding himself for hoping.

She didn't call. Not that week or the next. Charlie called her house once, hanging up when her mother answered, then did not call again.

On the street, at the drive-in, he avoided her, ostentatiously moving out of range, though he couldn't tell if

40

she ever noticed. She seemed totally absorbed in Mickey, cheerful, almost giddy. Usually she was the only girl in their group.

Charlie disliked them. They were loud; their humor seemed crude to him. It bothered him most to see her laughing among them. He noticed that all of them but Connie seemed to look to Mickey while they laughed.

6-

The Ford was gone. The fiberglass front end had come from Gardena. It took Vaca almost a week to install the chalky, primer-grey fenders and hood, and when he'd finished, he shipped it immediately to Bert Homan, the painter. When the paint was done, he planned to send it to Jamgochian, the Armenian motor genius, for fine-tuning.

The therapy center was a long interior room in the hospital's old wing. It was five flights up but had the feel and odor of a basement room. It was windowless with a single entrance. Mirrors were on both sides, the length of the exercise section. The walls were painted a bright apple green. The machines were mostly chrome. The weights, pads, and wood were all bright primary colors.

On his first visits, just after the cast and brace were removed, the machines had unnerved Vaca. Strangely human in their motion, irritating in their grace, they were a contrast to the hesitant or flailing movements of the newer patients. More experienced patients showed an economy in their movement, even when the motion itself was awkward. Now though, Vaca would have preferred them painted drab colors and the metal anodized to a dull finish. The constant motion of the chrome arms, joints, and curved bars, diminishingly repeated in the wall mirrors, irritated him.

Normally he went to the center twice a week. Since the car had gone to the painter, he had increased his visits. He enjoyed the feel of the weights and the rhythm of the exercises, and the time passed without the sense of loss he often felt.

He worked mostly with the weights, concentrating on his upper arm and chest development. From the waist up, including the therapists, he was the largest man in the gym.

Vaca's condition had been diagnosed as paresis, not paralysis; paresis was incomplete paralysis - a severe weakening of the muscles - but sensation was still present. He could feel and the chances of improving, as a paraparetic, were far better than those of paraplegics.

Vaca usually referred to himself, when he had to, as a paraplegic. It was easier than explaining a condition that most people didn't understand. In Vaca's estimation, when they did understand more was expected of him, and his injuries were not thought of as quite so damaging.

The therapists left him alone now. When he'd started therapy, they'd designed a program that would improve the coordination and strength of his legs. He'd stuck with it for two months. There was little improvement in his legs in that time, but the musculature of his arms and shoulders became impressive. He settled for that.

The therapists were upset. He'd put on twenty pounds, all in his upper body and looked like a composite photograph, his thighs and shins wasted and frail. They insisted his legs would improve, but none of them could say how long it would take.

At root, Vaca didn't care. He'd only wanted out. He had been in the hospital seven months and his suit would go to court the next month. His lawyer had warned him - hinting in the delicate, oblique conventions that lawyers were forced to use when giving expedient but improper advice - not to show too much improvement.

Above him, the barbell wavered sideways. Vaca could feel his face reddening from the strain. His forearms were dead white and the veins bulged out from the effort. He let out his breath with a slow whoosh as he lowered the bar onto the rack above his chest.

He felt good, loose and sweaty. He let his arms dangle, enjoying the tingling, swollen feel of them as the blood rushed back. The last lift had been 210 pounds, a good stopping point. Vaca called out for one of the attendants. The man helped him into his wheelchair and followed him to the whirlpool tank, a four-by-four tub set into the floor, surrounded by a gutter and sloping, roughened tile.

Vaca settled on the slatted bench. The attendant adjusted the height until his shoulders just cleared the water and then started the pump. Vaca eased back against the padded side and gave himself to the warm, swirling pressure of the water.

He had the tank to himself for the first ten minutes. He opened his eyes as the motion of the water slowed to a pulse. The attendant helped another patient, a thin, muscular man in his early forties, slip over the side and restarted the pump. The man's left arm ended in a knob, just below the elbow. His left leg was a stump below the knee.

The man leaned back, took off his glasses and then his trunks, and let them float in the swirling water. He pointed to the glasses, bumping against the side of the tank and said, "Plastic."

Vaca pushed the trunks away from his armpit. "You should take your pants off," the man told him. "Let your balls bob. What do you think the machine is for?" Vaca picked up the trunks with his thumb and forefinger and slung them onto the carpet, beyond the tile surrounding the bath. He called for the orderly to help him out.

While he waited, Vaca urinated, staring steadily at the man on the other side of the tank. The orderly moved his wheelchair onto the tile. Vaca stretched his arms out, gripping the gutter, and raised his chest clear of the water. The orderly grasped him by the armpits and lifted him out, lowering him into his chair. "Hey buddy," Vaca told the man in the tank, "don't drink any of that water."

The orderly brought him a towel. Vaca reached for it and the man tossed it in his lap. "Why don't you go to a regular gym?" the orderly said.

Vaca dried his shoulders and his chest. He hunched his shoulders when he was done, looking down at the pigeon-like swell of his pectoral muscles. He tossed the towel back at the orderly. "I like this gym."

He dressed. His thoughts were on the Ford again; the painter had promised it for the following week. It was time to call Brody. He didn't think that Brody knew he was still pissed. Vaca couldn't forget what Brody had done the night they'd raced Reinhard. That was the way he remembered what Brody had done. He'd sat alone in the car that night for a long time, waiting for the tow truck, and thought about Brody leaving. He'd thought about it then and a lot since. Vaca hated feeling helpless. Sometimes it couldn't be prevented, but he arranged his life so those instances were rare. Brody knew that. Vaca hadn't decided what to do about it yet.

Leaving, he caught the aide at the whirlpool staring at him resentfully. Vaca gave him the finger as he wheeled through the entry, where a nurse with a professional smile held the door back. The therapy staff couldn't decide about him. None of them thought he was lazy, which was the usual reason for minimal efforts in therapy. Some patients fought, some accepted their condition. The ones who accepted paralysis led more comfortable lives. Vaca wasn't comfortable. The consensus was that he had convinced himself that his settlement was still vulnerable, open to adjustment. He must feel that everything he'd earned, everything he'd achieved, could still be taken away from him.

7-

Lamont's voice, barely audible above the clatter of plates and the roar of a large fan situated near the phone, trailed off altogether. Charlie waited.

"Well, I don't know," Lamont said finally. "At least if I enlist they give me a choice of schools."

"Do what you want," Charlie told him. "What do I know?"

The clatter of dishes grew louder and someone yelled, "Lamont? Backin' up in here."

Lamont said, "I got to go. You be home later?"

"No," Charlie said. "Try Vandy's."

A tray of silverware clashed, dropped somewhere nearby. "I got to go," Lamont said.

Lamont was becoming a problem. Charlie had twice talked him out of enlisting; each time Lamont had gone home and had another argument with Dean, his stepfather.

The last time it happened, Charlie started thinking the Army might not be a bad choice for Lamont.

Lamont worked two jobs, bussing tables during the day and filling in as a janitor most nights. He could hardly afford to keep his Plymouth running and pay rent for his room. He ate out every night rather than face Dean across a dinner table. When at home, Lamont fought with his mother and was consequently battered by his stepfather, to her satisfaction.

Lamont insisted his time would come but this didn't seem likely to occur soon. Dean worked in a foundry, and at 50, looked like he could be welded on. His mother wanted him to stay but Lamont suspected that she was worried about who Dean would hit on when Lamont was gone.

Charlie suggested better jobs that could pay for an apartment but Lamont explained that he had no time to look.

Finally, he had enlisted. He'd waited a week to tell Charlie, and Charlie, unwilling to make him feel any more apprehensive, told him it was probably the best thing.

Lamont expected a month's grace, but the induction notice ordered him to report in a week. Time was so short that he reacted with complete indecision and didn't settle any of his affairs. He worked both jobs until the day before his induction and apologized to both employers for giving such short notice.

That night he drained the water out of his Plymouth's radiator, disconnected the battery and put the car up on blocks. Afterward, he went with Charlie to Van de Kamp's and hung out in the parking lot. He did not mention the occasion of the next day to anyone, and his only gesture toward leaving was the tip he left their waitress, clearing his pockets of pennies and silver.

Charlie drove him to the induction center. The interior of the building looked like it was designed to collect fire insurance, with narrow stairways and old wood everywhere. Nearly everyone there, soldiers and those waiting in the rows of folding chairs, was drinking coffee from styrofoam cups and smoking cigarettes.

Lamont's appointment was for ten a.m., but the sergeant behind the desk gave him a meal ticket and told him to report back at three.

They had lunch at the cafe designated on the ticket. Charlie guessed a retired army cook must have owned the restaurant. The food was spooned onto segmented metal trays. A limp, iridescent ham slice with raisin sauce was the entree. Everything else was instant or powdered, except the corn which tasted canned, and the two slices of dry white bread and pats of white margarine.

Belching, feeling bloated but still nervously hungry, they

walked out into the smoggy afternoon heat and wandered, never more than a few blocks from the induction center. They went into the dark and cool interior of a poolroom, the first place they saw that admitted minors.

They shot three racks, playing badly, tried most of the pinball machines in an adjacent arcade and had their pictures taken in a quarter booth. Both of them looked surprisingly tan in the pictures, squeezed together, solemnly giving the finger to the light and camera behind the plate glass. Charlie tore the strip of pictures in half and they tucked them in their wallets.

Lamont spent a dollar on a crane in a glass box of prizes but retrieved only candy-coated peanuts and an aluminum disc that said, *good luck,* on one side and the name of the establishment, *Kramers's Automated Amusements,* on the other. Then it was time.

They waited in the middle of the large room for the last ten minutes to pass, standing beneath a wall clock. A plaque underneath the clock said *Army Time.*

At three, Lamont shook hands; "Well, see you in three months," he said, and advanced, white faced, to the desk. After receiving his instructions and his folders he came back and surprised Charlie by borrowing cigarettes and some matches. "Give me something to do," he said, and then shook hands again.

Charlie watched him walk up the narrow stairs and waved when he reached the first landing. Lamont didn't look back.

For a moment Charlie envied him. A young sunburned sergeant, a neat compact man with a broad forehead and an olive-shaped birth mark on one cheek, came down the stairs, two at a time, and began bawling names. "Arenson, Audeh, Blaker, Chan, Clary, Cobb, Davis, Encinas, Harfenist, Harold, Johnson, Mackey, Mead, Nada, Pearlstein, Perez, Peyton, Resnick, Sachs, Shull, Skene, Taylor, Troise." Boys scattered through the rows of folding chairs, stood up and moved toward him. When they were assembled, he began yelling. Raggedly, they lined up. He continued to yell, giving instructions so rapidly Charlie couldn't understand him. His accent was southern but his cadence was rapid-fire.

"Gerenline," the sergeant shouted. "Shapeup. Gerenline 'n follahmee. Moo, Moo, Moo, you Pissants!"

The boys in line looked at each other. None of them seemed to comprehend what he was saying. The sergeant turned and started up the stairs, still yelling, and the line, after several shoves to the boy in front, started jerkily up the stairs behind him.

Charlie started for the door, listening to the sergeant. The whole place had begun to feel alien. Walking to the door, he felt he was being watched.

At Van de Kamp's, that night, Charlie spread the news of Lamont's departure, agreeing with everyone that there should have been a party.

Connie was there. He noticed her while he was making his rounds. Mickey and his friends were in their usual parking spaces. She was sitting by herself on the low lavender-colored cement-block wall cornering the property. She wore a broad-banded striped knit dress in aqua colors with half sleeves, one stretched and longer than the other, and oddly, a beach hat and sunglasses.

He studied her for a moment, shuffling memories, trying to recall a past image that was irritatingly reminiscent of the way she appeared tonight. He couldn't decide whether it was an attitude, or the way she sat, or what she wore that kept snagging in his thoughts. Charlie closed his eyes, concentrating. One image wavered and locked in place. He walked over.

She wouldn't look up. Gently he lifted the glasses and then set them back. Her left eye was nearly swollen shut. The puffed skin of the eyelid was rubbery looking. Below the glasses heavily caked makeup hid other bruises.

Connie pulled her floppy hat down tight around her ears and looked up at him.

"Richie do that?" Charlie asked.

"Richie leads with his left. He always got the other eye. This one's Mickey's. Nice, huh?"

"Christsake Connie."

"I know. I know." She touched the hidden bruises. "Does it show a lot?"

Charlie said no and sat down next to her. They looked at the cars across the lot. She lit a cigarette.

"I told you he was a pimp," Charlie said.

Connie coughed on her cigarette smoke, laughing. "If he was, he wouldn't damage the visible merchandise."

"You know what I mean."

"Yeah." She touched her cheek again. "It really pisses him off that I'm smarter than he is. I mean, he knows it, I know it, that's cool. I just can't help reminding him."

"Motormouth."

"Can't resist," she smiled wryly. "I mean he does leave himself open."

"I know it's a stupid question, but why are you staying with him?"

Connie shrugged, "I don't know, he's dumb but he knows me inside out." Charlie borrowed her cigarette to light his and they smoked silently for a moment.

Connie turned her head, watching Mickey in the middle of his friends. "He hasn't even looked at me. I mean, you've been sitting here five minutes and he hasn't even sneaked a look. Could you do that? I mean, if it was switched."

Charlie studied his cigarette, "No."

"Yeah, neither could I."

Charlie stood up to go. She looked up at him with her hand on the back of her hat. "Listen, I'm sorry I didn't call you back."

"Yeah, Well," Charlie said. "Same old, same old."

She dipped her head and looked up again. "You going to keep avoiding me?"

"You tell me."

"I wish you'd come by."

He felt she was watching him as he walked across the lot but when he turned she had moved. Connie stood in back of the group of boys around Mickey's car. Mickey was standing on the front seat of the Corvair, folding back the convertible top. He paused with the top half up, to illustrate some point to the listeners looking up at him. It looked like he was describing a wreck; his hands smacked together and one fell and the other veered to the right. Following the motion of his hand, outward, his eyes caught and focused on Connie. Connie raised her sunglasses and winked at him with her good eye.

8-

The Armenian himself, Matthew Jamgochian, delivered the Ford. He kept his assistant waiting while he lifted the hood off to show Vaca a few inspired modifications he had made. None of them, it turned out, were really visible. The tapering ports he'd deburred and expanded in the manifold were now hidden; he could only point out the areas of the carburetor where the fuel passages and jets had been drilled larger. His stubby fingers circled and pointed gracefully and his voice was filled with remembered pleasure as he described the work.

Vaca cut him short by turning the key, bringing the engine to raucous life. Jamgochian listened with a slack, happy smile, while Vaca revved it, reaching in to push the pedal with his hand. When Vaca shut it off, Jamgochian replaced the hood carefully and wiped everything he'd touched with a clean pink rag.

Leaving, he handed over his card, printing his home phone on the back. He told Vaca to call if he ever decided to sell the car or the motor.

The Ford's black paint, bottomless and crystalline, 23 coats and two coats of clear, shone in the late afternoon sun. The engine ticked slightly as it cooled, and a spot of fresh oil appeared on the driveway that had been clean for a month. Vaca wheeled around, looking the Ford over critically.

The only remaining work was the pinstriping, which would have to wait. Von Dutch was out of town or not answering his phone. In truth, Vaca was relieved. The pinstriping on the old hood had been ruined when they pulled the molds for the fiberglass one; he didn't know how the artist would feel about that, or whether he would recreate old work.

The paintwork, which he'd worried over, had been matched beautifully. The painter, Bert Homan, had also done the original paint the year before but had since acquired religion.

Vaca had been shocked and a little reluctant when he'd dropped off the car. Homan and his new assistant were wearing uniform overalls; his wife was typing receipts. Previously, Homan had worked out of a quonset hut in back of his house. The hut had been painted his favorite color, California orange-orange, the same shade as his mailbox, front door and four of his cars. The only bill Vaca could remember was a pencilled set of figures on a piece of brown paper bag. The cash had gone into one pocket of Homan's jeans, and the change had been dug out of other pockets.

The frame building he now worked in had none of the calendars that papered the rounded sides and ceiling of the quonset hut. Also missing were his projects - three old Ford trucks, in various states of finish, the refrigerator for beer to cut the edge of the paint fumes, and the five or six friends present every time Vaca had visited, sitting on old car seats. The trucks were now parked outside, covered with parachutes, and customers' cars were kept inside.

The new shop made Vaca uneasy. So had the stack of *Watchtowers* on a rack near the door and the realization that Homan was sober. But the paint was beautiful, un-distinguishable from the original.

When he arrived to pick it up, the car had been washed, the interior vacuumed, and the bill was less than anticipated. Homan had no time to talk, however.

The last time it had taken Vaca several hours to retrieve the car. Homan had seemed sorry to see it go, walking around the Ford while they talked, squinting along the fender line and hunkering down, beer in hand, to stroke the finish with admiration. This time he simply wav. from where he stood in the spray booth, mask up on his forehead while he unkinked the airlines running to his spray gun and pointed to where his wife waited brightly behind her desk with the bill.

Everything seemed to be moving Vaca's way. Brody sounded friendly. He swore that he'd just been ready to call. A team race was in the talking stage with Stan's drive-in, Van Nuys, for the unofficial championship of L.A.. Reinhard was up for it, so were the rest, and Brody had hoped that they would be ready.

It had all sounded good to Vaca. He hung up thinking about how everything seemed to be working out, and only peripherally about how he would get back at Brody.

9-

Charlie was organizing the team race and enjoying the details. He made five trips to Stan's. The first three were wasted trying to find out who to talk to. It seemed he had no opposite number there; agreement was consequently difficult. When a point was disputed, he was told typically, "Check with the guy in the blue Corvette and see what he says." After many similar referrals, consensus was reached.

The races would be held at a neutral site near Hansen Dam, ten ranked cars each and two back-up cars per team. Van de Kamp's top car would race Stan's top car, second against second, and so on. If a car broke, the back-ups would race in their place. The pot would be twelve hundred, one hundred per car.

There would be four rounds, a fifth if necessary. The starter, by unenthusiastic agreement, would be Arky Brazil. He was a long time street-racer from South Pasadena, so disagreeable that no one thought he would favor either side.

Charlie hoped to race himself. His Chevy wasn't fast enough for the top ten, but as a favor it would be the final back-up car. The races were set for Tuesday night.

At Van de Kamp's, Charlie looked over the other early arrivers in the parking lot; most of them were spectators. The only racers who had shown so far were parked together - Gilbert Chavez, in his new Corvette, and Willy Lum, the driver of a lightweight injected '56 Chevy. Charlie joined them, ignoring the greetings of several watchers sitting along the wall that separated the drive-in from the lot.

Lum, the owner and sole mechanic of a sporadically open garage in Atwater, was describing in intricate detail and without a trace of his usual Island patois, some recent work he'd completed on his Chevy's cylinder heads. Charlie listened respectfully, trying to remember the terms for future discussions, as Lum ticked off the list on his fingers.

"Milled twenty-thousandths," Lum was saying, "New seats, cut for oversize valves, sodium-filled. C.C.'ed. Ported. Polished. And machined for needle bearing rockers." Charlie understood most of the list only in theory; he listened mainly for brand names.

Other racers were arriving. They wheeled in with sweeping turns, revving the engines in place before shutting down. By five, everyone had shown except Brody and Vaca, and Reinhard.

Brody had parked his El Camino down the block, as close as he could get to the street lamp, and walked up the driveway at four o'clock, a half-hour earlier than expected. Vaca was already sitting in the car.

Brody rapped on the windshield and waved. Vaca's startled expression, with the whites showing around his pupils, gave his face a momentary quality of innocence. This was shortly replaced by a scowl. Brody didn't notice, absorbed in the new paintwork.

After circling the car, he lowered himself into the driver's seat. "Looking good," he said. "How's it run?"

Vaca reached across and turned the key. The garage exploded in noise. After the first burst, shaking the walls, the exhaust note settled into an unwavering idle, a tight thrumming bass sound, achingly loud in the confines. Brody's grin widened.

Vaca reached again and turned it off. In the silence, Brody turned to look at him, and Vaca leaned and swung backhanded, smacking Brody across the mouth.

Brody's head hit the window frame. As Brody rebounded, Vaca moved to brace his back against the door and raised his hands in front of him. Brody shook his head violently, hunched and set his neck like a stunned boxer. He looked at Vaca, amazed.

"Come on," Vaca said. His fists, clenching, trembled. "Come on, it's fair, you can't stand up."

Brody stared distractedly at the raised vein pumping on Vaca's forehead, blinked and backed away, reaching behind him for the doorhandle. Out of the car, he peered curiously through the windshield. He walked around the car - Vaca swiveled to watch him - and came back to the driver's window.

He wiped his hands on his shirtfront, staring in. Nodding, narrowing his eyes, he seemed to come to some decision. He pointed a forefinger. "That's for the night we raced Reinhard, right?" Vaca said nothing, still braced, opening and closing his hands. "For leaving. Right?" Brody straightened up and Vaca could no longer see his face.

"I'll kick your ass!" Vaca yelled.

Brody's stomach began to move. As Brody leaned down, Vaca could see his shoulders shake. His expression, behind a hand, was mirthful. He straightened up and when he bent again, his features, except for his eyes - which still held humor - were controlled. "That's fair," Brody said.

"Yeah, it's fair. I mean, what can you say? Anyone who waits two months, goes to all this hassle, gets the fucking car all set up, painted, and then risks the whole thing? What can I say? If it pissed you off that much, then it must be fair."

Vaca's expression softened for the first time. He lowered one hand. "That's right."

Brody said, "You need to hit me anymore?"

Vaca said no and shook his head, but kept his hands clenched as Brody got in. Brody locked his hands on top of his head. "We're even."

Vaca opened his fists. Brody brought his hands down slowly, nodding calmly, with half closed eyes. "If you ever," Brody said, "pull that shit again, I will kick your ass." When Vaca turned to roll down his window, Brody settled more comfortably into the seat and reached for the key.

Charlie was organizing, but no one seemed to notice. He drew maps, which were placed in glove compartments or tossed on back seats unread. As he handed out the maps, he went over the agreed-upon conditions for the match, but most of the racers waved him off before he finished while several onlookers heckled him for not speaking louder. After five o'clock he gave up, went to sit in his Chevy and wait like everyone else for Brody, Vaca and Reinhard to arrive.

A tap on the roof of the Chevy turned him around. Connie Ciccarelli was leaning forward to press her face against the passenger side window. Her eyes were crossed and her lips were smeared wetly on the glass. Charlie started and she cracked up.

Charlie reached for the doorhandle and let her in. "Jesus, Lucille. Scared me to death," Charlie said. "For a minute there you looked like Ciccarelli." She tossed her purse in his lap. Charlie opened the purse and rummaged through it, holding her away with one hand as she tried to reclaim it. "Ahh Ciccarelli, it is you," Charlie said. "Who else carries a roll of quarters and spare underwear."

"Keep it up," Connie said. "Maybe your big sister'd like to know about her girdle. Think she'd wonder what it was doing in your glove box? You still let it casually pop out and impress the boys?" She grabbed for her purse. Charlie let go before the strap could break. Connie sat back against the door and put her feet up on the dash. "You're in a good mood."

Charlie grinned back at her, "You can't touch me tonight, flying low. Car's running great. Got a race on. I'm running great. Got a hard-on. I've thrown three other women out of here tonight for putting their feet on the dash." His hand encircled one of her stockinged ankles. "How would you like to land?"

Connie laughed. She put her feet on the floor and smoothed the green pleated fabric of her skirt over her knees. Her sweater, a long-sleeved pink imitation mohair with fuzzy snarls, clashed with the skirt.

"So how's your ma?" Connie said. "She still making the-novenas-for-the-brain-damage or did she give you up to Saint Anthony?"

"Can't touch me. You want to go racing?"

"Sure. Where we going?"

"Out by Hansen Dam. We're racing Stan's tonight."

"Sure. As long as I'm home before noon."

"What about Mickey?" Charlie said.

"Didn't I tell you?" She pressed the back of her wrist against her forehead, mocking the dramatic gesture of a silent movie heroine. "I think I'm not in love."

Charlie pulled himself up by the steering wheel, alerted by motion in the crowd around the entrance. Brody and Vaca were pulling in. Brody inched forward, revving the engine. Unable to reach a parking space, he finally shut down in the middle of the crowd. He wedged open the door and stood on the sill, looking out over their heads.

Charlie got out and made his way through the bodies milling around the Ford. He reached up and pulled Brody's coatsleeve. "What?" Brody said; he cupped a hand behind his ear.

Charlie pulled him down and yelled in his ear. "I said, we're ready to go, just waiting for Reinhard."

"He's on his way," Brody said. "We went by his house."

They turned as a familiar roar sounded behind them. Vaca turned to watch as the nose of Reinhard's Chevy edged toward the back window of the Ford.

"Let's go," Brody said. "Tell Reinhard to back out and we'll follow him."

63

Charlie relayed the instructions to Reinhard and then ran past the cars of the other racers, shouting directions as they started to line up behind Brody.

Connie had the Chevy idling and Charlie was able to pull into line while most of the crowd was still heading for their cars.

The line of cars traveled down Fletcher to the freeway onramp, ignoring a red light that should have stopped the last six cars.

On the Golden State Freeway, they blasted out of the onramp one after another, and quickly sorted themselves out from the traffic in a long single file in the center lane, cruising comfortably at fifty.

By the time they reached Burbank, the crowd had caught up, at first flanking them on either side, then gradually backing off to join the line at the rear.

Charlie was euphoric. The Chevy was running smoothly; throttle response was instant. He goosed the pedal occasionally, surging forward then dropping back, and smiling to himself.

Connie smoked quietly, watching the cars ahead. At a bend she pointed toward the lead cars. "Do you know him?" she asked.

She had to repeat the question before Charlie looked over. "Who? Reinhard?"

"No. The one in the black car. Vaca."

"Sure," Charlie said, "I know all those guys."

"He was in my brother's class in high school. What's he like?"

Charlie looked at her distractedly. "He's a dick. Why?"

"I don't know. He seems interesting."

"He's a snake."

"Oh."

"Why'd you think he was interesting?"

"Just from what Cheryl told me."

"What'd she say?"

"About the same as you." Connie stubbed her cigarette and opened the windwing to toss it. "God, what a nice night to be driving."

Ahead, the lead cars' blinkers were flashing for the Pacoima turnoff.

At Hanson Dam they parked in a lot overlooking the picnic grounds and a fenced area enclosing a miniature train ride.

No one from Stan's had shown yet. Charlie walked the parking lot nervously, having to listen to baited questions from the dark cars, assuring the questioners that he had the correct date and hour.

Someone broke down a section of the fence and part of the crowd drifted down onto the railway. In the twilight haze, Charlie could see some beer drinkers lounging like passengers on a ship, their feet hanging out of the small open railway cars alongside the miniature station. Others wandered into the tar paper-and-plaster Alpine tunnel and shortly thereafter holes began appearing in the side, punched through, the punchers then waving to an encouraging group on the embankment above and shaking hands through adjacent holes.

Finally, a single car arrived, an emissary from Stan's with directions to a new location.

There was a hurried consultation between cars, with Charlie angrily insisting the change shouldn't be made. "They all agreed," Charlie said. "We shouldn't let them fuck with us." The emissary said, "The cops found out. We're just trying to lose them."

Reinhard and Brody conferred separately. Brody settled the question. He climbed into the back of a pickup and set his beer down on the cab roof. "Screw 'em," he said. "It doesn't matter what games they run. No way can they take us. Let's go do it." Ragged cheers came from the parking lot and the train, and a chorus of voices from the remains of the tunnel yelled, "Fuck 'em" in unison. The emissary gave directions and swore the rest would be there within a half-hour. "We all split up to lose the cops," he explained.

Brody was familiar with the new location and Reinhard said he would follow; the crowd made for their cars.

10-

The new site was a long empty stretch of two-lane road, between gravel pits, in Pacoima. The absolutely flat landscape was unbroken for miles in any direction, dark and windblown. To the south the county power plants were visible, three separate girdered frameworks housing pipes, catwalks, boilers, and machinery. Two huge smokestacks on opposite sides of each framework were ringed with red and white lights, the red ones on top blinking for aircraft. At that distance they looked like vast paddleboats, steaming toward them.

The cars parked along the unlit road were quiet; the groups out of the cars were small and subdued.

Brody, sharing another beer alongside Willy Lum's Chevy, passed the can to Charlie and pointed a finger toward a dimly visible signboard on the small shelf of land edging the gravel pit. "That guy's my godfather. I ever tell you about him?"

Charlie wandered closer to the fence and peered through; spelled out in gilt letters on a black background, with so many looping flourishes it was hard to read, the sign said: Vasek Norkus Enterprises.

"Shrewd as hell," Brody was saying. "He used to work with my old man. I bet I haven't talked to him in ten years."

"What is he?" Charlie said. "Does he run the gravel pit?"

Brody joined him at the fence. "Him and my old man drove trucks out here. Just after the war. The old guy that owned the place decided he was going to die and wanted to go back to Italy, so he offered to sell to Vasek and my old man."

"My old man didn't want to do it. He was going to school

nights, so Vasek did it himself. Mortgaged his house and moonlighted and came up with the down payment. It wasn't much.

"The first year my old man made more than he did, but after that Norkus worked out what was probably the only idea he ever got in his life and he just raked it in. It was weird, my old man was the one taking business classes and he laughed at him. Norkus figured it all out by himself. My old man told him he was crazy, but he went to the tax board and it turned out he was right.

"What he did. See, alls he's got is a hole in the ground, but he figured out that every year he's taking out so much sand, so much gravel, and every year there's less left. So he got them to allow for depreciation. Like the oil guys. Cut his taxes down to zero, next to nothing, right? That works great for about ten years, but then finally he gets down almost to bedrock and even with the tax break it's not paying its way.

"So he sells his trucks, shuts the whole thing down, just cools it for about a year, and then he reopens the place as a garbage dump. Wait, it gets sweeter. He sews up every municipal contract in the Valley. Now he's sitting pretty. It'll take twenty years to fill it up. They're paying him to fill it and then he goes back to the tax board. Now he gets another depreciation, because each year the hole gets smaller. They didn't even fight him. He made them laugh."

Brody took his beer back, shook it next to his ear, and stepped on the can. "He's got about ten more years to fill it up. Then comes the kicker. They get it all filled in, he smoothes it off a little, and he's sitting on a hundred twenty acres that can now get zoned residential. The last open land in the valley."

He squinted through the chainlink. "He lives in a trailer out there. Everybody always figures he's the watchman."

"Too bad your old man didn't get into it," Charlie said.

"Yeah. Norkus fired him the second year."

Several horns sounded faintly. Turning from the fence, they could see a line of headlights showing the contour of the road as they vanished and reappeared. People started to get out of the parked cars.

Walking back to the Chevy, Charlie saw a group of boys around Vaca, with Connie on the periphery, listening to them talk. Charlie was surprised; she'd declined to join him, preferring to stay in the car with the heater. The boys were asking about the Ford, the latest changes. Vaca was pissy with them, and his occasional answers were brief.

The string of headlights was growing larger and the sound of the engines more distinct. Charlie walked to the center of the road and waited.

The lead car, a primer grey '40 Ford with chrome Lake pipes, well ahead of the others, started braking a quarter mile away, swerving slightly each time the driver hit the brakes or downshifted, characteristic with dangerously lightened and overpowered cars. Charlie moved to the side and watched it coast in, the driver and the boy with him taking a long appraising look at the cars lined up on the shoulder.

They stopped beside Reinhard's Chevy and got out, two clean-cut looking youths in thin tee shirts and off-white Levis. Charlie recognized the driver, the taller of the two, long-backed and round-shouldered, as one of the negotiators on his last visit.

The other cars from Stan's were pulling in. Charlie walked down the line to inspect them, noticing particularly a red Corvette that had been towed in. The Corvette had a ladder frame and sat up so high the driver jumped to get out. A blower with dual quads on top protruded a foot above the cutout hood.

Charlie spotted the starter, Arky Vaughn, at the end of the line. Vaughn, a dour, hollow-cheeked man in his early thirties wearing thick-framed glasses, was easily identified at a distance by his odd-looking flattop haircut. It was cropped to scalp level on top, long and swept back on the sides like the wings of a nesting bird, a style known on yellowing barbershop posters as a "Chicago Boxcar."

While the mutual inspections went on, Vaughn opened the trunk of his Buick Riviera and began unloading black and yellow rubber safety cones, four tall tripods with reflector studs and a huge surveyor's tape reel.

Charlie and the driver of the '40 Ford assisted him as he laid out the quarter-mile course. Silently, he marked a line across the road with a chunk of chalk, tossed it to one of the onlookers, and told him to fill it in more plainly. He selected another to hold the end of the tape and started walking backward, playing out the reel. Charlie and the other boy followed him, carrying the reflector poles.

As they moved away from the cars, the darkness became intense. The second time Vaughn stumbled, he told them, "Next time pick a road with some streetlights. Assholes."

He slowed as the tape reached 1300 feet and had Charlie hold a flashlight on it. When he reached 1320, he set the tape down and marked on either side with chalk, then extended the line across the road. They placed the reflector sticks, two on either side, one right at the edge of the pavement, the other a few feet away. When Vaughn was satisfied, they started walking back, rolling up the tape.

At the start, Vaughn set out the cones marking staging lanes and then collected his money, twenty-five dollars from each side and the pot. He said he was ready when they were.

Numbers had been daubed on the cars' rear windows with whitewash. Charlie's Chevy was number twelve. The number one car for Stan's, as expected, was the blown Corvette. The '40 Ford was number three. An orange Austin Healey with a Chevy engine was the number two.

Arky Vaughn signaled for the number ten cars and the drivers began moving forward in the staging lanes. About a third of the crowd had moved down to the finish. Two of Vaughn's friends would determine the winners and had walked down with them, taking their places on either side. They blinked their flashlights to signal they were ready. Charlie stood with Connie near the starting line. This was the time he enjoyed most, the anticipation. His eyes traveled down the line, twenty cars; the variety was astonishing. At the back, the

70

shapes of Reinhard's Chevy and the Corvette next to him were brutally functional. Their lines were chopped by the cutout rear fenders and exposed wide tires and made stubby by their jacked-up stance. One car up, beside Brody, was the sleek and lowered symmetry of the Austin Healey, the lines unbroken and recurving. The colors ranged from drab primer to a roadster halfway back that glinted like a fresh-caught trout with iridescent greens, blues, and reds.

The noise was uniform. All of them were uncorked and the usual subtleties in the sounds of their idles, caused by differences in engine size, exhaust systems, camshafts and a dozen other factors, were missing. The only distinctions among the rasping, unmuffled bellows up and down the line were loud and louder, tight and tighter.

The first two cars moved forward, following Vaughn's beckoning arms. Charlie, arms crossed, hands tucked between arms and his sides, watched the flames dancing on the pavement from their open head pipes. He squeezed the flesh around his ribs as Vaughn began blinking his flashlight. The raw odors of gas, oil baking on exhaust pipes, and hot rubber were distinct and strong.

The familiar sawing roar began as Arky blinked for the start, both cars fighting for traction on the cold pavement. Smoke billowed from the tires and the waver in the roar ceased as they took off, becoming sharper and sharper until the note broke with their first, simultaneous shifts.

The crowd at the starting line sucked in toward the center of the road, watching them go. Shortly, only their taillights could be seen, and then the reflectors at the end, lighting in the beams of their headlamps. A second passed and the flashlight on the left side, Stan's side, blinked three times. A mild sounding cheer came from the crowd at the finish, and both judges' lights blinked to show the road was clear. Arky waved up the next pair.

After the first race, the crowd stayed on the sides. Arky ran them off rapidly, staging the next pair while their predecessors were still on the course. Halfway through the first round, it became clear that the top cars would decide the match. Each side had three wins as the number four cars rolled into the staging lanes.

Gilbert Chavez, in his new Corvette, was racing against a silver Ramcharger with taped-on racing stripes. The start was even, but halfway down something blew in the Corvette. The engine wailed, overrevved; there were sparks in back and under the car from metal hitting the pavement, then it was quiet. The Ramcharger sailed past the finish. The Corvette coasted through and disappeared.

The cars on the starting line shut down, and everyone waited while the roadway was inspected for oil and large pieces of metal. Charlie tried to figure the new order and how much it would hurt them. Everyone on the Van de Kamp's side would move up a notch and the number eleven car would go against Stan's ten. The Ramcharger looked fast and that match was probably lost, but the rest seemed close. There wasn't that much difference in the bottom six.

Willy Lum won the next race, blowing off the grey '40 Ford, which seemed to have shifting troubles, by ten car lengths.

Brody and Vaca rolled forward, accompanied by the strong sounding Austin Healey. The driver of the Healey looked cool. Vaca looked pale and fierce. Brody was grinning constantly and seemed to be enjoying himself.

As Arky waved them up, he appeared interested for the first time that night. The Healey was hanging back; the driver pushed the shifter and the car lurched up to the mark. Charlie guessed it was a hydro trans - a beefed automatic - from the sound and the way it idled forward, which meant it would be consistent and that there was some real money in it.

The hydro definitely helped at the start. As Arky started blinking the light, the Healey's driver pushed harder on the brake and brought up the engine rev's, to just below stall speed.

The front of the car lifted and quivered. When Arky blinked

the last time, the Healey driver yanked his foot off the brake and was gone.

Brody got a good start but had several car lengths to make up. It didn't take long; the Ford gained with each shift. Halfway down they were even, and the crowd relaxed. Winding out, the Ford built a sizeable lead, and its brakelights showed before the finish.

There was a lull as Reinhard and the driver of the blown Corvette prepared. Reinhard laid down a puddle of bleach in front of his Chevy and made several burnouts, spinning the slicks through the bleach, producing a choking white smoke, cleaning the tires and warming them up to provide better traction.

In the other lane, three people were starting the Stingray. It had been pushed through the line to this point. The driver signaled he was ready, and one boy standing on the opposite side leaned in to hook up jumper cables from a pair of truck batteries. In front another boy with a spray can of ether held open the carburetor butterflies and sprayed the starting fluid down their throats. Both backed away, and the driver closed his eyes tightly and turned the key.

The engine lit with a "whooomp," and the few faces in the crowd that hadn't been watching turned, startled. The Corvette vibrated like a tuning fork. All four tires seemed to dance. The throttle linkage, visible above the hood, moved back leisurely and the ribbed belt turning the blower drive blurred as the engine speed raised. The linkage kicked back as the driver revved it, and the engine and car flexed minutely to the right with the torque. A boy next to Charlie held his ears and yelled, "Sounds nasty." Charlie nodded dumbly. He'd never heard anything like it on the street. The people from Stan's, around the starting line, all had the same irrepressible grin on their faces.

Reinhard's head had whipped around when the Vette started. Now he was looking calmly at Arky and trying, with an ear against the glass, to sense his own engine against the racket of the Vette.

On the line, Arky took a deep breath and motioned them forward. He took his time staging them, moving once to the side, to be sure the front tires were dead even with each other and with the line. Satisfied, he took his stance in front and pointed the light at them.

The crowd around him held their ears. The engines were equally loud, but the intensity of sound from the Stingray was different, higher in pitch and idle, with more variation. Arky blinked three times for the staging and then again quickly, on about a two count.

Reinhard's Chevy surged and then snapped off the line. With the Corvette it was more of a lunge, as though all four tires left the ground. It seemed to be nearly out of shape, veering to the left, bouncing. The driver backed off a little, corrected, and the Vette roared out in a series of shuddering fishtails.

Reinhard's start had given him a decent lead. It was surprising, because of the noise and awesome acceleration of the Vette, how gradually it diminished. It wasn't until they were through their shifts, two-thirds of the way down, that the Vette began visibly closing in. The crowd stretched, trying to see if Reinhard would hold him off, but it was impossible to judge at that angle and distance.

The flashlights on both sides of the reflectors blinked three times. There was a pause, and then they both blinked again. The crowd came down with a murmur. Arky announced a five-minute break between rounds as pairs of racers started returning from the other end.

Charlie checked his scoring against Arky's and found it agreed. Five wins for Van de Kamp's, four for Stan's, and the tie. He tried to figure, best and worst, what could happen the next round. The best he could anticipate was five-five. He couldn't imagine Reinhard beating the Stingray. If things went wrong anywhere in the bottom six cars, it could easily go six-four Stan's or even seven-three. He went to talk to Brody.

Brody was ebullient, laughing and talking, finishing another beer. Vaca looked cheerful for once. Brody didn't seem

74

worried about the Stingray. Charlie told him it was because he only caught the finish and hadn't really seen or heard the car.

Brody told him, "Don't give up on Reinhard, my man, it's not fast that counts, it's quickest." Charlie looked dubious; Brody continued, "I don't doubt the Vette's carrying more horses, but he's not getting them all on the ground. You saw how he was frying all over the line. He's pushing it too much for a short wheelbase. If Reinhard gets a better start, he'll beat him. Besides, you ever see a blown street car that lasted?" Vaca dug into the bag of beer on the floor; Charlie could see the side of the bag moving and guessed that Vaca was shaking the can. Vaca held the can out to him on his palm and smiled politely. Charlie said no and went off.

In back of the staging area, the hoods of most of the losers were up. The driver of the Austin Healey was nearly inside the engine compartment, reaching to turn the distributor, while a friend leaned in aiming a timing light at the crank pulley.

The second round began with a loss for Van de Kamp's.

The driver of the first back-up car, anxious, overrevved at the line and blew his clutch coming out. The car jumped once and then trailed off to the side, while his opponent made an easy solo pass, looking back most of the way.

Stan's won five of the first seven races in the second round, then suffered their first breakdown of the evening. The '40 Ford matched against Willy Lum got its transmission locked in gear and had to scratch. Brody and Vaca won easily again. As Reinhard and the Stingray came to the line, Stan's held a five-four edge.

Reinhard got a great start this time; he'd dropped the air pressure in his slicks by two pounds, and it made a difference. The tires bit instantly and sent him off almost without slippage or smoke. The Vette's driver was still slipping the clutch to get traction. The Van de Kamp's backers, recognizing the hole shot, began to yell, already sensing the outcome.

Just before Reinhard reached the outer range of the headlights around the start, there was a bang, then a chinking whine, sounding like a fork tossed in a blender, and then the heavy flop of a tire kicking around under a fender. Reinhard's Chevy hobbled off to the side with the right rear slick at an angle, bumping against the wheelwell. The Corvette was already by him and coasting for the finish.

The Stan's enthusiasts at both ends were jumping up and down and yelling. "Fuck," Charlie said, "he broke an axle."

Next to him, Connie shivered in her light sweater, her hands balled up inside the sleeves. She asked if that meant it was over.

"Might as well be," Charlie said. "I'll be back in a minute." He started walking towards Reinhard's Chevy.

The Stan's cars and drivers were already back from the finish line and celebrating. The Van de Kamp's cars were parking near Reinhard, ranged in a semi-circle with their lights on. Reinhard was lifting a toolbox out of the trunk.

As Charlie arrived, the right side was already up on jackstands. The tire, still bolted to the brake drum and the broken stub of the axle, was in the roadway. Someone rolled it closer to one of the cars, wedged it against a bumper, and began loosening the lugnuts with a crosswrench.

"What's it look like?" Charlie asked the quiet group behind Reinhard. Willy Lum turned, looking irritated, and then recognized him. "No way, bruddah," Willy said, "Dah slick's holding air but he got some bad cuts in the sidewall. He got a spare axle but it's dah kine stock, won' take no strain. He gonna slap it togeddah an slide home."

"We're screwed," Charlie said. He went to watch Reinhard working. Brody was squatting beside him, shining a flashlight, while Reinhard, lying on his side, reached into the axle tube trying to extricate the remaining sheared-off portion of the axle. He wiggled something inside and drew back, bringing out the axle end dripping with heavy oil.

Reinhard brought the jagged end under the light and turned it slowly, examining. Brody pointed to a small recess where the metal glinted whitely like powdered glass. Charlie

76

caught the word, "crystallized" and Reinhard saying something about someone buying it back or wearing it.

Tossing the axle end behind him, Reinhard stood up, wiping his hands. They continued their conversation in tones too low for Charlie to overhear, seeming to reach agreement on something near the end and then laughing together. Charlie had edged closer until Brody shone the light on him and he moved away, embarrassed.

Some of the Stan's racers had drifted down to watch and finally one of them moved forward to ask, "You guys going to race or what?"

Brody came over to join the Van de Kamp's racers. "Hell yes," he said. "We're ready. You ready?"

"Yeah. We're lined up," he pointed to Reinhard's Chevy, "He going to make it?"

"He's done," Brody said. "I'll race the Healey and the Vette." From behind the Chevy, where he was refitting the brake drum, Reinhard yelled, "Kick his ass Brody."

There was a hurried consultation among the Stan's racers and near immediate agreement, surprising Brody, who had stood nearby muttering "chickenshit." The boy in front spread his hands and said, "Sure. Sure thing."

The Stan's racers walked off. As Brody eased behind the wheel, Vaca handed him what was left of the last beer and asked, "You want to go for a side bet with the guy in the Vette?"

"Naw," Brody told him, "I don't want to push them too much, they might get antsy. The way it was set up, they don't really have to let us run. They're just figuring it's in the bag anyway, and there'll be less trouble about the pot if we run."

Watching the Stan's cars lining up, it suddenly hit Charlie that with Chavez and Reinhard sidelined, he would be racing. "Damn," he said and started to run.

He arrived, red faced and wheezing. Connie was sitting in the car. She looked at him quizzically as he leaned against the door. "Is that it?" she asked.

He grinned at her, between gasps, "... I'm racing."

77

When he was breathing easier, Charlie got the toolbox out of the trunk and slid under the car to unbolt the cutouts. Connie stood in front, kicking absently at his soles and watching. He pushed out when he was done and opened the hood, checked the water and oil and leaned in over the fender to remove the air cleaner from the carburetor. "Jesus," Connie said, "you're filthy." She brushed at the dirt and grease on his back, stopping when she looked at her hand. She wiped it on his pants as he straightened up, but Charlie never noticed. He tossed the air cleaner in the back seat and fired the Chevy up.

Arky was waving for him, looking irritated. The other car, a black 1959 El Camino with the tailgate down, was already waiting. Charlie took his time moving up, making sure the engine was warm. Arky's beckoning motions became more insistent.

When they were staged, Charlie watched Arky intently. His expression was sour, and his eyes showed impatience. Charlie eased the clutch out a fraction and rolled across the starting line by a foot. Arky's face tweaked with rage; he yelled something as he walked over. Pushing on the Chevy's hood, he rolled it back across the line, still yelling.

Arky turned as soon as he walked back to his spot and started blinking the flashlight at them. Three blinks for staged. Charlie anticipated a quick start and was right. A second after Arky had them staged, he blinked again for the start.

Charlie was already raising his foot from the clutch; the Chevy lifted nicely and surged forward, leaving the startled driver of the El Camino at the line.

Charlie wound it up in first, concentrating on the tach and the tightening sound of the engine. The shift was crisp, the exhaust note hardly broken. Charlie was insensible to everything but the tachometer needle and the noise. His feet and the hand on the shifter and the hand on the wheel were in motion or preparing for motion, without thought. Going into third, his best gear, he could feel the torque, the force, in the pit of his stomach and the small of his back.

He never saw the El Camino pass him. He was close to the finish, then past the finish, and for the first time he saw the taillights beside him. He had to look back to see the blinking flashlight in the other lane, to know he'd lost.

He couldn't feel bad. The start was good; he'd never shifted better. The car was running the best it had ever run. He patted the seat beside him and geared down, drifting to the side of the road as he braked. Charlie rolled in next to the El Camino, almost a quarter mile beyond the finish.

The other driver turned off his lights and got out, lighting a cigarette. The match revealed a turquoise blue tee shirt, a sweep of red hair above a high forehead, and pinched features that might have been caused by the smoke. Charlie left the engine running and got out. He pushed in the headlight switch, noticing for the first time his shaking hands.

"Damn good race," the other boy said.

"Yeah it was," said Charlie. The exhaust burbled fatly, flickering under the cars. "What're you running?" Charlie asked.

"348, tri-power."

Charlie stretched, feeling even better, "Mine's 283, punched thirty over to 301."

They turned as the flattening exhaust notes of the next pair of racers grew louder and watched them through the finish. The lights bobbed, coasting towards them.

"Jesus, it's dark out here," the El Camino driver said. Charlie looked up, noticing the surprising number of stars overhead for the first time. He couldn't remember ever seeing so many. They were almost down to the horizon around him. He suddenly felt tiny. There was an accompanying sensation; he now felt the chill of the night air on his arms, face, and the back of his neck. Two cars pulled in. Another pair were winding out behind them, closing in on the finish.

After Brody had demoralized the driver of the Austin Healey for the third time, there was a break and all the cars came back from the finish line to watch the race with the Stingray. Van de Kamp's led in the third round, five-four. The match was now even at fourteen and the draw.

Brody walked around the Vette while they were starting it, stopping once to drop to one knee and examine the undercarriage. He stood up and shrugged for Vaca, watching him through the Ford's back window. The Vette fired up and Brody jumped backward a half step. He took a long look at the car and walked back to the Ford.

In the Stingray, the driver was easing a helmet down past his ears. He buckled the chinstrap and put it in gear; the car shuddered forward to the line.

It sat there, rocking each time he revved it. Brody started the Ford and the crowd spread out around the starting line, holding their ears.

Arky went through his motions, looking from one driver to the other. Brody signaled O.K. with a circled thumb and forefinger. The driver of the Vette nodded. Vaca braced himself.

Arky went with a long count, seven or eight, before flashing the light. Brody popped the clutch; both their heads jerked backward and the Ford came out hard, the front end almost lifting. The Vette came out the same way, but moving more side to side; the wheel hop was more pronounced.

The Ford's lead was slight. It increased a little with the first shift. Brody powershifted, keeping his foot on the throttle while he slammed back into second. The Vette's driver shifted early, before the engine had peaked. It looked like he was fighting the wheel, and the early shift was to regain some control.

The margin stayed the same through second and third. In fourth, about the point that everyone sensed the Vette would begin pulling, there was a visible change. It looked like Brody had been holding back or suddenly found a little extra throttle. The Ford seemed to lift a little higher and surged away from the

Stingray. There was no question at the finish; the light on the Ford's side was blinking as it passed.

The Stan's people stared down the strip in disbelief. They gathered in quiet groups, apart from the Van de Kamp's celebraters, and awaited the Vette's return.

Brody had turned right around. The Ford came flying back, straight down the centerline. The last half he coasted, putting the clutch in and continually revving the engine. The Vette followed him back at a distance.

The crowd from Stan's surrounded the Vette. The driver jumped down and threw his helmet in back. He shook his head to the questions and began pulling the lockpins holding down the hood. One of the boys who'd helped him start it took a side of the hood and they lifted it and placed it on top of the car. The other was returning from the trailer, stooped over with the weight of a four-drawer tool chest.

Still ignoring the questioners, who were now retreating to watch, the driver began changing to smaller diameter pulleys to raise the blower's boost.

The final round began with Van de Kamp's leading 15-14. Charlie made it even, losing again to the El Camino. In the next race, the Stan's car sucked a valve halfway down. It backfired like a machine gun and coasted gently into the fence beside the road as the driver tried to put in the clutch, brake, shift into neutral, shut down the engine, and steer at the same time. Thereafter, all the luck seemed to ride with Van de Kamp's.

Willy Lum drove for the owner of a '55 Chevy that had lost three straight, by hood ornament margins, to the fishscale roadster. He took it cleanly, then was ferried back and won again in his own car. Brody beat the Austin Healey for the fourth time. The Healey driver made an easy pass, resigned, wishing only to save his engine, and the final race became meaningless to the match, with Van de Kamp's holding a 21-17 lead.

No one seemed to mind. For the Stingray owner, a win still meant a split with Brody, a two-one edge for the match, and bragging rights. The fastest car would be remembered.

The changes he'd made in the blower settings affected the sound of the Vette as it approached the line; it roared like the throttle was stuck, with a whistling, keening note.

Brody smiled, listening, and Vaca waved as Arky started the staging process. The Vette's driver kept his eyes locked on Arky. The flashlight's batteries had failed, and this time Arky started them with hand signals.

Arky closed and fanned his hands, instead of three blinks, then raised them overhead. Brody slowly raised the engine speed, until its pitch was even with the Vette's. Arky swept his arms down, turning sideways. Brody came out cleanly.

The Vette jumped, the front end lifting skyward. There was a clear foot between the front tires and the road. The wheelstand continued for three or four car lengths as the crowd scattered. The Vette touched down gradually, picking up speed, and seemed to dig in. The crowd was looking ahead, measuring Brody's lead, when the Vette's blower belt let loose, taking out a chunk of the hood and sailing beyond the fence into the gravel pit. The engine died with a "Whump".

Brody was already hitting the brakes as the Vette wheeled around in a wide U and coasted silently back toward the start line. Brody had his head out the window, watching. He put the Ford in reverse and began backing up, weaving as he came.

The Vette, aided by a tangled mob of volunteers, had been pushed almost to its trailer by the time the Ford parked at the starting line.

Brody turned the engine off and stepped out with a flourishing gesture for himself, for the car, and for the crowd. Walking over to where Arky stood holding the money, he sang at the top of his voice, "Whennn yoou lose your money, learn to lose." He accepted the money with another flourish and held it up facing the crowd.

"Glad you could all be here," Brody said, "I 'preciate you all coming. Nice letting you see me again." In the Ford, Vaca laughed with his head thrown back and clapped vigorously.

The crowd thinned as the Stan's people filtered back

toward their cars. The racers were coming back from the other end. Brody walked down the track to meet them, still holding the money aloft.

11-

On the freeway home, Charlie couldn't stop smiling to himself or fingering the shirt pocket that held his share of the pot, four twenties and two tens. He still couldn't feel bad about losing his two races; the car had simply been overmatched. The hundred would go toward a set of headers that might make a difference.

Connie was asleep, slumped with her head against the window. During the celebration following the races, she drank several beers, her teeth chattering, and when the wind came up she went back to the car.

Charlie had stayed until it broke up, savoring the closeness and good feeling among the racers. Races were rerun with much hand motion and embellishment. Charlie found himself describing in detail the way the other car had crept up on him, their margin at the finish, and the El Camino which was now a 409 with dual quads. His second race, lost by five car lengths, was not discussed.

A party, to be held at Cheryl's in a few weeks, was casually mentioned. Everyone else seemed to know about it. Charlie acted as though he did, without resentment, understanding that he was now included.

He ignored the cold, though he shivered with his hands jammed in his jacket pockets, knees and shoes pressed together, and hoped the others would ignore it also.

Around two, there were only eight left in the circle. The beer was gone and their breath misted when they talked. Someone stomped a can flat and sailed it towards the gravel pit. It hit the fence and fell back to the pavement with a clatter.

One of the bent-over, shivering figures said, "I'm afraid to look. I think my balls just broke off and fell down my pantleg. I'm going to go home and piss in a light socket to thaw out. I'll send someone by tomorrow to chip the rest of you assholes out." The group broke up, with much hawking and spitting, and there was a general movement toward the cars. Some walked slowly, huddled up; others sprinted, yelling as they went. Charlie walked back to his Chevy, turning as he walked to fix the spot as a memory. With the engine warming and the first blasts of air from the heater eddying around his feet, he sat rubbing his hands dreamily, thinking through the sequence.

There had only been one unpleasant occurrence the whole evening. Brody had given the money to Vaca to pass out. Vaca sat there, with the door open, handing it out like it was his.

Reinhard was the last to collect; at the end there had been two or three waiting, almost a line, and he'd stayed away until they were gone.

Then Vaca was left holding one last sheaf of bills, looking in Reinhard's direction. As Reinhard reached for his money, there was a tiny hesitation on Vaca's part, a little hitch as though he would hold it back, and he asked, "So when you going to run us?"

Reinhard snatched the money from him and for the first time in Charlie's experience, appeared to be genuinely angry. "You think you're ready for me?" Reinhard said. "Shit. This is the first time you've been on the street in three months."

"Two," Vaca said.

"Two months, three, I don't give a fuck. There's a few ahead of you. You've got to do a little racing first."

"We're ready for you now," Vaca said.

Reinhard was walking away; he turned and came back and leaned in close. "I'm through fucking with you Vaca. When I decide, you'll get a shot. When it happens, and it'll be soon, it'll be three out of five. And it'll cost you a grand."

Vaca appeared to draw back a little but he said, "You got it."

"I know it," said Reinhard, and walked off.

Then the beer arrived and the tension was gone. Brody sat atop a fence pole, kicking his feet against the chainlink, alternately singing and waiting for his echo to come back across the gravel pit for a chorus. "Bright lights," Brody sang, "...bright lights, Big city...big city. Went to my baby's head." The echo wasn't bad, Charlie thought.

The two a.m. traffic was light, an occasional truck, a Highway Patrolman who'd whipped by without looking and turned at the next exit. When they passed the San Val drive-in a few cars were climbing the onramp, a lowered '57 Ford with fogged windows and a station wagon with a playpen in back.

Connie was still asleep. Charlie drove, following his hood more than the road. He loved looking down that hood. It was the best feature of '57's, the one former owners always remembered. The Chevy was dented at one rear fender and there were rust spots along the rocker panels, but looking out over the hood, with its two perfectly proportioned tubular welts and the bullet shaped chrome ends with the small fins, he could feel the car was perfect.

Charlie reached to adjust the heater and cracked the wind wing. He moved his head to the restoring flow of cold air.

Tomorrow he could sleep in. After a late lunch, he would price headers. That was something to talk over with Brody. Charlie tripped the blinker and eased over two lanes, heading for the Riverside exit.

Jogged by the stop and turn, Connie stirred and woke, blinking. "What time is it?" she said. Charlie reached and pressed the button on the glove box. The little door kicked down. Connie found the watch, peered at it and frowned, "Jesus," she said, "I hope I had a good time." She lit a cigarette and considered Charlie.

"I'll write you a note," Charlie said. "You want the flat tire or a dead battery."

"Richie went to Vegas for the weekend."

"I'll take you all the way to your corner then."

Connie laughed. After most of her late nights, she walked the last few blocks so Richie couldn't get the license number.

Connie rolled her window down and held out the cigarette until the ash blew off. "You're still feeling pretty good."

"No complaints," Charlie said. He dug into his shirt pocket and held up the bills.

"Yeah, you showed me," Connie said. She stretched languorously, flicking her nails on the vinyl headliner. "I'm glad you guys won. You'd be crying if you lost your money."

"Nope. I'd still feel good. I couldn't have done any better than I did."

"No. It'd be different if they'd lost the bet. You'd blame yourself."

"I guess."

"It's true. You get too wrapped up in it. You take it too serious."

"What? Racing?"

"That. Your cars. I swear, I can tell how your car's running by looking at your face. If something's broken on it, you walk around like you're lost."

Charlie nearly missed the street that led to her house; he crossed over a lane and turned without signaling. He couldn't think of an answer.

"I know. Bitch, bitch, bitch," Connie said, "I just think there's more important things in life."

Charlie tried to think what they might be. It seemed unfair to him, being placed on the defensive over something that couldn't really be talked about. It was the life. You were in the life or you weren't. If you were, there was nothing to talk about; if you weren't, there was nothing to talk about. "I guess," Charlie said.

They reached her house. As she collected her things, he remembered that he'd planned to mention Cheryl's party. A slight resentment made him hold back, then regretting it, he thought about how he could introduce the subject.

88

There was a moment. She retrieved her purse from under the seat and turning back, she steadied herself. Her hand touched his shoulder. He almost reached for her. He thought she might have leaned toward him. For an instant, there seemed to be more weight on his shoulder. Then his door, already ajar as he'd planned to accompany her to the porch, nudged open and the dome light winked on.

The kiss was perfunctory, heads held forward, lips closed and the only things that touched. He watched her walk in. The porch light went off and he sat in the dark, thinking about how good he'd been feeling, just a little while before.

12-

At Cheryl's, the party had spread to the lawn and the street by the time Charlie arrived.

Charlie paused on the sidewalk, joining a small crowd looking into the open hood of a car parked on the grass strip between the sidewalk and the curb.

Two of the Orozco brothers, John and Ray, and their cousin, Rudy Camarillo, were sitting on the fenders. The car was a dumpy pale yellow '56 Chevy, with a broken leafspring that tilted it to one side. The engine was immaculate. It was jointly owned by the trio, built during two years of auto shop. They specialized in sleepers. When one of their cars became well known, they would acquire a new hulk and install their engine.

Sitting across from John and Ray was Donny Calcagno, a shortlegged tubby boy, with thin frizzy hair and a badly pockmarked face, partially covered by mutton chop sideburns.

Listening to the bantering conversation, Charlie surmised he was coming in on the end of a chop fest. Donny was saying, "Yeah, Esse, this is a fine car." He looked around, nodding, including the crowd, "Got all them fine options, even gots a special lubrication system so they don't have to use a grease gun." Donny paused for effect. "Every six thousand miles, they drive over one of their cousins. Lots of Vaseline on those boys."

Someone said, "Oooh, down to the ground," and the crowd sucked in a little. The mention of family was rare and usually a last resort.

Rudy snapped out of what had seemed an intense yawn

and stretch. "Hey, that's alright Scarface," he said. "At least nobody hit me with a bag of nickels."

Ray leaned in, "No, man, that's not what happened. Tell the truth, Donny. I heard someone set your face on fire and put it out with a ice-pick."

"Yeah," Rudy said, "and the other thing I heard, I heard you fell down in the middle of a track meet, an' all them guys got to you with them spike shoes."

Making an attempt at profound indifference, Donny was considering his nails, but his face was beginning to redden. He sensed the crowd was not with him. John, who had tried to interrupt from the beginning, had their attention.

John was going, "Hey, hey, no, I know. I got the true story. ¡Digame! You know how he got all them holes in his face?"

Rudy slowly turned to him. "You'll have to tell me, Cuz." His cadence was assured and delighted, like a preacher finding his rhythm. "How did he get those ugly holes in his face?"

John shouted, "It was when he was learning to eat with a fork!"

The crowd exploded with hooting laughter. John repeated the line. Donny attempted a reply but couldn't make himself heard. His face and ears bloomed red. He boosted himself off the fender and backed away, throwing up the finger in all directions.

A mock soprano voice responded, "See you later, 'Chopper Don'."

It was a nickname he had once unsuccessfully promoted for himself. Donny whirled and fled into the house.

When he stopped laughing, Charlie moved over next to Ray. "¿Que paso?" Charlie said.

"Nada, y pues nada, y nada mas. You want a beer?"

"Sure," Charlie said. "You seen Brody?"

"Yeah," Ray told him. "He's inside someplace. You'll probably trip over him, man, he's all fucked up."

Charlie pulled a can out of the sixpack sitting on the air cleaner. "Thanks. I'll see you when I come up for air."

"Orale pues," Ray said.

Charlie started up the walk. Every window in the stucco duplex was lit and filled with silhouettes. The doorway and hall were jammed. He squeezed past an arguing couple; she had one arm in her coat sleeve, her boyfriend had wrapped the other sleeve around his hand and was trying to pull her backward.

Just inside the entryway, Charlie was confronted by a small, drunken uniformed sailor with sandy red hair and a mass of boils on his neck. The sailor was reaching out to shake hands with everyone entering or leaving.

"I'm really glad you could come," he told Charlie. "Really good you could make it. I'm Tex. What's your name?"

Charlie, trying to see past him, avoided his hand. The sailor was insistent. "Say, how the hell are you? My name's Tex."

Charlie shook his hand briefly, "Glad to know you Tex," and pushed on by.

The sailor followed, trying to shake hands from behind. "Say, I didn't catch your name," he said.

Saint and a blonde couple in matching white sweaters were standing in the hallway. Charlie jerked a thumb in the general direction of the sailor, "Who the fuck is this guy?"

"He's supposed to be Cheryl's cousin," Saint said.

Charlie stepped to one side. "Tex," he said, "I'd like you to meet Saint. Saint's been looking all over for you." The sailor stepped forward, offering his hand, and Charlie sidled into the living room.

The room was so packed he couldn't see the faces of the people seated on the couches and chairs along the wall. The only open space was in the center, where the start of a beer can pyramid reached waist height.

The stereo was playing the garbled voices of Huey "Piano" Smith and the Clowns on their biggest record, *Don't You Just Know It*. The bass was set so loud it fuzzed over even Huey's crashing piano chords.

After adding his can to the pyramid, Charlie bumped back through the crowd. He found his way blocked at the kitchen, where a knot had formed, waiting for ice.

Looking for a way in, he noticed Donna. She was seated in a folding chair next to the doorway. He didn't recognize her at first. Her hair was done differently, rolled and tucked up in back, showing her neck. She was wearing a beige suit and lace front blouse. Charlie stood there for a moment, admiring her legs, before he realized who she was. It was the first time he'd seen her out of uniform.

She raised her punch cup towards him and smiled, "Hi Charlie."

"Hi Donna, I didn't recognize you. You really look nice."

"Thanks a lot," Donna said, "I think."

"Yeah, I really like your hair that way. What do they call that?"

"This? It's sort of a chignon."

"Oh. Well it looks really nice. I guess you can't wear it like that at work."

"No," she said. "It wouldn't fit under a net."

Charlie asked if she had been here long. "Since about eight," she said. He asked if she'd seen Brody. No, she hadn't, not for several hours. Charlie nodded; their conversation was running down. He was impressed; he wished he could say something charming but the noise around them precluded all but the simplest conversation. He noticed her cup was empty and offered to bring more punch. "If you can find it. I said, if you can find it," Donna told him, "They've got the bowl on the other side."

"Don't go away," Charlie said. He started pushing through the crowd, holding the glass cup aloft.

The party took up both sides of the duplex. Cheryl's neighbors had been evicted the previous week. Some of the early arrivers had broken down the boarded-up doors between the apartments.

94

The punch bowl was set up on a draped card table in the other living room. Someone handed Charlie the ladle. He dipped and filled Donna's cup and a highball glass for himself. The punch was purple, with floating orange sections and maraschino cherries bumping around the bottom. Charlie lifted out two cherries and added them to their drinks.

The punch seemed to have grape Kool-Aid for a base. Charlie could detect rum and a slight aftertaste of mint, probably peppermint schnapps, probably Cheryl's, he thought. She liked schnapps because everyone at work assumed it was breath mints they smelled.

"Not too bad," Charlie decided, and filled his glass again.

In the other living room, Brody slumped contentedly in the armchair he'd claimed several hours before. He had seen Charlie when he came in but hadn't felt much like talking.

Brody was comfortably drunk and planned to get drunker.

The remains of two sixpacks were strewn around the chair. The third was half gone, stacked on top of the fourth he planned to finish.

Brody and Vaca had arrived early, so Vaca could get comfortable. The wheelchair was hidden before any of the other guests arrived. Brody had helped Cheryl put out bowls of chips and crackers and had mixed the punch, stirring and testing it with a straw until Cheryl caught him.

Vaca, in the next room, was talking loudly to Brody, going on about Reinhard, cocky and full of himself. What they were going to do to Reinhard and how sick Reinhard would look when he'd been beaten.

Cheryl carrying a tray of glasses in from the kitchen,

caught the end of the conversation. "Reinhard?" she said, "Oh yeah, that was a bad bust."

Brody looked up questioningly from the punch bowl.

Cheryl stared back at him, "Wasn't that who you were talking about? Reinhard?"

"What'd you say before?" Brody asked.

"Where've you been. It's all over the drive-in. He's in sixty days for non-support."

"Whaaat?"

"Yeah. His ex got pissed off 'cause he showed up to pick up the kids with a brand new set of polished mags on that Chevy of his. She says about three hundred bucks worth, and he hadn't made an alimony payment in two months. She got on the phone to her lawyer and that was that. Thursday morning they came and got him."

Brody made shushing motions with his hands and listened. He noticed that the other room was quiet. "Vaca?" he said.

"He's down at County," Cheryl finished.

Vaca had his head resting on the back of the sofa, looking straight at the ceiling, if his eyes had been open, and was laughing softly. He lowered his head as Brody approached. His eyes snapped open. "That asshole," he said.

Brody sat down on the couch. Vaca wouldn't look at him. "Get away from me, man, I don't want to talk about it." Brody started to say something and Vaca cut him off with a hissing noise.

"There's nothing to talk about, there's not a fucking thing we can do. Just leave it alone." Brody stood up and Vaca tilted his head back again. He kept his eyes closed until Brody left.

Cheryl peeked around the doorway when Brody came back. "What gave him the red ass?"

"He's been waiting a long time," Brody said.

"So? It's only sixty days. He just has to wait a little longer."

"Yeah."

Brody made a beer run and when he got back the party

was rolling. Vaca shared the couch with Cheryl and two older guys who sold supplies to the drive-in. He seemed to be alright. Drinking steadily and still keeping his eyes shut most of the time, but alright.

Brody started on his beer and forgot Vaca for a while.

Some time later, on his way to the bathroom, he passed the couch and felt his arm gripped. Vaca leered up at him, "The bastard is ducking us. He knew." Brody pulled his arm away. "He knew."

Brody jiggled in his chair, bouncing in rhythm and slapping the sides, to the first booming piano notes of one of his favorite songs, *Big Boy Pete* by the Olympics.

"The Joint was a jumpin' on the corner," the Olympics sang, "Down on a Honky Tonk street/ When all of a sudden/ Up pulls a Cadillac/ An' out steps a cat named Pete."

The news about Reinhard didn't bother him too much, now that he'd absorbed it. There were some other people he'd like to race and two months wasn't that long. Mainly, he thought, it boiled down to what he would have to put up with from Vaca.

Brody dismissed the subject and rejoined the Olympics. "Walkin' on a through the doorway, aye yeah/ Right at the people's feet/ He pulled out a pistol/ He turned around/ He said mah name is a Big Boy Pete."

As the record ended, Brody dug around the sides of the armchair and retrieved his can opener. He lifted a beer up and opened it. In the pause, as the record changer made its moves, Brody raised the can to the people around him. "And remember, boys and girls," he said, "Blotto, our motto."

Charlie stood in back of the card table, ladling punch into a double row of paper cups. About half the liquid made the cups.

He had stayed for a third glass, an hour ago, talking to Ray Orozco. Some time after that, Donna's cup had been knocked to the floor. He had to sweep it up and then the shaky leg on the card table had folded. He'd been holding the punch bowl, glorying in his reflexes, when Cheryl slammed in, screeching about crystal. She'd made him responsible for her heirloom and made him mix a new batch of punch. Donna had been forgotten.

After mixing the punch, a long, judicious process that involved much sampling, he acted as bartender. A small crowd had congregated around the table. Ray and Saint were telling stories. When they ran down a little, they prompted Charlie to tell his most recent, an embellished account of his and Brody's adventure the previous month at a local junkyard.

Looking up, after another pass over the cups, he discovered his audience had tripled. He started over, for the benefit of the latecomers.

"You all know the Broken Drum junkyard on San Fernando? He's got a big sign out front, says 'Broken Drum/Can't be beat!'

"So," said Charlie, "We were going by there on a Tuesday, just cruising, and Brody slams on the brakes. I damn near mashed my nose all over the windshield.

"They were towing in a brand new Corvette, brand new, and the sucker's totaled. Brody's eyes get big. He says, 'Know whose that is? That's Burchmore's new Vette.'

"'Too bad for Burchmore', I said.

"Brody says, 'I know for a fact that's got the new fuel injection setup on it.' I swear he was drooling.

"Sooo, we come back that night. Walked around to the side yard where they put it and Brody started looking for the dog. The owner there has a German Shepherd. It's supposed to be an Army dog, big bastard and meaner than sin.

"Brody shook the fence and you could hear him running. You wouldn't believe how fast he got there. He's big as a pony and all covered with grease and shit from sleeping under the cars. It was weird, the whole time he was coming for us he didn't even bark.

"Then he hit the fence and went crazy. It was a chain link and he bulged it out about a foot trying to get at Brody, snapping and frothing, just nuts.

"Brody stepped back a little, casual as you please, and then he sails this piece of meat over the fence. The dog wouldn't pay any attention to it at first, but finally he goes up and sniffs it. It's got rat poison on it, right?

"He sniffs at it and pushed it with his nose, but he won't eat it. We waited at least a half-hour. Every so often he'd come over and snarl at Brody and then go back and paw at the meat some more, but he wouldn't eat it.

"Finally, Brody says, ' fuck it.' He figured it must be the Army training the dog got and we get ready to leave. Then, he starts worrying about the meat. He thought if the old man that owns the place finds it, he'll know someone's trying to burn him. So nothing's gonna do but Brody has to get the meat out of there.

"He found about a ten foot stick. When he goes to put it through the fence, the dog really goes bizarro, chewing on it and breaking it up. I don't think he wanted Brody to have the meat either.

"After a few minutes of this, he's got about four feet of stick left but he finally gets the meat close enough to flip it back over, while I'm pretending to climb the fence at the other end.

"Cracked me up, he made me drive home so he can pick the splinters out of his hands, swearing the whole time. He was really pissed at that dog. You could see him scheming, trying to figure a way around him."

Charlie paused to refill his glass. "Yeah? So what happened?" someone said.

Charlie continued dipping; his movements were deliberate. He no longer felt fuzzy from the punch. There was only a glow, and the anticipatory pleasure he felt from his waiting audience.

Vaca dropped the empty pint bottle behind the couch. It bounced noiselessly on the carpet and he wished he'd thrown it at the wall.

The rest of the couch was empty. Cheryl and her suitors had been driven off by his rudeness and needling comments. The couple that took their place left after listening to a short monologue on the worthlessness of everyone present. They had laughed at first and then realized he was including them and getting increasingly particular.

Several times during the last few hours, he'd given money to people for liquor. One had returned. Vaca opened the fresh pint and threw the cap away. He steadied the bottle between slack thighs with one hand and rubbed his eyelids with a thumb and forefinger. His eyes burned from the smoke.

A voice beside him asked for the second time, "Can I sit down here?"

Vaca opened his eyes. A thin, long-nosed girl wearing an unflattering sleeveless dress stood in front of him. Her face was red and shiny and she held her beer can at a careless angle.

She repeated her question.

"I don't give a damn," Vaca said. "Sit on my face if you want to. Free couch. Free country." He closed his eyes again and was surprised to feel the cushion bulging beside him as she settled. Her perfume reminded him of a hair pomade he'd used once, Trés Flores.

"You're Vaca, aren't you?" Vaca didn't say anything. "You don't know me, I'm Connie Ciccarelli." Vaca heard a crackle of cellophane and the pop of a match. He pinched his eyes tighter as the smoke reached him. "You went to school with my brother, Richie."

"Richie Ciccarelli?" Vaca said. "Yeah. He's a punk."

He heard her cough and take another drag on her cigarette. She seemed to be blowing the smoke towards him.

"Yeah," Connie said, "he is."

Vaca squinted at her. She was flicking ashes all over the couch and smiling at him steadily.

Vaca laughed a humorless single exclamation and lifted his bottle, "Here's to your family." She raised her beer in return.

Charlie was saying, "So Brody thought it over for a couple days. He really had the hots for that injector setup, you can't find them for less than three bills, so Friday we went back."

Charlie's manner was assured. His gestures were sweeping and confident. His voice, to his ear, was deeper, reminding him of times he went to church. His voice always felt an octave lower by the time mass was over.

"Same thing as before, Brody shakes the fence and the dog comes tearing out. Only this time, Brody's brought along a Collie bitch that he picked up at the pound, and he's backed her up to the fence. You got it, she's in heat. Brody made sure before he got her. That Shepherd stopped, just dead, and then kind of sidles along the fence, whining and sniffing around.

"Now that Brody's got his attention, he waits a little while and then lifts the Collie up and shoves her over the fence. She made a little run for it but the Shepherd was right behind her and bit her on the neck until she settled down.

"The bastard acted like a puppy, frisking around and making little barks. Then he figured out what he was supposed to do. We watched them for a while. Brody figured it must have been his first piece because he'd been in the Army and locked up since.

"So Brody jumps the fence and the Shepherd never looked up. He made a big circle around them and disappeared.

"About ten minutes later he comes back, the Shepherd's still going at it and doesn't even notice. 'I found the Vette,' he says. 'Jesus Christ,' I tell him, 'you'd better hurry up.' Brody says, 'It's all set except I need a three-eighths socket. I dropped the sonuvabitch and can't find it.' So I ran back to the car and got one and he disappears again.

"He's gone about twenty minutes this time and I notice the

101

dogs have stopped. They're just laying there side by side but God knows what'll happen when Brody gets back. I'm just about ready to whistle when I see Brody coming out from behind some cars. He's got the injection unit in one hand and a pipe in the other.

"I point to where the dogs are and he nods and starts tiptoeing over to the fence. The Shepherd lifts his head up off his paws and he looks at Brody but he's cool. He puts his head down again, kinda sighs.

"Brody reaches the fence and hands the injection unit over. He's giggling like a madman. ' Like a charm,' he tells me. ' Like a fucking charm,' and about then I see the Collie has gotten up and she's walking toward him, and right behind her, just mooning along and sniffing her tail, is the Shepherd.

"'Move slow Brody,' I tell him and he freezes. The Collie is looking up at him and whining. She wants to go. Brody's got one hand hooked in the fence, but he's afraid to pull himself up. The Shepherd moves in next to him and nudges his head at the pipe and Brody drops it like it's on fire. Then he nudges Brody's hand, like a cat does, so Brody reaches down and scratches his head. Man, you should've seen his hand shake, but that was all the dog wanted.

"Brody scratchs his ears and the dog wags his tail a few times and sits down. Brody figures he can go now, so he gives him one final pat and then rubs the Collie too. As soon as he touches her, that Shepherd gets up again and lets out the wickedest fucking growl you ever heard. He showed about six inches of teeth. It looked like a piano out there in the dark. Brody snatches his hand away and he's over the fence before the bastard starts barking. You would've thought he was pole vaulting.

"We beat it back to the car, Brody's still giggling like crazy. All the way home he was cracking up, wondering what the hell the guy that owned the junkyard would say when he sees the Collie in the morning and tries to figure out how she jumped a nine-foot fence.

"Then, we're home. He's pounding on the steering wheel, laughing like hell, and tells me, 'Jeezus Charlie, can you imagine what's going to happen if he tries to take her away from him.' We damn near died.

"Crazy night. The old bag next door finally came out and yelled at us to shut up. I'm still tempted to go back over there, just to see if the owner's got a cast on.

"Brody got two bills for it, next day, from some kid in Bell Gardens." Charlie sipped his punch. He looked at his audience with a joyous smirk. "You guys should have seen it. I wish you could've been there."

Brody was nearly asleep. Two cans remained of the last sixpack, but he felt too comfortable to open a fresh one. He breathed gently through his mouth; a cigarette with an inch long ash glowed between his fingers.

The room was almost dark. A dim blue light by the record player hazily outlined the nearest barely moving couples. They'd played nothing but slow songs for some time. *Summer Place,* over and over again, what seemed like several dozen records by The Platters, all hits and all at the same dreamy tempo, and a few by Ivory Joe Hunter.

One of these was playing now. Brody listened to Ivory Joe's gentle, sad voice. He belched and sighed deeply.

"Since I met you baby/ My whole life has changed/ Since I met you baby/ My whole life has changed/ And everybody tells me/ That I am not the same..."

Brody watched a couple near the blue light, heads bowed on each other's shoulders, hands stroking on the back facing him. He dropped his cigarette in the beer can and smiled, feeling foolish and pleased with himself and finally, as he closed his eyes, a sweet sadness he identified as contentment.

Charlie wandered from room to room, stopping to look into dark doorways and to peer at the faces of dancing and embracing couples.

Halfway through what had suddenly become a pointless story, he had realized that the punch had caught up to him and that his audience had been slipping away. Charlie had focused on what remained of the group - two teenaged boys who had nodded dully at every pause and the bored date of one of them, a plump girl in knee length jeans and a sweat shirt, concentrating on her chewing gum - and he stopped in mid-sentence.

Walking away, he'd remembered Donna. He returned to the chair near the kitchen, but she was gone. He started walking through the house, trying to find her.

The kitchen was empty. The refrigerator door hung open, stopped by a pile of icetrays on the wet floor. Someone had fried up bacon and eggs, using an electric skillet over a gas burner. The plastic legs were melted onto the stove.

The party was fragmenting, breaking up into separate parties throughout the house.

Charlie paused in a doorway. Connie Ciccarelli was sitting on the couch, talking animatedly to Vaca. She was using a beer can held between her knees for an ashtray. Her dress was covered with ashes and beer spots.

Charlie's throat constricted as he watched her. Her face was flushed, and her hands moved constantly as she talked. He thought momentarily of walking in and guiding her away someplace so they could talk, but he knew she would resist, probably loudly and with sarcasm. His throat tightened again. He backed out of the doorway and went the other way.

Saint was acting as bartender at the punch bowl. Absently, he dipped a glass in the bowl for Charlie, listening to a girl seated next to him. The girl, a wispy brunette, perhaps eighteen years old, with tight ring curls surrounding a pretty oval face, was leaning towards Saint with her elbows on the card table.

She was saying, "I gave him more love than any man

deserves..." She paused, losing her train of thought. She stared at Saint intently, as though he knew what should come next. Saint stared back blearily, until she regained her focus and spoke with renewed enthusiasm. "More love than any man deserves!" She paused again, this time for effect, "For two whole months!" She held out her cup for a refill. "And then he goes and does that to me. I just don't feel he showed me much consideration."

"No," Saint agreed; he squinted at her. "That's not. That doesn't seem like much consideration. I guess he just didn't appreciate what he had."

"Damn rights!" She straightened up proudly, spilling her punch.

Charlie dipped his cup and walked away. He nearly tripped on the carpet coming into Cheryl's side of the house but kept going, leaning forward.

Connie and Vaca were gone. Cheryl was sitting on the lap of one of the salesmen with her hand inside his coat. The other sprawled at the end of the couch, holding his necktie up in front of his face, staring at the shiny fabric with interest.

Charlie tossed off his punch with much head and arm motion and regretted the gesture instantly. He stared stupidly at the people on the couch waiting to see if his stomach would settle. He belched tentatively, relieved when it came up air, and stumbled off. He felt he had to stay in motion.

Bumping off walls, around furniture, and through doorways, he made his way to the front porch. He stood there, breathing deeply, carefully, through his mouth. His vision, when he didn't concentrate, was doubled. Closing his eyes made him rock back on his heels.

Walking made him feel better. He kept at it, walking a bowed square around the lawn, ignoring an urge to lie down on the wet grass. His feet flopped ahead of him, feeling disconnected, and he stubbed his toes on the sprinklers. He kept going until he started to sweat. He stopped to light a cigarette and continued at a slower pace, shivering.

The cold and an overwhelming need to urinate drove him back into the house.

He found the bathroom after a hurried search and crashed through the door, almost falling into the shower stall. He turned the light on and stared, blinking at the muzzy face in the mirror, before sidestepping over to the toilet. He struggled with his zipper and finally used both hands, banging a shoulder against the wall. His pants around his knees, he relieved himself with a groaning sigh.

He raised his zipper cautiously, sucking up his belly and peering down, concentrating. Reaching to flush, he stopped, listening. There was a regular thwacking noise coming from beyond the other bathroom door, leading to Cheryl's bedroom.

He put his ear to it. There was the heavy slap of a hand somewhere soft. Then a voice, Vaca's voice. "Move," was the only word Charlie caught.

He flicked off the bathroom light and lowered himself to his hands and knees. Slipping the lock, he eased the door open and moved his head into the bedroom.

In the faint light from the window behind them they were softly profiled. Vaca was on his back with his lower legs dangling over the end of the bed. Connie was straddling him. Her dress was rolled down off her shoulders, bunched around her waist. Her small breasts bobbled a little each time she shifted.

Vaca's legs were swinging weightlessly. His heavy shoes hit the bedframe each time Connie moved back. His hands were stretched out, reaching for her shoulders.

Connie threw her head back. Charlie heard a low, recurring sound from deep in her throat. She reached behind her, slipping her hands under Vaca's legs and strained, pulling herself down and tighter, moving frantically until she shuddered, her shoulder wings twitching, and collapsed, pitching forward onto Vaca's chest.

Charlie backed away when she started to cry. As he slowly closed the door, his field of vision narrowed until he could see only a corner of the bed, then just the bedpost, and for the first time he noticed the peach-colored panties hanging on the knob. He stared at them, knowing it was what he would always see when he thought of her. The door latch snapped noisily but he didn't care. He felt like crying himself, flooded with loneliness and self-pity.

He stumbled out of the bathroom and made his way to the living room, walking with an outstretched hand against the wall.

Only two dancing couples remained, shuffling slowly, out of time, to a Rolling Stones' song, *Lady Jane*. Other couples were crushed together on the couches and chairs around the room.

Charlie found a whiskey bottle with a few swallows left, lying on its side on an end table. He carried the bottle with him out the front door, dangling it loosely by the neck.

Standing on the lawn, he looked up at the house and raised the whiskey. He swallowed, coughing as the last few drops burned down. He sailed the bottle into the street and it burst with a satisfying crash.

Charlie felt some irretrievable loss had occurred. He concluded, with pleasurable sorrow that some part of his youth was now sealed off. There was a melancholy sense that he would no longer be so open and trusting. He wondered if this would harden into cynicism, deciding solemnly that it would probably be for the best.

The whiskey was reviving the worst effects of the punch. He sat down heavily on the lawn and fell over on his side. He rubbed his cheek and arm against the cool wet grass. The clean smell soothed him as he closed his eyes and curled tighter. He drifted into what he thought was sleep.

He awoke from an unsettling dream filled with spinning lights, crying out as someone tugged at his arm, trying to turn him. He pulled away violently.

Donna looked down at him with worried eyes. "Are you alright?"

Charlie sat up, nodding dumbly.

She reached for his hand, "Come on. Let's get you on your feet." Charlie struggled up and immediately fell over. The leg he'd been lying on was asleep.

She helped him up again. "Leg's asleep," he said.

"You'll have to walk it off. Lean on me."

They walked to the corner and back, his foot dragging and scuffing until the circulation came back.

"Feeling better?"

Charlie nodded, eyes closed.

"Let's get you some coffee then."

They drove with the windows down and Charlie held his head into the wind. Donna pulled into O-Boy's on Glendale Avenue, a small hamburger stand with a black and white concrete cow on its flat roof.

Theirs was the only car on the lot. In one corner was a searchlight on a trailer with flat tires. The restaurant's owner ran the searchlight all night, every night, attracting disappointed carloads of kids who sometimes stayed to eat and watch the machine.

Charlie pulled himself out of the car, shading his eyes as the white flare rolled in his direction. The driving generator was laboring, a hollow pounding sound, and the heavy gear wheels turning the lamp grated on every tooth.

Donna was waiting at the order window. Charlie sat down at the first table he came to in the open patio fronting the building. He slumped forward, leaning his head against the metal umbrella pole coming up through the center of the table.

Donna carried a tray over, lining up five cups of coffee in front of Charlie and one for herself.

He scalded his tongue with the first mouthful and sipped after that. He crushed the cup and picked up another. The coffee steamed in the cold air, cooling rapidly. He swallowed half of it and sat up straighter, convinced the worst was over. *I'll be hurting tomorrow,* he told himself, *but I'm not going to get sick tonight.* It seemed like a victory.

He swallowed some more and considered Donna over the rim of his cup. She was watching him.

"I think I'll be alright," Charlie said. "Yeah, and I really appreciate you helping me out. I still owe you a cup of punch." Charlie was feeling better by the moment, nearly giddy. Before, he'd been sure that he would get sick in front of her and it had subdued him.

"Yeah. You do. And five coffees. Did you want something to eat? I'm going to get another cup." Charlie told her no, not yet. He watched her walking to the counter and thought about what might happen.

She bent to talk through the screened serving window and he studied the gradual rise of her skirt, his gaze lingering on the dimples in back of her knees, the heft of her calves and thighs, the white lacy line of her blouse and a smaller line of skin, exposed as her suit jacket rode up.

What was wrong with her ex-husband, he wondered, *Lord, she had a nice ass.* She sat down again and he was prepared to ask if she would drive him home.

With what he thought was casual grace, he reached for his third cup of coffee. His fingers brushed it before it was in his grasp and the cup tipped. Lunging to catch it, he knocked over the other two and watched, stricken, as the coffee pooled and ran into Donna's lap.

"Oh shit," she said, and slid over on the bench, dabbing at her skirt with a handful of sopping napkins. She stood up brushing at her front and went to get more napkins. Charlie put his head in his hands.

He wouldn't blame her if she left, just drove off. In a way he hoped she would. He had an urge to bang his head on the table, but somewhere inside he was already sneering at the gesture as self-serving.

The caustic edge of his anger was directed inward for himself, for his unfounded confidence. Arrogance, he decided. Connie had something to do with it he knew, but in the contemptuous mood he was in, he refused to accept that as an excuse. Atonement was not possible. He couldn't remember feeling lower. Tears were dripping from his nose to his hands. He looked at them bitterly, unaware until now that he'd been crying. He scrubbed at his face, angered at what he felt was another sign of self-indulgence.

He discovered he was still crying and tipped his head back, as though it were a nosebleed. He rubbed his eyes, blinked and finally noticed Donna sitting quietly, watching him. He put his head down again.

Donna reached across and brushed his hair back over his ears. "It had to go to the cleaners anyway. Really. Charlie?"

Charlie restrained a bitter laugh, staying resolvedly silent and miserable, but as she continued stroking his head he was soothed and then overwhelmed by what he perceived as unaffected kindness.

He caught her hand and held it against his cheek. Charlie's voice was low and fiercely emotional. "You're so good to me."

Donna smiled wanly. She looked tired. Her chignon was loosening and the hair was slipping down her neck. Charlie stared down at the cardboard cups stirring with the light wind and the initials, names, and messages carved in the heavy wood table. None were recent; a thick coat of dark green paint covered them all.

He pressed her hand tighter against his cheek. "No one's ever been so good to me."

The trundling spotlight in the parking lot groaned like a carnival ride. The column of light rolled, probing the flat yellow-grey underside of a seamless bank of clouds and haze.

13-

Kenny, the night manager at Van de Kamp's, called Cheryl and asked her to give him a few weeks warning the next time she planned on a party. Half of his crew - Cheryl, Donna, two other carhops, one of the cooks and two busboys - had called in sick.

One of Cheryl's salesmen brought a dozen roses by that night. Kenny deep fried them and stood them up in her locker.

Cheryl missed the next night as well, but Donna and the rest returned and enjoyed a slow night because of rain.

Charlie brought flowers also, Shasta daisies tinted red, blue and green, with further apologies that Donna cheerfully dismissed. She accepted his offer to pay the cleaning bill, after some argument, to make him feel better.

It stayed slow and the rain curtained the cars from the kitchen so Donna was able to sit in Charlie's Chevy, sharing coffee and talking, between customers. Before leaving, he hesitantly invited her to a movie, and she accepted. "You sure?" Charlie said.

Donna replied, "Sure. Saturday? Sure."

Charlie departed in an ebullient mood, broken only by a momentary uncertainty as he considered what now, should be the proper amount for her tip.

It took Brody a day to rebound also. He sat at his house, a notch roofed imitation adobe opposite the train yards, and watched the switch engines and slowly passing freights, preferring their slow rocking to television and the frantic motion of the cartoons. He went out, once, for aspirin and milkshakes.

Vaca stayed home. It was a hard time for him. Brody had talked about getting some races but Vaca wasn't that interested; he considered parking the Ford for the next two months, just waiting until Reinhard got out, avoiding the risk of breaking something, in races he couldn't care about.

From Connie, Vaca had heard nothing. Following the party, he'd anticipated at least a call and had answered the phone warily, waiting for the caller to speak before responding, but only Brody and a man offering to demonstrate a home care product whose name he could not reveal over the phone, called that week.

Vaca was relieved when the first week passed and there seemed to be no obligation. Then he got pissed because she didn't call.

Sex for Vaca wasn't complicated. Mostly it was blowjobs, bought in Hollywood. His regular was a skeletal junkie called Laurel who commanded a premium because her top teeth had been knocked out.

Vaca had run into a few freaks over the years, women who preferred him paralyzed, but he treated them like hookers and they didn't last. He didn't know if Connie was a freak. Sex with her had been frantic, almost desperate, but the situation was complicated because she knew him and knew that he had money. What Vaca had particularly liked about their encounter was that he hadn't paid for it. He'd gotten away with it and avoiding her phone calls was part of the package, a victory ruined by the fact that she had not called.

He considered calling her, considered not calling her. Finally, without any idea what he would say, he dialed her number, but her father or brother answered and Vaca hung up without speaking.

It had been a short penance. Three Hail Marys and an Our Father. Connie rose easily without touching the altar rail. She adjusted her mantilla, fiddling with the bobby pins for a moment, and genuflected.

Someone opened one of the vestibule doors and the votive candles behind her flickered in the dimness. She turned to regard the candles, ten stepped rows of them on a wrought iron table, in front of the first pews.

They still reminded her of bleachers - the unlit candles, empty seats. She picked up one of the long waxed wicks from the tray beside the coin box and dipped it to a lighted candle. She carried the flame to a candle on a lower rank that was half burned, but out. She patiently melted the wax, burying its wick. The flame caught and swayed steadily. Sputtering, the wick bent in the middle and went out. She put it down in the sand and selected a new one.

"Father," she'd planned to say, "my life's a mess," but when the shutter slid back, she caught the scent of aftershave and knew it was Father Galvin, the younger priest.

So instead she slipped into the responses. "Bless me Father, for I have sinned," then paused long enough that he asked, "And how long has it been since your last good confession?"

She gave up. "It's been two weeks since my last confession," she'd said, and the rest of the lies came easily.

The priest listened silently, interjecting only once, when she had admitted entertaining impure thoughts. "How many times?" he asked. "Twice, Father," she told him.

He'd given the easy penance and suggested she pray to Saint Maria Goretti should impure thoughts present themselves again.

Facing the candles, Connie tried to remember the recommended saint. The name was familiar. A virgin and martyr, as Connie recalled, and the two facts were somehow related. Her mother would probably know.

Christ, Connie thought, *Who can you talk to?* She held the wick up and watched the flame. *Cheryl, maybe, except she had*

113

such a big mouth. Or Charlie. Except it would kill him. There was no one, really.

Even if it had been the Monsignor, instead of the younger priest, she knew she probably would have done the same thing. Coming in, walking up the steps of the church, she'd sensed her visit was a mistake. Unexplainable. A vague and contradictory longing for a stability, an order and constancy she had not believed in since around the sixth grade, the time of her last honest confession.

She wondered if Saint Maria Goretti would understand or accept a prayer that began: "If you let me get away with this one, I promise I'll never fuck around again."

Absently, Connie had continued to fill in the gaps in the bottom row of candles, until the whole rank was lit. The flames wavered and swelled; they seemed to burn higher than the candles in the partially lit rows. She smiled. At the altar rail, one of the old women that haunted the church was turning to stare at her. She watched Connie, fingering her rosary and muttering.

Connie stared back, setting her jaw, and lit a new wick from the stub of the old. She worked quickly, across and down, lighting every candle. She began to feel the heat, and the glow was becoming almost cheerful, illuminating the first rows of pews and the small side altar.

The woman at the altar rail stood up. "You. Girl..." she hissed.

Connie looked at the flames and waved the lighting wick until it went out. She placed it carefully on the sand tray as the woman advanced. "You, girl..." she said again.

"Make a wish," Connie told her and headed for the side door.

14-

Charlie sat on the edge of the sofa regarding his hands. There were several faint half moons of grease around his cuticles that had not been apparent when he'd inspected them under the dome light of his Chevy.

Donna's mother, Dolores, a trim, short-haired blonde with a deep tan, sat across from him in a sling chair. Charlie avoided looking at her legs, after an unavoidable glance. They were excellent. She lifted a glass of bourbon on the rocks from the end table beside her. "Did you go to high school with Donna?"

"Uh, no," Charlie said, "I went to a different high school." Charlie folded his nails under. Donna had told him her mother, a hostess at a supper club in Phoenix, was visiting. Charlie had envisioned someone much different. Though her makeup was precisely applied and her neck faintly lined, she did not look much older than Donna.

In the bedroom, Donna was talking with her daughter, "Grandma will be in, in a minute," she was saying.

"How come you're going out with him?"

"Lizabeth. Shut up."

"Well? How come?"

Donna's mother walked into the kitchen and opened the refrigerator.

"Because he's nice." There was a rustle of sheets. "Jump into bed."

"Aww, he's not nice. He's just fat."

Donna's mother stayed in the kitchen, running water in the sink, stacking dishes and glasses.

115

Charlie heard the bedroom door shut firmly and Donna came into the room looking at him. "Did you hear?"

Charlie cocked his head and shrugged.

"Kids just love me," he said. "No one knows why, they just do."

"I'm sorry, Charlie. She's a smartmouth. Someone's convinced her it's cute."

"Tell her I'm built for comfort, not for speed."

"You're not fat."

"Tell her my chest slipped."

Donna's mother laughed in the kitchen.

"I used to have a huge chest," Charlie said.

Donna went to change.

Charlie gawked when she returned. She wore a blue and white checked wool skirt and matching blue turtleneck. She tilted her head to the side and reached to tighten an earring, a pearl drop. Her mother came out from the kitchen, "You look nice, Hon."

Charlie nodded dumbly.

Donna reached for her coat, stopped, and smiled radiantly, "Thank you."

Charlie helped her put the coat on and walked before her to open the door. Donna kissed her mother. "Have a good time," Dolores said. "Nice meeting you, Charlie."

The front light winked on behind them as they walked down the apartment stairs.

Donna slid over on the seat, her hip touching his. She put her arm on the seat back, her hand touching his shoulder. "What's the movie we're going to see?"

"*Grand Prix*. It's about Formula One Racing. That's what they do in Europe. James Garner is in it. The guy that used to be on *Maverick*. Did you ever watch that show?"

"I liked that show," Donna said.

"He was Brett," Charlie said. "I always thought he should have been Bart. He just looks more like a Bart."

"Thanks for asking me out," Donna said. "I'd been hoping you would for a long time."

Charlie looked over, momentarily unnerved by her closeness, the light flowery scent of her perfume and the admission she'd wanted to go out with him.

The Cinerama Dome was on Sunset, near Vine Street, a large geodesic dome that was spectacular under construction but now looked too large for the space it occupied. Displays for upcoming movies hemmed in one side and the view the other way was blocked by new buildings.

As they walked toward it through the parking lot, Charlie had to check himself, shorten stride, so Donna could keep up. The lights, the buzzing roar of racecars played over outside speakers, and the sight of other couples streaming through the lot made him impatient.

Waiting in line after purchasing their tickets, Charlie held Donna's hand and fidgeted with the coins and keys in his pocket. He looked at the couples around them. "I hate lines," he announced. "You know?"

"If I ever get rich I'll never stand in line again." He stretched to look over the heads of the people in front, "I like to keep moving." He bounced on the balls of his feet, rocking back on his heels occasionally to regain his balance.

Donna squeezed his hand. "I meant to tell you before," she said, "you look nice tonight."

Charlie looked down at his clothes, a long light-colored car coat of a heavy canvas-like material, non-bleeding madras shirt worn outside his tan corduroys and black slip-on shoes with tassels. He stopped bouncing and squeezed back. Ahead, the line began to move.

Once inside, he'd moved them quickly through the crowd to secure seats in the middle, which he preferred. Seated in the darkness, Charlie relaxed further. The movie began startlingly, with an earsplitting roar of revving engines, while the screen remained blank. The exhaust noise continued; then the screen burst into life with the bright single image of an exhaust pipe tip that multiplied, and Charlie put his knees up against the seat in front of him, prepared to enjoy himself.

Walking back through the parking lot, they listened to the comments of other moviegoers, all of whom seemed to like the film. Charlie, a few technical quibbles aside, had liked it also. Donna had enjoyed it unreservedly and argued lightly with him over the technical points, linking her arm through his and pressing it against her side to emphasize the teasing.

"You can't say it absolutely wouldn't happen that way," she was saying, "it could be a freak thing."

"Well, if it was an explosion or something, yeah, but it just fell off. And then it just happens to fall thirty feet, directly in front of the guy? That kind of stuff is always safety-wired."

They reached the car and she disengaged, poking him with a forefinger. "Someday, you can make a movie just for mechanics."

"Well, I'd get it right." He held the door for her.

"You'll get it exactly right," she said reaching to unlock his side, "and they'll show it on Sunday morning television."

Charlie was delighted by her bantering tone. She seemed spirited to him, independent, qualities he had not strongly sensed in her before. Without thinking, more in admiration and simple gratitude for her presence, he leaned over and kissed her. He felt her face go slack, and then she kissed him back.

The kiss became serious. They broke, looking into each other's eyes and then down at their hands, their fingers twined in Donna's lap.

They retraced their route home on Los Feliz, Charlie driving slowly, timing the lights to avoid shifting and removing his hand from her knee. She curled against him and he leaned toward her, holding himself at an uncomfortable angle to maintain the contact. She appeared to be nearly asleep.

Donna stirred, placing her hand on his knee as he braked.

Charlie reversed and backed into a parking spot a block away from the front of her apartment building, the El Dorado, and its red, green and white spotlighted tropical landscaping - banana plants, mock rubber trees, Schefflera and Giant Bird of Paradise.

Charlie shut off the engine and set the emergency brake.

"Well..." he said. Donna cupped her hand behind his head and drew him toward her.

She kissed his neck and moved to his chin. "I had. A wonderful time." She looked into his eyes. He returned her gaze, wonderingly, closing his eyes as she kissed him on the mouth.

Moving slowly, he shifted, turning toward her. She pressed against him and her hands fluttered on his neck. Charlie wrapped his arms around her, pressing back as her tongue touched his teeth. They strained against each other, broke, and kissed again, more gently, learning each other, moving more and more slowly. Charlie shivered as her fingers traced the short hairs on his neck.

Donna sighed as they separated. She leaned against him and nestled her head under his chin. They sat silently for what seemed a long time. Charlie stroked her back.

A slowly passing car broke the moment. They straightened, Donna tucking in her blouse, Charlie moving his hand back over his hair. She ran her nails over his shirt buttons as the car's taillights dwindled.

The same car returned, a moment later, its lights off. Charlie watched it move toward them in the mirror. Several heads crowded the lowered windows on their side. As it approached, Charlie swung his door open and got out. The car swerved and sped away, the boys inside anxiously cranking up the windows and yelling. Donna collected her purse and coat. She slid across the seat and joined him outside the car, linking her arm solidly in his as they crossed the street and advanced toward the stairs.

Dolores had thoughtfully left the outside light off. They

kissed again and Donna squeezed his hand, hard. "Call me," she said.

15-

Vaca made the call. He'd cruised Connie's house with Brody. He'd hung out at Van de Kamp's for hours. She never showed. As far as he could tell she'd never left the house so a coincidental meeting, which he would have preferred, wasn't possible.

He made the call and Connie answered. "Connie," he said, "it's Vaca." There was a long pause.

"I don't want to see you," she said.

"Look I just want to talk."

"I don't want to talk with you."

Vaca began to wonder if Richie was listening. "Is there someone else there?"

"I just can't talk," Connie said.

"Look, why don't you come to Van de Kamp's. I'll be there tonight and we can talk."

"I can't talk right now."

"Okay, Okay," Vaca said, "I get it. You don't have to say anything. Just come by the drive-in. I'll buy you a burger."

"I've got to go," Connie said, and the line disconnected. Vaca listened to the buzz in his ear and then slammed down the phone. "Fucking bitch!"

He calmed after a bit, deciding that someone was in the room with her. His hopes rebounding, he called Brody and said to come get him.

Brody was puzzled. For the third night in a row, Vaca had called wanting to cruise the drive-in and around Atwater. They'd been hanging out at Van De Kamp's most of the evening.

It was raining, a steady drifting fall, the slant visible against the lights. Vaca peered out the windshield, staying in the car alone. Brody was tired of sitting and walked through the drive-in, stopping to talk with friends and sit in their cars.

Earlier they'd prowled through Atwater, concentrating on several blocks of a residential area. Vaca refused to talk about it. Brody couldn't determine if there was a particular house, or even block, that Vaca was interested in. He never asked Brody to slow, stop, or speed up, just told him where to turn.

Walking back to the car, Brody pulled his coat tighter around the bulky sack containing cheeseburgers, fries and coffee. He stepped delicately along the slick tile walkway beside the coffee shop, moving closer to the wall at corners to avoid the splash from the downspouts. Approaching the car, he saw Vaca swabbing the fogged windshield with a balled towel.

They ate silently, Vaca stopping frequently to clear the windshield that kept misting again from the warm food.

"You about ready to go?" Brody asked. "In a while," Vaca told him. Brody shrugged, "When?" but Vaca didn't reply.

Brody lit a Lucky Strike and turned on the radio, punching the buttons between songs, wondering how much longer and why.

Vaca finally showed some impatience as a disc jockey signaled the headlines for the upcoming ten o'clock news.

He looked over, "Did he say ten o'clock? He did, didn't he? What a ration of shit!" Wringing out the towel, he told Brody "I must be nuts. It's the only explanation. What else can you call it, putting up with this shit."

He fell silent and Brody grew hopeful, but after angrily wiping the window Vaca seemed to settle down again.

Brody watched Vaca, mystified, and Vaca watched the cars drifting through, circling, parking in the half empty drive-in and the carhops running across the lot in their clear plastic ponchos, menus held above their heads to ward off the steady rain.

Connie stood before her bedroom window looking out at the tangled foliage in the overgrown back yard - morning glories shrouding the fence, a thicket of bamboo, knee-high bermuda grass and a bare persimmon tree with the last wizened fruit hanging long-stemmed from the branches. Everything glistened, dripping from the evening's rain in the lights of the used car lot beyond their fence.

She touched the pane and moved her finger down, watching the water bead, form rivulets on either side and run off.

There was a light knock on her door.

"Yeah Ma," Connie said.

"Are you asleep, honey?"

"Not yet."

"I just wondered... the light was off."

Connie waited.

"Are you alright?"

"I'm fine, Ma. Really." Connie listened carefully, until she heard the scuff of slippers going away.

Her mother had been hovering the last few days. Connie had mentioned Maria Goretti one morning at breakfast.

That night Connie found a copy of Lives of Modern Saints on her pillow and the chapter about Maria Goretti was marked by a holy card. Her mother had probed hesitantly, sure something was wrong, but unsure how to proceed with a daughter who had not confided in her since grammar school.

Connie was firm in her denials, adopting the technique - a brusque tone, minimal responses - her father and brother used when they didn't want to explain. It was the only thing she was firm about. Indecision, wistful daydreaming, and bouts of silent

123

crying and aimless drives ending at the ocean had marred the past week.

Once she'd read the chapter on Maria Goretti, Connie decided she didn't have enough in common with the Saint, who had died defending her virginity from a rapist with a knife, to pray to her. Instead she'd tried Saint Mary Magdalene, but even the Magdalene couldn't help.

Her period, now, was four days overdue. That had happened before, but this time she knew with absolute certainty it wasn't late. It wasn't coming at all.

Scudding clouds, loose and vapory, were passing quickly across the moon. Connie swung her window open. The air was chill and clean, carrying the fragrance of the wet earth and greenery. A movement in the branches of the persimmon tree caught her eye.

The bird moved into the light, a scruffy looking linnet, hopping to a lower branch. She couldn't remember seeing a bird feeding this late at night. The linnet pecked desultorily at one of the persimmons. The orange fruit dropped into the tall grass. The bird hopped to another branch, then flew off.

Connie tightened the belt on her bathrobe and dried her face. Returning from the bathroom, she sat on the edge of her bed and reset her alarm. Tomorrow she would have to get up early. It was time to look for work.

16-

"Hang on a sec." Charlie put the receiver down and felt his ear. Moving the phone to the other side he held it awkwardly, propped against a hunched shoulder, and rubbed the sore cartilage.

"I'm back. I think I got a cramp in my ear. How long have we been talking?"

"I don't know," Donna said, "an hour?"

Charlie turned the clock in the window to face him, "Jesus, closer to two." There had only been three interruptions in that time, two gas customers and one elderly drunk, very polite, seeking directions to a bar Charlie had never heard of. He was parked now in a dark corner of the gas station lot, sleeping it off or awaiting inspiration.

"It can't be. Really?"

"Almost eleven now. I know, it doesn't seem that long." Charlie switched sides again holding the receiver a careful distance from the sore ear. "I guess I'd better get started on clean-up."

"I'll let you go then..." There was a pause.

"I wish I didn't have to hang up," Charlie said.

"I know." There was another silence.

Finally, Donna said, "One of us has to hang up."

"I know."

"I miss you. I wish you were here right now."

"So do I."

Donna's voice grew wistful. "I had such a nice time last night. Thank you again."

"I did too."

"I talked with Lizabeth today. I still feel bad about that."

"It's alright. Really."

"She gets kind of weird when there's a man in the house."

"Oh?" Charlie said, "Hunh."

"Well, anyway."

"I miss you," Charlie said.

"One of us really has to hang up."

"We could count to three," Charlie suggested.

"No. I'm going to hang up. I am, I really am. Are you ready?"

Charlie sighed deeply. "I guess."

"Don't listen. Just put the phone down."

Charlie waited.

"Charlie?" Donna's voice was wistful again. "Why don't you call me when you get home. Not to talk, just ring twice, to let me know you're home safe, and hang up."

Charlie thought. "Okay. But if you feel like it, you can pick it up. Just to say goodnight."

"A deal."

"Well, maybe later then."

"Goodnight, Charlie."

He laid the phone down on the countertop, snatching it up again when he thought he heard her say something more, but it was quiet when he listened and then the connection was broken with a click. He listened to the silence for a moment and put the receiver back on the cradle.

Charlie splashed solvent on the floor around the lube racks and scrubbed the worst patches with a push broom. He rinsed the solvent with water, pushing it toward the drains with a long-handled rubber wiper. Waiting for the floor to dry, he stayed to the edges of the room. He wiped down tools and the workbench. He felt buoyant, energetic. As he worked, Donna's words, "... a man in the house," kept recurring. It had been a small shock said so directly, almost casually. He could not recall hearing himself described as a man. He did not think of himself that way, had seldom applied the title to others. It seemed a vague category that shifted with age. At fifteen, he had thought of it in terms of the legal requirement; at twenty-one you were a man. Now, approaching that age, those he would describe as men were closer to thirty and the category was still vague; it appeared more a matter of responsibility than age.

She'd said it so easily. It was obviously how she thought of him, and the small shock he'd felt when she used the word was in part, he now realized with a thrill of humility and pride, the shock of recognition. If Donna felt that way, it was likely that others regarded him similarly.

One other comment she'd made, early in the conversation, now came pleasingly to mind. She'd interrupted a description of her afternoon at work in mid-sentence, saying, "Oh. Did I tell you what my mother said about you?

"Dolores said," Donna told him, "that she didn't care how old you were and if I had any sense at all I'd snap you up."

Charlie lowered the lube racks and switched off the lights. Sauntering toward his car he sang, his voice reverberating strongly under the metal canopy, "Duh doo-tuh-doo, Yes it's me and I'm in looove again..."

At home he studied the clock beside his bed, undecided. It was after one and he knew she worked a morning shift tomorrow. She also might be awake, worrying.

Charlie dialed her number. He hung up on the second ring, before she could pick it up.

He turned out the light, thinking about his considerate gesture. These thoughts swelled as he stretched happily under his blankets, his sentiments assuming a character of near nobility. The covers and bed warming around him, he drifted into sleep filled with pleasurable anticipation of his dreams and the morning.

17-

One of the trustees came down with the message. The man walked the corridor, bawling, "Wayne Reinhard. Wayne Reinhard in here? Reinhard, Wayne." Reinhard had rolled off his bunk and gone to the bars, calling out, "You got him."

The news was good. One of his former employers, Paul Povich of Paul's Machine Shop, had gone to his ex-wife's lawyer with an offer of immediate employment and an advance to cover the back alimony payments. He would be released tomorrow morning, twenty days short of his two-month sentence.

The trustee let him keep the message, shrugging when Reinhard tried to hand it back. "They didn't say." Reinhard shrugged as well and tucked it into his shirt pocket. He reread it during dinner and again just before lights-out. The switch was thrown as it was every night, without warning, while he was staring at the paper. In the unexpected darkness the image of the words he'd been staring at, "Suspended sentence" lingered. He laid back on the bunk and put his hands under his head.

It was a good description he thought, not for the leaving, but for the time, the forty days. Suspended. Tonight was the first time he'd had to think about the future.

Jail hadn't been bad, but better than he had expected. It was the first time for him and he had been able to float. "Gravytime" they called it; he bothered nobody - nobody bothered him.

For forty days everything had been done for him; he wished he had an extra day, to think things out.

It would take a while to catch up. There was the advance, the alimony, child support and his own bills. The Chevy needed work. Running right, it could make some money for him, but first he would have to put some money into it.

Before this, there had always been a cushion. He had been broke occasionally but, until now, had never felt pressed. He'd always had what other people called luck. He had never thought of it that way; he just assumed things would work out because of his talents, because of who he was.

Staring at the empty bunk above him, thinking about the past, he wondered if dues, long delayed, were now catching up to him. He wondered if his age had something to do with it. He was closing in on thirty, an age that he had previously seen as a barrier. He'd begun to think of it as a dividing line, the age at which you were caught and had to settle for what you were.

At fifteen, Wayne Reinhard had owned the quickest flathead Ford in Tulsa, Oklahoma. A boast he later realized did not mean much.

In Tulsa, in the mid-fifties, everyone else was interested in stock car racing. The competition, mostly new Chevrolets, Pontiacs and an occasional Hudson was best at top end racing on long stretches of country road, not stoplight duels.

A visit to a cousin in Bakersfield - a thriving, ugly farming and oil city a hundred miles north of Los Angeles - had ruined him for circle track racing. There he had accompanied a cousin, two years older and the owner of a fenderless Model A with an Oldsmobile engine, to the annual Smokers Meet - a wild, unsanctioned three day event held at Famosa, just north of Bakersfield. The drag racers took over the city, and the parking lots of every motel on Union Avenue were blocked with trailers and a variety of race cars Reinhard had never known existed.

At home the racecars he knew were stripped, battered, but recognizable versions of cars to be found at any dealer. Here

130

there were an anarchic variety of classes - Altered Roadsters, Altered Coupes, gas and fuel dragsters, competition class cars - and generally he could only guess at their origin.

His cousin enjoyed competitor's status because of the Model A and they spent most of the evenings, after attending races all day, on motel row in the company of other racers.

At the Bakersfield Inn they assisted the crew of a AA Altered Roadster in pulling the car's engine. It took the four crewmembers plus Reinhard and his cousin to carry the engine to the living room of their suite. There, on the carpet, the engine was disassembled. The bathtub was partially filled with solvent to wash the engine parts and sheets were torn in strips to dry them.

Dazzled by their ease and company Reinhard scraped parts most of the night, spurred on by casually offered beers and the next day, the day of the finals, the newly rebuilt engine held up through four rounds and the championship round. They set a new meet record and won four hundred dollars. Reinhard, considered a mascot by now, was given twenty-five and an honored place at the celebration that followed. It ruined him for any other kind of racing.

Returning to Tulsa he dropped his woodworking classes for auto shop and began building his first car, a hand-me-down '40 Ford that his older brother had been unable to sell before joining the Coast Guard.

He had a hard time building the car the way he wanted. The kind of speed parts he needed were mainly available by mail and the expertise of the shops around town centered on track racing - building engines and gearing the cars for mid-range and top end response, not the instant acceleration demanded in quarter-mile racing.

He read catalogues and Hot Rod magazine ads like textbooks, trying to pick apart the design and function of the equipment from photographs, tiny drawings and the enthusiastically written but seldom informative text.

His father, a welder with a storage tank and pipeline manufacturer, had taught him arc and gas welding. This skill got him an afternoon and weekend job at a well equipped machine shop.

The owner let him experiment evenings in exchange for cleaning up and in a few months he had duplicated some of the equipment pictured in the speed catalogues. Most of it worked, some didn't. He knew little of the theory behind their design.

The car ran reasonably well. It seemed to strain, top end, but came off the line like it was catapulted. The start and low gearing was enough to beat everything he met at the stoplights of Tulsa.

It didn't impress Tulsa much. The Ford was considered a novelty, and so was he. But it was hard to generate races in town. The only people who seemed interested were the police who shadowed him from parking lot to parking lot, pulling him over at least once a week to check for equipment violations.

In Reinhard's junior year of high school his father made a bad mistake, trying to braze a patch on a holed gas tank belonging to a neighbor. They had left a water hose running in the tank but there were enough fumes left to catch a spark and when they exploded the acetylene did too. The blast was so fierce that brown glass shards from the case of beer the neighbor had brought to pay for the favor rained down through trees at a city park two blocks away.

Reinhard heard about it from a policeman who came to the school. He remembered telling the policeman that his father was a better welder than that. Reinhard could only conclude that his father had been in a hurry since he hadn't used the usual cheapjack method, running a hose from the exhaust pipe of an idling car, pumping carbon dioxide into the tank to inhibit combustion.

There was no insurance. The house was rented. The pipeline company offered him his father's job but Reinhard said no, he thought he'd try California. The neighbor who'd owned the gas tank had survived, but was still hospitalized. When Reinhard visited him the man appreciated the visit but mentioned a court suit, further incentive for Reinhard to move on.

He wrote to his brother in the Coast Guard. His mother hadn't written for a while. She was married now or said she was, to the country singer she had followed to Baton Rouge. He traveled, so there was no way to reach her.

Reinhard left word with the neighbor on the other side, asking that any letters from his mother be forwarded to the cousin in Bakersfield. He sold his father's tools and fishing gear, for traveling money. The landlord had already claimed everything else to cover the cost of paint, three windows and the rent.

Years later he remembered that leisurely trip west with a clarity he could not summon for his father, family or hometown.

He stopped in every little town on the way, seeking out the drive-ins, and could still recall most of the names, the way they looked, the carhops, whether the food was good and the cars that had singled him out.

The kids he met were awed by the vision of his trip. California was a magic name to them. If he stayed more than a day he was treated as a celebrity, shown their secrets - the meeting places, landmarks, lover's lanes. He was used as the occasion for parties, fed, invited along to football games. He generally learned everything worth knowing about a town in a day or two and never stayed longer than that.

The parents, even those that liked him, were glad to see him go. More than once he had police escorts to the county line. He sensed, most places, that he left a restlessness behind him.

The Ford was charmed, the whole way. It lost only two races, nothing east of the Rockies and never broke down, never missed a beat. In Reinhard too, there was a steadiness, an appreciation with each day's travel of his worth.

The night he came down the Grapevine, with the lights of Bakersfield below him, he had a sense of completion but felt no loss. He smelled his first orange blossoms. Then onions. The gathering heat and wind from the valley that grew with the descent seemed like a greeting to him, a skin feeling to complement the thought that he was exactly where he should be.

Reinhard yawned and stretched, pushing with his palms against the metal webbing that supported the mattress above him. Two or three cells away someone's coughing fit subsided in suppressed choking bursts. Reinhard put his knuckles to his mouth and pictured the man down the row doing the same, to hold in the coughing.

"Goddam it," someone yelled, "knock off the noise. I'm going to kick your ass in the morning."

Down the hall, his neighbor was now hiccuping, between sporadic coughs.

18-

Drowsily, Charlie stretched, clenching his toes. He turned onto his right side, tugging the coverlet up over his head.

Morning light was filtering through the curtains above the bed, making a warm yellow square, reaching almost to his knees.

As he shifted, Donna turned sleepily behind him. She reached out, touching his back and moved closer, nestling in with her arm over his shoulder. They dozed.

The sun was on his chest when Charlie stirred again, wakened by the touch of Donna's fingers following his ribs. She was pressed against him. Her leg rode up on his thigh and she reached around his stomach, cupping him gently.

He pressed back against her and was startled by the heat he felt on his back and buttocks, a baking warmth that dried the sweat there. She kissed his neck. "Merry Christmas," she said. He turned to her.

It was the first week of December but this would be the only Chrismas they would get. The kids were gone, visiting their grandmother in Phoenix. Donna would be leaving tomorrow, to join them.

How long her visit would last, was undetermined. There was the possibility of a job opening; a hostess was quitting at the supper club where her mother worked.

Donna had mentioned it only once, and described her

chances as slim, because the money, location and hours were so favorable. Charlie tried not to think about it.

Her luggage, gradually packed over the last week, was stored out of sight. Train tickets, left in view on a kitchen shelf, were hidden on Charlie's next visit.

As the day of her departure neared, they spent more time together. Charlie skipped work for two days, calling in sick and switched shifts to have the weekend free.

They made love. They clung to each other. Donna was quiet, her face paler and sad, evading his eyes when he became serious.

Charlie considered the possibility of marriage, wondered if the trip to Phoenix was the result of that unasked question. He even speculated, surprising himself as the thought occurred, whether it might be to force the issue.

He did not ask. Between them, growing stronger through that last week, there was a bond of kindness, a mutual solicitude and neither seemed to want any disturbance in the pattern of the days, to break the mood by speaking of the future.

At the Glendale train station, a sunfaded rose adobe structure, with a roofline reminiscent of the Alamo, they sat on a bench in the open sided waiting area, watching a man stack mail bags and suitcases on a linked row of baggage carts. The loading finished, the man climbed into the rattling Cushman hauler at the head of the line and drove slowly off, watching behind him the steel wheeled carts, jouncing and shaking, and the sway of the overstacked luggage.

Charlie looked from the tiled floor to the thick walls and lashed beams supporting the roof. "Houses in Phoenix look like this?"

Donna glanced around her. "Not where my mom lives. It's all apartments." She sighed. "It's not my favorite city. Mostly, it's just brown and dry, dry, dry."

Charlie's spirits rose at the unhappiness in her voice. "Lots of cactus?"

"I don't know. I guess I'll find out." They sank again.

Down the track, the circling reflector on the nose of the engine flashed in the sun and the horn blared as the train crossed the Los Feliz bridge. They got up from the bench and stood beside the tracks as the train eased in. The engine and first cars passed them, white coated porters standing at the back of each car, hands on the half door, gazing impassively at the boarding crowd. The train bumped to a stop, with a crash and groan of couplings, jets of steam hissing under the cars, and rolled backward slightly.

Donna smoothed her hair along her cheeks, drawing it down between her thumbs and forefingers. Her face was puffed from lack of sleep, circled under the eyes. Her nose looked red and sharp. Charlie reached to touch her hair and looked down fondly at the front of her beige suit. "I'm glad they could get the coffee out."

She hugged him tightly and breathing into his shoulder she said, "I'm going to miss you so." Charlie patted her back and then clutched the fabric of her suit. "Ahh Hell," he said, tearing.

He held her elbow as she ascended the metal stairs. She turned on the top step and gripped his hand. "I'll write as soon as I get there."

Charlie walked alongside, looking through the windows, as she made her way down the aisle to her seat. He pressed his hand against the glass and she matched it on her side. The train's horn sounded twice and a porter, leaning out, asked him to stand clear.

He stayed in step with the train, until he was striding, and then relaxed his pace, as her window slid away. Stopping at the end of the walkway, he watched the train out of sight.

He sighed and then raised his head, looking across the tracks, up at a row of slim palm trees lining an adjacent street, the waving crowns of fronds eighty feet above the house-tops.

Charlie kicked a chunk of gravel, a stray from the roadbed, ahead of him, all the way back to the car. His regret was tinged with relief; it had been an effort to sustain unfailing sweetness, those last two days. He was glad he'd maintained it, but also glad to have it end, to be alone with his thoughts.

If she came back, he didn't know what would happen. The last two weeks had been nearly perfect, but demanding, and at the heart of it had been a sadness and nobility of sentiment based on his relinquishment. It was necessary, only fair he'd decided, to give her up. He did not feel he had that much to offer.

She would probably have more choices in Phoenix. He hoped the town would treat her well. If she did return, their relationship could be better, or worse; he didn't know. It would be different.

A month or more would pass, before he could know what would happen and he appreciated having that deferral. He felt he had learned a lot with Donna. Grown up some, changed, and gained experience that would affect him in the future. At times in the last week, he could almost believe he was older than she was.

Charlie kicked the rock under the car and got in. He would have to work straight shifts the next few days. After that however, the holidays stretched before him. He'd have time to hang out at the drive-in and catch up on the racing scene and Lamont was scheduled to get back from Army Boot Camp with money, he said, to burn.

19-

A balding man in a pale blue polo shirt, rust colored cuffless slacks, and a textured grey houndstooth sport coat, Paul Povich of Paul's Machine Shop, was there to meet him when Reinhard stepped out of the doorway, county jeans rolled under his arm.

Paul turned towards him, legs well apart, hands thrust into his back pockets, and looked Reinhard up and down. "Call, next time. You could've been out a month ago."

Reinhard tilted his head to one side and shrugged. "Where's your suitcase?" Paul said. "Jesus. Didn't they make you bring nothing with you? No wonder I'm paying the taxes I'm paying. Every wino in the county must check in when he needs a shave and new clothes."

Reinhard followed Paul to his T-Bird, listening to a lecture on the uselessness of lawyers, the courts and ex-wives (his three and Reinhard's) that continued to Reinhard's apartment.

Standing on the steps, Paul unwrapped another of the clove-flavored toothpicks he claimed as the cure for a three-pack-a-day habit. Sucking on it reflectively, he went through his wallet for a further advance to cover Reinhard's rent and walking-around money.

As he handed it over, he told him, "Take today off. You come in when you're ready."

Reinhard said he'd be there in the morning. Paul said, "Whatever's right. But don't come in unless you're sure you're ready. It's going to be eighty-hour weeks." He rolled his shoulders under his jacket, nodded emphatically and pounded down the stairs.

"Hey," Reinhard called after him, "should I stick a broom up my ass so I can sweep up while I'm walking?"

Paul waggled a hand without looking back. Reinhard went up the stairs. The apartment was stuffy. The kitchen smelled foul.

Reinhard cranked the windows open and started the ceiling fan. There were three beers left in the refrigerator and what looked like a brain in a plastic bag. It might have been a cantaloupe once.

Reinhard settled on the couch and opened his first beer. He raised the can in the direction of his window and settled back deeper on the couch so the power and phone lines disappeared from view and he could see only the top of the ginkgo tree in the next yard and the grey-yellow haze of the sky behind it. "Forty days," he said, and swallowed. He felt the first cold taste, almost metallic, where his head joined his neck and then all the way down his back and had to sit up, shuddering.

Paul wasn't kidding about the eighty-hour weeks. Anticipating Reinhard's return, he had stopped turning down work and built up a backlog. Reinhard didn't mind. Paul didn't pay overtime but the extra hours would help pay the advances back sooner.

The shop employed four other machinists and was large enough to keep them out of each other's way. It was dark, with pockets of light over the machine tools. They kept the overhead door open to let in the breeze and to give them a view, the open side of the cabinet shop next door. They rotated every so often so no one got stuck on the boring bar or the crankshaft lathe for the whole day.

For Reinhard, the days ran together. He was accurate, he kept up, but he took no pleasure in the work. Paul favored him and tried to funnel the more interesting jobs his way. The antiques, some tricky aluminum heads and an injection unit from a 300 SL Gullwing Mercedes, so rare that it was cheaper for the dealer to have the parts machined than to order them from the factory, but they failed to intrigue him.

Reinhard did the work but seldom thought much about it; he simply progressed. The job was different for him now because there was no end in sight. Before, he had worked seven months in one stretch, twice for four months, once just for two, but each time he'd known that in a pinch he could give two weeks notice, anytime, and be able to float.

Driving to work each morning was an irritant; the Chevy was running rough now and getting worse. He suspected a burnt valve but tried not to think about it, knowing that it would be some time before he could afford the overhaul.

When he did think about it, it worried him. Each time Reinhard thought on the problem, because there was no solution, the same question came to him: Was it worth the hassle anymore? He'd never felt that before. The street, the life, had always meant independence to him. Now, in these gloomier moments, he thought he might be seeing it the way it probably always was, a break-even kind of life. One that could be a steady loser with a run of bad luck - an accident, a bad bust, anything.

He had friends that got out. They just stopped racing. Something had usually taken the place - water-skiing, judo lessons, weekend gold mining - some excitement with less risk. He'd never understood before how they could simply give it up.

Paul sensed his mood. He asked Reinhard to stay on later than usual one night, to help recalibrate and repair some of the shop's equipment, a job Paul usually did on his own.

While they worked, Paul asked how the Chevy was running; Reinhard said O.K., just needed a few things. Paul asked when he wanted to shop. Reinhard said he didn't know. In a month maybe, but he really get started, explaining that he would have the run of the wasn't sure.

Paul didn't press further, but a few days later the sales rep for a piston company stopped by. After taking the usual order from Paul, he walked back to the shop, approached Reinhard and spoke to him for several minutes about a new line of racing pistons his company was experimenting with. Reinhard gradually realized the man was offering him a free set, for testing.

Reinhard agreed and gave him the bore size. The man was back the same week, bringing a wooden case with eight boxed and numbered pistons. After Reinhard had signed for them, the rep, somewhat apologetically, passed on several window decals explaining that he didn't really expect Reinhard to put them on, only if he liked the parts to pass the word.

The aluminum pistons were lovingly finished, balanced to within a quarter gram. The skirts and crowns were radical in design, unlike any others he'd seen.

That afternoon, he started thinking about the Chevy. The pistons would have been a major expense; getting them this way meant he could move his schedule up a month and he was starting to see other ways he might scrape by.

That weekend Reinhard pulled the engine and started tearing down the heads. Monday, on the cleared bench where he had pieces of the motor laid out, he found a package with new, oversize intake and exhaust valves and a note from Paul, telling him that new seats had been ordered. The parts would be billed at cost, deducted from future paychecks if he preferred.

Phone calls came from people he hadn't heard from in some time. Jobbers, partsmen, other machinists, an old racing adversary who'd given it up and now owned a junkyard. He had advice and a freshly crated 409 block, out of a burned Impala, that he was ready to hoist over the back gate - for insurance reasons - on any dark night Reinhard chose. They all had something to offer - labor, parts, loans.

Thursday, some of the Van de Kamp's regulars stopped by, with encouragement and unkind words for Vaca. Reinhard realized that he had become a crusade for a lot of people. He appreciated it. He also realized, with a returning sense of worth, that a lot of those people needed someone like him to survive.

Friday, at an early impromptu Christmas party, Paul and the rest of the shop staff presented him with their contribution, a stroker crank that he knew represented forty or fifty hours of shared work and at odd hours, necessarily; he had never suspected.

Paul had welded the journals himself. They had taken turns on the grinding, finishing, and balancing. The crankshaft, perfect and gleaming under a light coat of machine oil, was set upright on a table. Christmas tree ornaments dangled from the throws and counterweights.

An iced tub of beer was dragged out from under a blanket and the party started. The ornaments were broken in the first half-hour as the crankshaft was picked up and passed around. Each of them had to touch it, reinspect the perfectly machined bearing journals and feel the smoothness of the ground welds.

When it was Reinhard's turn, he held it up, suspending it with his fingertips under the top throw, and lightly tapped the bottom counterweight with a small ball-peen hammer. It rang like a bell, a clear true note that continued in the approving silence until the weight was too much to hold and he had to grasp the bottom, muffling the fading ring.

It was a lovely freakish sculpted prayer of metal, a risk no sane Chevrolet engineer could countenance. Any sound engineer would recognize the crank for what it was: a grenade waiting. Added to the oversized pistons in the sleeved and rebored block, the stroked crankshaft would bring the engine displacement to over 500 cubic inches.

Paul closed the office, bringing back cups and Christmas whiskey from their parts suppliers.

The men in the cabinet shop behind them filed out of their building, raising goggles, brushing the sawdust from their jeans and blinking at the smoggy sunlight. They waited for the coffee truck and watched the party enviously. It was only three o'clock. Paul invited one of them, who had walked over to the fence for a closer look, to join them when he finished work. By four, a half-dozen had climbed the fence.

Around eight, the take-out pizza and chicken were gone and while they waited for more beer to arrive, Paul painted a sign with a tube of Prussian blue and a parts cleaning brush. When he was finished, he propped it up on the bench that held all the parts for Reinhard's engine. The sign said: "Running by New Year's."

All six of them stood behind the bench and the sign, grinning, holding up fresh cans of beer and one of the cabinet shop workers took the photograph.

20-

The television set in back of the bar streaked, and the picture began to slowly roll upward. "Third and twenty-two for the Rams this time." The announcer's voice was cheerful, conversational. "And I believe the Packers will be coming."

"Hey Kelsoe", someone called, "adjust the damn set will you?"

The bartender reached for a knob, turning it left, then right, until the picture held. He readjusted the color to a level of artificial brilliancy. The uniforms of the teams sharpened to hues of gaseous blue, orange, and yellow, against an emerald felt-like field, fuzzing as they went into motion.

"Better," someone said.

"Kelsoe?" Vaca held up his glass. "Same again." The bartender lifted a bottle of Old Crow by the neck and looked at him questioningly. Vaca nodded.

The table beside him was littered with the remains of a chicken dinner from a Chicken Delite take-out restaurant two doors down - napkins, an empty pitcher and smudged beer glass, full ashtrays, change and crumpled bills.

Kelsoe, a heavy man in his fifties with seamed brows, a spread nose and a puffed, ruddy face, rounded the bar carrying a large tray. He had a wide rolling walk, placing his weight on the sides of his feet. His expression was placid, except for a weariness around the eyes.

Setting the tray down, he handed Vaca his drink and began clearing the table. Vaca swallowed half of it and held the drink up before his eyes. "That's a little light," he said.

Kelsoe, wrapping a napkin around the chicken bones, told

him, "I'll double up on you next time." He turned, distracted, as one of the men in front of the television pounded his glass on the bar, yelling, "*Jee-zus!* Did you see that?" The Ram punter, hurrying to avoid an attempted block, had shanked the ball out of bounds. "That's about a net ten-yard punt," the announcer said cheerfully.

With an eye on the men studying and bitterly commenting on a replay of the punt, Kelsoe said, "We haven't seen much of you lately."

Vaca downed the rest of his drink and set the glass on the tray. "Yeah. I been out spinning my wheels." Kelsoe looked at Vaca and his wheelchair, to see if it was a joke. "Wasting time. Chasing pussy." Vaca separated two bills and tossed them across. The bartender pushed them back. "I'll get that one."

"Forget it," Vaca said, "I don't mind paying for it. You got your overhead like everyone else."

Kelsoe wrung his towel out over the empty beer pitcher and wiped the table again, "I'll get the next one."

"Up to you. I'm not complaining. Everybody makes mistakes."

Kelsoe gave him a long look as he picked up the tray. Vaca turned to watch the group at the end of the bar, their faces aimed up at the television. "What's the score?" he shouted.

Kelsoe returned, bringing the fresh drink and a brimming shot glass. As he set them down, Vaca turned back, looking up at him. One of his eyelids drooped slightly. "Everybody makes mistakes," Vaca said. "These are on me," Kelsoe told him.

"I wasted the last three weeks on a mistake." He sipped delicately from the shot glass and then from the drink. "I don't know. I guess it's not a total waste if you learn something."

Kelsoe wiped the table absently, "Yeah. It's all experience."

"I did. Know what I learned? From now on I pay for it. That's what." Kelsoe nodded. Vaca nodded solemnly back, a little longer than necessary.

"All the time, you hear some jackoff go: 'I've never paid for it in my life.' And he's proud of it." Vaca's palm smacked the

146

table. "The hell they haven't. You pay. One way or another." He nodded again.

"Sometimes that's true," Kelsoe murmured.

Vaca continued, his voice suddenly raspy with conviction and outrage. "I'd rather pay all at once. Get it over with and Get On. Fuck it. I mean, you think it's free but that's if you don't figure your time's worth anything. That's a crock. My time's worth something."

On the television, the credits were rolling over a view of an emptying stadium. The men watching came to life, leaning away from the bar, hands pressed to their backs, stretching, lighting cigarettes, and looking down at their glasses. "Kelsoe," one of them called, "get your ass over here and ease the pain."

Kelsoe straightened, folded the towel and laid it neatly over his shoulder. "Did you want another?"

Vaca pushed the glasses forward. "Why not? And bring me the phone if it'll reach." Kelsoe brought back the phone, unspooling the cord behind him, set it on the table, and returned to the crush at the bar. Vaca, after several moments of overfocused concentration, brought a worn slip of paper from his wallet. He studied the slip, then dialed. He winked at Kelsoe, who was busy and didn't notice.

"Hey Laurel," Vaca said, "It's me. Your favorite... Your favorite ... Vaca ... Yeah. You got it. Take out your teeth, I'm on my way." He slammed the phone back in its cradle triumphantly.

Someone at the end of the bar unplugged the television set and plugged in the Christmas tree lights that encircled the long back mirror, woven through tinsel, small plastic wreaths and boughs covered with what looked like fluorescent salmon eggs. The lights stuttered as the man fiddled with the plug and then began to blink steadily. Vaca focused on them with difficulty, finding it hard to anticipate the sequence. He shook his head violently, as though something were loose, and then steadied it on his palm, his elbow on the table, staring at the other patrons with interest. "So who won?" he yelled.

21-

Charlie sat stiffly in the Greyhound terminal on Main Street. The orange fiberglass chairs, bolted in rows to the floor, looked comfortable, but after switching chairs and positions for the last twenty minutes, Charlie had concluded that they were designed to prevent loitering or at least to encourage waiting passengers in the direction of the padded booths in the terminal restaurant. He was bored and nervous from too much coffee and too many cigarettes. The bus from Monterey was late.

How much longer it would be was not clear. He had waited two hours already. Lamont had called early that morning. He had a six day leave after finishing basic training at Fort Ord and planned to spend most of it, including New Year's, with Charlie.

The depot was high ceilinged and dark and smelled like a bad bar under new management: an odorous mix of fortified wine, beer, bleach, harsh cleansers, ancient urine, and mildew. Charlie had exhausted its amusements quickly. The pinball machines were short, three balls instead of the usual five, and easy tilts. The prices in the restaurant offended him.

After the pinball games and three sour cups of coffee, bought at intervals from three different machines, he'd spent his last fifty cents, purchasing what he thought was a pack of topless playing cards from a vending machine in the men's room.

Opening them in the shelter of a stall, he found it was only half the deck and the cards were the size of a matchbook. The reproductions were disappointingly fuzzy; the garish colors bled into one another, blurring the profiles of the arch, coy, and pouting models.

He looked through them once and was ready to throw them away but decided to save them for Lamont.

The public address speaker in the corner of the room crackled and announced that the express bus from Monterey and Salinas had left the North Hollywood terminal and would arrive in twenty minutes. Stretching, Charlie stood. His hands and face felt gritty; he decided to wash up.

Charlie pushed open the door of the men's room. Halfway down the row of stalls there was a heavyset black man, kneeling on the tiles with three playing cards laid out in front of him. He was well dressed, wearing pale yellow slacks of a soft-looking fabric, a checked sports coat, and grey turtleneck shirt. The light gleamed on his scalp and a gold tooth as he looked up.

The men surrounding him were bent forward to watch the cards, money in hand. Charlie took a place behind them and watched for a time, picking out the shills, two scornful acting black youths. They seemed too young and too obvious to Charlie, hurrying their bets and snatching their winnings from between the man's fingers.

The dealer was good, his movements were unhurried and smooth, and his voice was a curious and effective sing-song.

As Charlie watched, he paid off thirty dollars in bets and tore up the old cards. He drew three from a deck with a rubberband around it, creased them down the middle and flipped them onto the tiles, calling out each one, "Ideekay Queen, Red Queen. Deekay Ace. Beefay King."

Then he started to move them, dropping and crossing, occasionally turning up an edge to show the location of the queen.

He chanted while his hands circled and crossed, "Shufflem, shufflem. Roday. Modo, modo, shufflem." The red queen had acquired a bent corner.

He stopped, squared the cards, and looked up enquiringly. "Ideekay Ofay, wheredeekay Queen? Red Queen?"

A man in front, not one of the shills, Charlie thought, pointed to the dog-eared card and won five dollars.

A Filipino man who stood next to Charlie grinned at him skeptically, but moved in closer for the next hand watching intently, jingling change in his loose-fitting pleated bronze slacks, and by the next hand he was in. Charlie noticed the bettors followed the exchange of money as intently as the cards.

The Filipino man won twice, sat out a hand, then doubled and redoubled, winning both times and backed away, looking shaken, holding eighty dollars. He refused to continue and the game went on. Nearly all the watchers were betting now.

It seesawed for a while and Charlie noticed, on a particularly large pot, that there were now two cards with bent corners. Neither, it turned out, was the queen. The next hand there were no corners and the dealer was suddenly up over a hundred dollars.

He was laying the cards out again when the swing door opened halfway and an unseen lookout yelled, "Cops!"

The crowd scattered for the door and Charlie was standing alone with the dealer, and the no longer dazed-looking Filipino.

The dealer handed his roll and the cards to the Filipino man, who immediately headed for the door, slowing to a pained looking shuffle as he approached it. The dealer winked at Charlie, turned, and then almost as an afterthought, handed him a squared five-dollar bill. He backed into a toilet stall. Charlie watched the man's trousers drop around his ankles, still open-mouthed, and then gathered himself enough to head for the door. On the way out, two broad shouldered men wearing nearly identical brown suits bumped him. One grabbed him by the arm and held him for the other's inspection. The other man said, "Naw," and Charlie was shoved aside while they hurried into the restroom.

Charlie pushed through the terminal, deciding to wait

outside, and hid himself in a crowd on the sidewalk where a tattered evangelist was pointing to a long furrowed scar on his bald pate. He waved his Bible with his left hand and pointed to the livid scar with his right. "I was a Sinner!" he shouted, "I was the worst of the worst. A Fornicator! A Drunkard! A Drug Taker! God Saw Me in My Wickedness! And Bless him. He did the merciful thing. He Smote me with his Golden Axe! You can see the results for yourself. I am a living Testament to his work! Look at what his Golden Axe did to me. How can you doubt what you see? If you doubt, like Thomas, run your finger down this holy wound!"

Charlie watched, fingering the bill in his pocket, grinning at it all, until the bus from Monterey arrived.

Lamont swung down from the bus, the last one off. Charlie looked at him, amazed. Lamont was wearing his dress uniform; he looked like he'd gained twenty pounds, most of it in his chest and neck. His face was bright red, the shade of a skier's sunburn; the sides were contrasting, pale between his ears and the rim of his hat from a recent haircut.

Lamont shook Charlie's hand gravely and with considerable pressure. "Thanks buddy. I appreciate you coming to get me."

"You look great," Charlie said. "What'd they do to you up there?"

"All that they could," Lamont said. "Just what the D.I. said they'd do. Knock the shit out of us and stack it back up the way the Army likes it. You wouldn't believe it. Run? Man, you run everywhere. Every morning, I get up and my bedding was on the floor. I was trying to run in my sleep." He pointed to his shoes. "Look at the gunboats. I jumped two shoe sizes."

Charlie showed the way to his Chevy in the parking lot. "You look like you put on some weight."

"About ten pounds. I was the only one in my platoon that gained anything. The first three weeks I was too scared to shit. They're always yelling at you."

They reached the car. Lamont slid in and tossed his bag in

the back seat. He patted the dash. "Man, it is good to be home. I'm ready to sell my soul for a decent cheeseburger."

On the way out of the parking lot, Charlie spotted the Filipino man from the card game, idling in front of a newsstand. He pointed him out to Lamont, "See that guy over there?"

"Who? The Gook?"

"What?"

"The Gook," Lamont said, "Looking at the magazines."

Charlie was unfamiliar with the term. "The Filipino guy."

"What about him?"

Charlie told him about the three-card monte game in the men's room, digging into his pocket while he drove with one hand, to produce the five-dollar bill.

"Lucky," Lamont said.

"That's dinner," said Charlie.

On the way to Van de Kamp's, Charlie brought him up to date. The match race against Stan's, Reinhard's marital problem, a brief account of Cheryl's party, Charlie and Brody's Midnight Auto Parts operation, and he mentioned offhandedly that he and Donna were going together.

Lamont looked shocked. "She's got a couple kids doesn't she? What is she, twenty-five, thirty, or so?"

"Twenty-four," Charlie said. "She's in Phoenix right now. Be back in a couple weeks."

"Lordy, Lordy," Lamont said.

At Van de Kamp's, Lamont ordered and ate three cheeseburgers and ordered another to go with his coffee. He took off his uniform hat for the first time and lounged back, looking at the cars and people around them.

A pearlescent white Corvette with fat tires and dual hood scoops cruised through and Lamont nearly stood up to watch it, eyes bright. He closed his eyes when it was past and inhaled loudly. "It's just like I remembered," he said.

He offered Charlie a cigar when their coffee came and smoked luxuriantly, talking about Army life.

Listening, Charlie sensed changes the Army or the time away, had made in Lamont. There was a new hard edge, a bitterness in his tone, and a smugness about him.

He mentioned politics, which Charlie had never heard from him before, and seemed to have unyielding opinions. It might be, like the cigar, just Lamont's way of showing he'd been away, but it was irritating.

"Yeah, they're all in on it," Lamont was saying. "They've got us handcuffed. If we got the green light, we could mop the place up in a month. See, we have to play by the rules. Believe me, Victor Charlie don't play by the rules."

After a pause, while Lamont puffed enthusiastically, Charlie said, "Well I don't know."

Lamont told him "You can take my word for it," and he went on to describe the photographs he'd seen of an overrun firebase near the Mekong Delta.

Charlie finally interrupted him, yawning to emphasize his claim of an a.m. prowl with Brody the night before. Lamont insisted, with his more usual politeness, that they leave immediately. On the way home, he admitted to some nervousness about his reception. Neither parent had answered his letters, so he couldn't be sure they were expecting him.

Charlie dropped him off, waited until he was on the porch, then drove slowly around the block. Lamont was still sitting on the front steps smoking another cigar with his feet propped up on his duffel bag.

When Charlie arrived the next morning, Lamont's mother answered his knock. A gaunt, hollow-chested woman with small sharp features, she spoke to him through the screen, patting at her curlers and drawing her bathrobe tighter, "You'll find Soldierboy in the garage but I don't know that he'll talk with you. He's very high and mighty this morning." She sniffed and closed the door.

Charlie walked around the house to a two-car garage opening onto an alley. Lamont was there, his legs splayed out from under the front of his Plymouth.

Charlie looked at the car. There were some new dents near the trunk and one of the rear doors was roped shut. The paint, which had never been good was always waxed, was oxidized to a chalky white. Old newspapers, empty bags, bottles, opened emptied cans of cheap bulk oil, sardines, fruit cocktail and balled up cigarette packs filled the back seat.

The hood scoop was gone, leaving a jagged hole in the center, and the engine compartment was covered with dirty oil. The hose between the radiator and the engine was wrapped with friction tape and there were rusty water marks on the underside of the hood.

Charlie kicked the sole of one of Lamont's tennis shoes and heard a thump from under the car. Lamont rolled out, swearing and rubbing at a red spot on his forehead. "Damn it, don't sneak up on a body that way." Lamont's baggy green fatigues and thin tee shirt were splotched with fresh oil and grease.

"So," Charlie said, "what're you doing?"

Lamont tossed a crescent wrench and pliers back under the car and stood up; he wiped his hands on his pants. "I don't know. I really don't." He looked the car over and kicked gently at a tire. "My dear old stepdaddy's been driving it back and forth to work for three months. Shithead. He just drove it until it wouldn't go no more."

"It's got no water, no gas, battery's dead, crankcase is dry, he ran it out of oil. If I get it started I guess I'll find out what else he ruined."

"Why don't you forget it? Enjoy your leave, man. You only got a week. Don't waste it on this heap."

Lamont pushed his chin out and narrowed his eyes. "No, I'm going to get it going and move it out of here. That bastard won't touch it again. I don't know what I'll do to it. I'll drive it off a cliff or give it away but he'll never see it again."

They made up a shopping list of parts needed to get the car

155

running and Charlie left, taking the battery with him to be charged and a gas can.

They had it running that night, after five raddled hours, tracing and fixing one problem after another. They poured fresh gas in the tank and found the fuel pump was shot. The first replacement pump, purchased at Pep Boy's, worked no better than the original. When they got a good pump, they found the fuel line leaked.

Beer and the necessary detached patience got them to the point where Lamont once more doubtfully turned the key, and it caught and ran. It ran roughly, but it was loud and Lamont revved it, again and again, as though he could shake loose the remaining problems. The garage filled with black smoke.

They stood in the doorway, finishing the beer, watching it idle. "Well, it's running on about six cylinders, but it's running," Charlie said.

Lamont lit his first cigar of the day. "I guess we can sort out the rest tomorrow. We're over the hard part, don't you think?"

The engine was rocking on its mounts, idling roughly; as they watched it started shaking harder, backfired, and then died. "Yeah," Charlie said, "that's enough for tonight."

Charlie cleaned his tools and Lamont lifted the trash out of the car's interior, filling a barrel. He was still digging around under the seats when Charlie was ready to leave.

Charlie leaned in, "Listen, I'll see you tomorrow. I've got to help Brody put in a clutch, so it probably won't be till after dinner. O.K.?"

Lamont said something that sounded like, "See you." He had his head nearly under the front seat and his feet hanging out a side window. Charlie tied his shoelaces together and left.

The clutch Brody's friend had provided was the wrong size and the job took longer than expected. It was nearly eight o'clock when Charlie arrived at Lamont's.

Lamont was waiting out front, sitting on the curb. He got in the car as Charlie parked. "Why don't you pull up the block," he said. Charlie looked over, drawn by a bruise on Lamont's cheek. A corner of his mouth was puffy and smeared with blood.

"What happened?"

Lamont looked in the mirror and wiped at the blood. "Dean."

"Your stepfather?"

"Yeah, he doesn't look too hot either."

"What'd he do it for?"

"He got up this morning and his pickup wouldn't start. So he took the Plymouth and drove it to work."

"Ahh man, that shows no class."

"I was still in bed when I heard him start it up. So I hitched out to Covina, where he works, and drove it back. He didn't come home until after seven and then we got into it. You suppose I could stay with you for the next couple days, just till New Year's."

"Sure," Charlie said. "What about your car?"

"It's parked about five blocks over. Just let me get my stuff."

Lamont walked back to the porch and got his bag and his uniform, encased in a long clear plastic laundry wrapper. Charlie saw a corner of the front window blinds move as Lamont came down the steps.

They picked up the Plymouth, hidden on a nearby supermarket parking lot. Lamont nervously hot-wired it, worried by the blase scrutiny of two boxboys collecting shopping carts, and followed Charlie to his apartment. They had to park on the street and Lamont removed the battery, and carried it inside.

They went out for dinner and as the evening wore on Lamont grew quieter. Just before bed he told Charlie, "It's strange, I'm gone three months and a lot of things changed. I wonder what it'll be like after three years."

"Well I hate to be the one," Charlie said, "but I told you not to enlist, man. Three years is a long time."

157

"I didn't look at it that way before, I mean, going in, you figure three years, it'll be gone in a hurry. Look at high school, I was a sophomore and bang, I was a senior. What the hell, I didn't have anything to keep me here when I went in and I sure don't now. Still, it's weird, inside a week I'll be in Kansas. In six months I'll be overseas."

Charlie was startled. "Is that for sure? I thought when you enlisted you got a choice."

"Not really. Not in infantry anyway. I think you have to have some college or something. You don't make any money, though, unless you get overseas."

"Did you volunteer?"

"It just sort of happens. See I qualified as an expert Rifle in basic. When I get to Fort Riley, I can get on heavy machine gun if I want. But even if I was a clerk, I'd still be going over. I'm ninth division and we're scheduled to go. The difference is that if I come out qualified on machine gun, I make rank faster and the money's double."

Lamont stretched and smiled dreamily, "By the time I hit the street again I'll be able to buy any car I want and fix it up the way I want and have money left to pay the speeding tickets."

"That's a long ways away," Charlie said.

"Yeah, but it'll probably take me that long just to decide what I want. Anyway, like I said before, there sure wasn't anything to keep me here."

Lamont stretched again and blinked. "I got to turn in. You really get used to going to bed early."

Charlie stripped the couch and went to find some blankets. Lamont was asleep when he returned.

The next morning they ran through a tune-up on the Plymouth, with little effect. Charlie finally checked the compression and found three cylinders were bad. "That settles it," he told Lamont.

Lamont looked at him helplessly. "Do you want it? I haven't got a pink slip 'cause I had to put it in Dean's name. I got it when I was seventeen. Maybe you could sell it for parts."

Charlie considered and shook his head. "Naw. The engine's shot. I could get maybe twenty bucks for the tires and rims, five for the battery. It's not what you'd call a hot model. Best bet's a junkyard." He closed the hood while Lamont nodded gloomily.

Over coffee that evening at Van de Kamp's, they were discussing New Year's Eve and Lamont got an idea. They planned to go to the Rose Parade, not really for the parade, but for the night preceding it. Thousands of kids swarmed Pasadena and took over the streets, and it struck Lamont that it might be wise to take the Plymouth. "Look, we'll both be drunk probably and if we're not, there'll still be plenty of drunks on the road. Why risk your Chevy. If we crack up mine, who cares?"

Charlie thought that made sense and had an idea of his own. "And afterwards, if you want to, we can just park it, grab the plates and the registration and walk away."

"Great idea. If there's no I.D., they can't trace it. Dean never gets a paw on it." Lamont said, "We can hitch home, pick up my stuff and run me down to the bus station. Neat and simple."

Their enthusiasm grew over the next day as they added refinements. They stripped the car of all identification; Charlie ground away the engine number on the side of the block. Lamont chiseled loose the chassis number plate and rigged the license plates with wire. They left the registration in the glove box, in case they were stopped.

Neither had ever seen the Rose Parade, but they had both heard rumors of the supposedly wild night that preceded it.

"I heard they turned over cop cars last year," Charlie told Lamont, "but they wouldn't say anything in the paper because they didn't want it to happen next year."

"Yeah. I heard that too and I heard they tore down some of the stands for bonfires. This guy I know was there two years ago and he met this girl from Muir High. She was wandering around drunk, carrying a sleeping bag. Anyway, he swears he

159

got laid on the lawn of one of those big mansions on Orange Grove."

"Could be," Charlie said. "They come from all over. I can see it, they get away from home, they know they'll never see the guy again. I mean, why not?"

"What time you think we should get there?" Lamont asked.

"We should be fairly early. I heard they block off the streets before midnight. I'd like to be there by eight or nine."

The car was packed with blankets and bags of food and liquor by late afternoon. They waited as long as they could stand to and a little after seven got in the car and headed north on San Fernando Road, turning at the beginning of Colorado Boulevard.

They rode across Glendale with the Plymouth dying at stoplights, breezed through Eagle Rock - Lamont finally had the signals timed - and dipped down on the other side for the approach to the Arroyo Seco Bridge, leading into Pasadena. Already traffic was backing up because of the barricaded side streets. People were parking on the Eagle Rock side of the bridge and walking across. Kids, mostly high school age, in couples, threesomes and small crowds, were streaming across the bridge carrying ice chests, blankets, folding chairs, sleeping bags and sacks of snacks and liquor. They walked between the motionless stalled cars, some laughing and talking among themselves and to the drivers and passengers. Others moved more hurriedly, intent on securing the best curbside seats along the parade route.

At the end of the bridge, the cars were waved left by a waiting policeman onto Orange Grove.

Caught in the flow of traffic, they followed Orange Grove to the first signal, Walnut, a street paralleling Colorado, and went right.

The side streets between Walnut and Colorado were blocked off along the parade route. As they drove past, looking down the long flare-lit blocks, they could see the crowds swarming Colorado, the bleachers and police cars parked crosswise in back of the barricades.

160

They followed Walnut for five miles, a half-hour drive in the traffic, before they were able to turn for Colorado. They came out by Pasadena City College, near a Bob's drive-in, and decided to have dinner before bucking the traffic again.

The line at the drive-in was long and it was almost nine before they found a place, nearly ten when they left.

They were several miles from the start of the parade route but cars were backed up from there to the college. "This is worse than the Sunset Strip on a Saturday night," Charlie said. "Look at it, no one's moving."

They remained in the middle of an intersection through two lights and then the lines began to creep forward. With the side streets blocked off, there was no cross traffic and the drivers ignored the traffic signals.

The Plymouth's engine was laboring badly and Lamont shut it off when they were stopped. He would wait for a gap to develop, not much more than a car-length to prevent people in the other lane from cutting in, start the engine, rush forward, hit the brakes and shut it off again.

During one of these surges, Lamont kept his foot on the gas a little too long and they nearly rear-ended the car in front. When he slammed on the brakes, something bumped forward on the floor from under Charlie's seat and hit him on the ankle. He groped under the seat and lifted out a brick.

He regarded it for a moment and looked over to Lamont. "You gonna break the windows when we're done?"

"Better than that," Lamont said, "You'll see."

Charlie looked at the brick again. "What are you going to do with it?"

"You'll see."

Charlie couldn't get him to tell what the brick was for. He tried direct questions, needling, and guessing, but nothing worked. Lamont was uncharacteristically resolute.

The sidewalks were now as packed as the street. Opposite them, a middle-aged couple had set up folding chairs and were resting contentedly watching the cars creep by. A line of boys in green lettermen's sweaters walked five abreast with their arms linked, causing people walking the other way to duck or walk around them. As Charlie watched, they neared a muscular young man with a Mohawk haircut. The man, dressed in a light sport shirt and baggy slacks, had been lounging in the doorway of a bar when he saw them coming and planted himself in their way, staring. Ten feet from him, the line split neatly, walked past and linked up again. They moved on, at a quicker pace, while the man stared at their backs and then walked back to the doorway.

They were nearing the starting point of the parade, where the cars had to turn off, and as they moved up Lamont grew more nervous, repeatedly stalling the car.

Approaching the next to last light, Lamont asked for the time again. Charlie told him a quarter after eleven.

"I wanted to wait for midnight but this is the best place," Lamont said. "I don't want to get too close to those cops."

"Are you talking about ditching it here?" Charlie asked.

"At the next light," Lamont said, "just lock it up and walk away and we leave the brick on the gas pedal."

Charlie started laughing. "You think of that by yourself?"

Lamont nodded, flushed with pleasure.

Charlie hauled the bags of food and liquor into the front seat between them and put the blankets on top. He locked the back doors and checked the windows, cranking them tight. They were two cars away from the intersection. Charlie opened the glove box to find the registration.

"Let's leave that," Lamont said. "I started thinking about all the trouble we were going to so the cops wouldn't know whose car it is and then I thought, why?"

Charlie read the form. The legal owner was *Dean E. Jackson*. "He had to sign for it," Lamont said. "Maybe they'll stick him for the towing and storage."

"That is simple. But nasty," Charlie said. "You sure you thought this up by yourself? Must be that Army training. We might as well leave the plates on then."

"You ready?" Lamont said. The car ahead of them was edging into the intersection. Lamont waited until it reached the other side. He eased the Plymouth to the middle of the intersection and set the parking brake. "Go ahead," he told Charlie, "I'll wait till you're off the street."

Charlie stuffed the blankets into the bags and backed out of the car, carrying one under each arm. He kicked the door shut and walked to the curb.

Lamont leaned across to lock the door. He opened his door, pushing down the button lock, and got out. No one seemed to be paying attention. He leaned in and set the brick on the accelerator pedal. He had the door locked and was crossing to the sidewalk before the turning heads had identified the source of the engine roar.

Lamont shoved his way into the crowd next to Charlie. They backed up until they were behind the crowd and could see over them.

The noise the Plymouth made was amazing; a tortured "WAAAAAAAAAAAAAAAAAAAAAAAAAAAAAAH..." worse than race track noise, because it was sustained. The whole car was trembling. People in front were beginning to hold their ears.

The noise went on and on, unchanged in pitch, and the people in front were beginning to look nervous. The press of the crowd behind was forcing them into the street and some of them were trying to move back, acting like it was a wounded animal in front of them.

The cars behind hadn't moved, but windows were going up all along the line as the exhaust smoke began to fill the intersection. Finally one of the cars in the other lane made a move, shooting past with the curious faces of the passengers pressed against the glass. Other cars pulled out after that, sweeping wide into the empty oncoming lanes to get around, and a space developed around the Plymouth. Drivers who judged they were far enough away hung back, watching.

The Plymouth was death-smoking now, sometimes blue, sometimes white, and the fumes reached even Charlie and

163

Lamont, well back from the street. They looked at each other; neither of them had expected the car to last this long.

The bellow of the Plymouth grew more distinct as the drivers in front and behind shut off their engines to wait. Masses of people were moving down from the parade start to find out what was making the noise and with them, pushing through, were the first three policemen.

Just before they arrived, two small boys raced out to touch it, tagging the Plymouth on the trunk and running back to the curb, head down and arms wrapped over their heads.

Charlie and Lamont backed into a doorway as the police burst through. In a minute there were ten of them. One of them got close enough to see the padlock securing the hood and backed away. They conferred, shouting in each other's ears, and laid down a circle of flares. There was a brief moment of tension when a mounted officer galloped up. He unholstered his revolver and was clearly ready to shoot the Plymouth, was in fact aiming at the hood, when a sergeant prevailed, grabbing the horse assuredly by the bit and swinging the pair away from the car. The police finally settled for more flares, pushed the crowd back and waited with everyone else.

The wail of the engine had altered only minimally from the beginning, but suddenly there was a hitch, then two more, and the note began to falter. White smoke was rolling out from under the fenders.

At the back, oil began to dribble out the tail pipe, then oil mixed with water and after the first of a series of backfires, a gush of water and steam. The pitch went lower and lower, the front end shaking, and the crowd began to press back.

The rods began knocking, clearly one, then two, then all, and then heavier and louder, the mains. The Plymouth started to rock and something let loose with a cracking noise, a bulge appeared in the hood and metal started dropping in the street. There were two more bangs, the engine seized and everything stopped. Only the eerie hiss of the radiator and a sizzle of hot oil and metal remained.

A curious singing hum started under the hood and continued until the police had emptied several fire extinguishers through the front end fenders.

Charlie and Lamont looked at each other. They were both sweating. "Fucker lasted a lot longer than I thought it would," Charlie said.

Lamont nodded solemnly in agreement. "Chrysler makes a good engine," he said. "I thought they were going to have to shoot it."

Charlie handed him a sack and one of the blankets and they started walking. Halfway down the next block they were still turning to look. At that distance the smoke and steam hanging at the intersection were more obvious. One of the policemen was breaking a front window. They saw him lean in to turn off the ignition and then the Plymouth was hidden again by the crowd.

They made their way around the barricades at the start of the parade route, avoiding the gazes of the policemen who stood by their cars, watching the crowd for obvious drunks and the overly nervous. Most of the crowd was about their age, there by the thousands, as they had anticipated. None of the stories had mentioned so many cops. There seemed to be hundreds of them, fully in control and making spot checks for liquor and I.D.

On Orange Grove there were fewer police, and they kept to the side streets. The crowd was less active here; most of them were already sitting or looking for space along the curb.

Charlie and Lamont had just settled in a space in front of a spotlighted mansion, Tournament of Roses Headquarters, when a ragged chant went up all over the street, counting down to midnight. "Five, four, three, two, one." Firecrackers started popping, airhorns sounded and a cheering roar came from the crowd. A couple next to them rose up in their sleeping bag in an athletic-looking kiss. Charlie struggled with his shopping bag, trying to reach a bottle of vodka in the bottom, but the yells of "Happy New Year" were over before he had it uncapped.

He and Lamont passed the bottle ceremonially and wished each other a happy New Year. They watched the convulsing sleeping bag beside them for a time. There was a shudder in the bag and it went still. "Happy 1968", Charlie said.

"Year of the Monkey," Lamont said, "I learned that in Basic. In the Asian Calendar this is the year of the Monkey. It's not usually a good year."

The drawn-out wail of a Klaxon siren down the street distracted them. They stood up and saw a stirring in the crowd there. A boy in a white suit, wearing a sandwich board with Greek letters on it, came into view. He wound the Klaxon again, holding it over his head. Behind him, rushing through the crowd, was a long costume dragon with twenty legs. The Greek letters were repeated the whole length of the dragon, red on the green background. A tall boy, occasionally visible inside the head, was clapping the mouth of the dragon at people along the curb. On a clear stretch he started running. The boys behind him took some time to catch up. Just when they were moving well, one of them got out of step and fell. The dragon sprawled sideways. At the tail, a boy's head popped through the fabric.

They tried to get up again, shouting and kicking at each other and finally got on their feet in unison at a count of three.

They started off again, more slowly. The boy at the tail, whose head was exposed, yelled directions, acting like the driver on the rear end of a hook and ladder firetruck.

"What college were they from?" Lamont asked.

"I don't know. I can't read Greek, man." Charlie passed the bottle back and began looking through the bags. He opened two bags of chips and cut up a salami.

Lamont didn't eat. He kept the bottle, getting quieter and shiny-eyed as the night wore on. He was asleep by two, curled in his blanket with his shoes under his head.

Charlie lasted an hour longer, tapering off on beer.

He woke up around nine o'clock. The parade was in progress. He could hear it, but couldn't see. He saw shoes and then a mass of legs. Blocking his view, directly in front, were three grey-haired women with sweaters on their shoulders, sitting in lawn chairs. The nearest one had set her chair down on Charlie's toes, waking him when she sat down. As he struggled to pull his blanket out from under, she turned glaring and lifted the back a little. Her friends turned around too and stared at him blankly while he gathered up the blanket.

Charlie touched his ankle and Lamont started up, face pale and frightened, marked with red creases from the shoes he had slept on. "No!" Lamont said, "I don't have to," and then he blinked at Charlie, lay down again and asked what time it was.

"Just about nine o'clock," Charlie told him. In a moment Lamont sat up, shading his face from the sun, and wrapped the blanket around his shoulders. A loudspeaker somewhere behind them announced the imminent arrival of the Sheriff's Mounted Posse, directing their attention to the nearly solid silver saddle of the lead rider. The clop of hooves and snorts of the horses reached them. After the posse had passed, a mock gunfight was staged. It sounded like six or seven gunmen were involved. The announcer noted coyly that the villains were choosing their resting spots carefully because of the horses that had preceded them. He raised them by name, introducing each to heavy applause and scattered hissing. They walked off, reloading. In a short time, the sound of gunfire started again several blocks down, partially obscured by an advancing band.

Charlie looked at Lamont. "Let's get out of here." The remaining food and liquor were scattered amongst the legs of the crowd and they left it. Exhausted, heads throbbing, red-eyed and cotton-mouthed, they walked away, trailing their blankets, without looking at the parade.

They found a gas station, two blocks over. The gas station owner was sitting on a cot in the driveway beside a sign reading: $5 - Parking - $5. After brief haggling, he agreed to open the restrooms for a dollar apiece.

They waited in the office for the cab to arrive. Charlie was willing to hitchhike, but Lamont said screw it. He had money left over and there wouldn't be time to spend it.

They dozed in the cab, scarcely hearing the driver's account of the difficulties and hazards overcome to reach them. At the apartment, Charlie showered and Lamont fell asleep on the floor. Charlie set the alarm for two-thirty. He awakened before the alarm and heard Lamont being sick in the bathroom. He took water, two shuddering gulps, until he felt well enough for coffee.

Lamont shaved in the shower, yelling above the rush of the water, got in his uniform and they left the apartment. They stopped on the way so Lamont could get cheeseburgers for the bus ride and drove the freeway at seventy-five with Lamont watching behind them. They arrived at the depot five minutes early to learn the bus was running late.

Sitting in the waiting room, they quickly ran out of conversation as the weight of the occasion bore down on them. Charlie was beginning to wish the bus had been waiting. In one of his jacket pockets, he felt a small packet and brought it out. He looked at the forgotten topless playing cards, and handed them over. "These are for the trip."

Lamont opened them and fanned the cards. "I'll be damned. I think I had the other half of these and I threw 'em away."

"Lot of stops between here and Kansas. You'll get the rest."

The bus arrived and Charlie carried Lamont's bag out to the driveway. There, with wistful solemnity, they shook hands and Lamont put his hat on. He stopped on the steps and called back, "It was a hell of a New Year's, wasn't it?" Charlie waved and nodded. "Let's get there earlier next time," Lamont said, and went up the steps.

Charlie followed his progress down the aisle and stood by the window where Lamont took a seat. Lamont pressed his nose against the glass and made faces, then stopped abruptly, sat back and lit a cigar. Charlie was puzzled until he followed the rolling motion of Lamont's eyes and the pointing cigar across the aisle where a young woman in a pink suit and matching scarf over her rollers had seated herself. She had a makeup case open in her lap and was staring into its mirror, the fingers of both hands spreading one corner of her mouth.

The bus's engine started and settled into a rattling idle while the driver walked back and made Lamont put out his cigar.

Lamont waved until the bus dipped into the driveway and then made a motion like a salute. Charlie watched the bus turn onto Main Street and followed it for a few signals, standing on the sidewalk with his hands in his back pockets, until the bus's interior lights winked off.

He walked back toward his car, thinking about the general future, something he rarely did, wondering when he would see Lamont again and what Lamont might be like in a couple of years. It was hard to imagine. He had no sense, himself, of where he would be and what he would be doing.

Preoccupied, searching his pockets for his keys as he walked, Charlie bumped against an elderly Chinese man in a heavy black overcoat wrapped about him like a robe, standing beneath the marquee at the Fifth and Main Follies. The man gasped as Charlie jarred him and struggled to stay upright, pushing on his canes. Charlie apologized, but the man wouldn't look at him. He shuffled a half step away and gazed ahead at the grainy, sepia-toned photograph of the theater's featured entertainer, a large-breasted blonde woman curled on a hassock, looking down with apparent admiration at a sign crossing her open fringed vest that read: "Held over".

Charlie glanced at the other photographs, the empty ticket booth, and walked on. Approaching the next intersection, he found his keys and started digging through his pockets for change, hoping he had enough to pay for parking.

22-

Connie was starting to show. Her reckoning was that it had been nearly five months. For the first four, she'd hardly had to bother with camouflage.

Now, even the loose-fitting waitress uniform and apron couldn't conceal what had happened, what was happening.

She'd hidden her condition as cunningly as she could, but her mother had been weeping since November. Richie had gone weird on her, silent but nearly sniffing at her, since December. Even her father had figured it out in January. She dealt with the havoc at home, but now it was becoming a problem at work. And that had to be solved. She needed two more months of tips to pay for the trip to Florida, where she would stay with her aunt.

Corio's Café was a great place to work. Tips were excellent, increasing now that her pregnancy was visible, and the owners, Reuben and Alma Corio were warm, kind people. They were also Pentecostal Christians and once Connie started to show, they'd pushed to meet her husband. A husband was preferred. They would settle, it seemed, for a father. Someone they might talk to about fatherly obligations. But Someone, a body to address, was required. Mrs. Corio had made that clear. A father, if not a husband, was going to be a condition of employment. They loved her, Mrs. Corio said, but they were not fools.

Desperate, Connie was working up the courage to make a phone call she dreaded. Charlie was the only one she could think of who would understand, who would go along with the goof.

Charlie was working the Saturday morning shift at Jesse's Mobil, a small two-pump station in Atwater, filling in for Ray Orozco.

Ray, planning to attend his brother John's wedding the night before and planning on a severe hangover or luck with a bridesmaid, had asked Charlie to open for him. There was some doubt in Charlie's mind whether Jesse knew or agreed to the substitution, but since Ray had prepaid him twenty dollars, he hadn't asked.

Charlie had unlocked the pumps at six, sleepy and irritated, but the corner was a slow one and with no commuter traffic. He was able to start a pot of coffee, walk down the street to pick up donuts, and read most of the paper before the first customer came in.

By seven, no other customers had appeared, and he was starting to enjoy the day. He sat at the owner's desk in the glass-fronted office, watching the occasional car glide by and reading through Jesse's employment application file. Some of his friends were in there; he read their forms idly, sometimes intrigued by the odd middle names, references, and past employment descriptions he knew to be lies.

The day had a slow, soothing feel to it. The air was crisp, still cool. Around eight, a young boy with a bright striped scarf trailing back over his shoulders walked by, bouncing a brand new basketball. His second customer came in, a friendly man in a glass company truck, who talked sports with Charlie and told him to take his time.

It felt, Charlie decided, like the day after Christmas. The weather, everyone moving slow, comfortable and still full from big dinners.

The day continued like that. Charlie took each customer as they came in, cheerfully washing all the windows, checking tires and under hoods without being asked. He found a frayed alternator belt on a Chevelle and changed it in less than five minutes. The belt was right there in the back room. He picked the right sockets on the first try.

By three, Ray Orozco hadn't showed and hadn't called, so Charlie decided to close. As he rolled the equipment and tire displays into the lube bay, Charlie reflected on how nicely the day had gone. He had dreaded getting up but now had to admit it was probably the best way he could have spent the time. He wrote down the opening and closing gas pump numbers on the daily sheet and locked the doors at four.

At home, the phone was ringing as he walked in. He rushed but it stopped as he picked up the receiver. He hung up and waited. The phone remained silent.

He was in the bathroom when it rang again. Pulling up his pants, he hurried into the front room and jerked the receiver out of the cradle. "Hang on", he said. He buttoned his pants and zipped up, the phone tucked under his arm. Stuffing in his shirt, he dropped the phone; a tinny voice reached him from the floor. He retrieved it and said, "Yeah?"

A dim, feminine voice said, "Charlie?"

"Donna? I'm sorry, I dropped the phone."

"It's Connie."

"What?"

"Connie Ciccarelli ... Were you expecting a call? I can call back."

"Oh, Connie. No. Not really. It just sounded like long distance."

"No. I'm still in town."

"I haven't seen you for a while. How're you doing?"

There was a slight pause. "Can I come by and talk to you for a minute?"

"Sure. You know where I live?"

"I'm right around the corner." The connection was broken. Charlie stood, listening to the buzz, and put the phone down. He wondered what she wanted. It had been about five months since he'd seen her, since the party.

He went out on the balcony, beside the stairs, to wait for her. Her dented blue Valiant rounded the corner, swung into the garage and emerged, to park along the front. Connie got out.

Leaving the door open, she leaned in. She backed out, struggling with a bulky grocery sack. Holding the sack against her, she kicked the door shut and walked toward the stairs.

Charlie met her halfway down and took the bag of groceries from her. "Hey," she said, "I can handle it." On the landing Charlie turned around, saying, "I know you can," and got his first real look at her. Her small, swollen stomach pushed out the front of a lint covered black jersey that bagged and hung everyplace else. He stared, wishing he wasn't, until her eyes dropped. "Come on in," Charlie said.

In the front room, she took back the bag of groceries. "There's some frozen stuff. I didn't want to leave it in the car. Is it okay if I put them in the fridge?"

Charlie nodded dumbly. "Where?" she said. He pointed to the kitchen and plopped down on the couch.

He caught himself rubbing his hands together and shaking his head. He clasped his hands and looked at them, anticipating her return. It was quiet in the kitchen for too long. Stepping quietly, he went to the doorway. Connie stood by the refrigerator, her hand still on the unopened freezer door, crying noiselessly.

He reached across and took the bag from her, set it on the counter and put his arms around her. He held her, careful not to press too hard against her stomach, and rubbed her back as she sobbed. She tried to stop, pushing away from him to wipe her face, and then sagged forward, her whole weight on him, limp, and her shoulders pitched and heaved uncontrollably.

When she'd quieted, he tried to lead her into the living room, but she resisted, breaking away to rummage through the bag on the counter, pulling out fish sticks, frozen vegetables, and ice cream, which she placed in the freezer. She tossed a roast, milk, and a carton of eggs onto an empty shelf in the refrigerator, banging the door shut behind them. She leaned the top of her head against the refrigerator door, looking down.

She sighed, shoulders lifting, and still looking down, said, "Half that stuff's probably gone bad. I've been driving them around for hours."

She turned to face Charlie. Her eyes, still tearing, pouched and red, showed enough anger to relieve him a little. "The only time they let me out of the house is for work and to go shopping." She looked down at her stomach and shook her head. "Real sharp folks, my family. Sometime, I hope they'll explain what kind of trouble they're supposed to be keeping me out of now."

"Have they been pretty shitty?"

Connie shrugged. "About what you'd expect. My dad yelled, went to work for two weeks in Fresno, came back and yelled some more. My mom cried. Now she just watches me.

"My fucking brother tells me I look like an olive stuck on a toothpick."

"Richie?"

"Richie, yeah." She sobered. "He cried when he found out. Then, he was going to kill the guy. Then, when I wouldn't tell him who, he was going to kill me."

Charlie said, "He never found out?"

Connie shook her head. "Nobody knows." She was silent, then catching Charlie's glance, she nodded, her mouth setting in a firm line. "Yeah. I know who."

"I didn't <u>ask</u>," Charlie said.

"Come on." She pushed away from the refrigerator and preceded him into the front room. They sat together on the couch. Charlie shook out a cigarette and offered her one.

"I quit," she said. Charlie opened his mouth in mock astonishment, allowing the cigarette to drop onto his lap. "It's hard on the kid," Connie said.

Charlie lit up, blowing the smoke away from her after she began fanning in front of her face.

"I can't tell you who it was."

"I didn't ask."

"I know. It doesn't really make any difference. You don't know him anyway." Charlie thought he did but stayed silent. She pinched the hem of her jersey and rolled it between her fingers. "Christ, I hardly did."

She looked up, managing a wobbly grin, "The nuns would love it. It was exactly what they said. One time. Boom! That's all. God gets you."

"One time?" Charlie said.

"Yeh ... to tell the truth, that first month? I thought I caught the clap, too. Would've rounded it off nice, you know?"

Charlie laughed and put out the cigarette. He opened the front door, to let the remaining smoke escape. He sat back down, studying her face smudged with mascara, still wet, but lively again.

"Are you going to keep it?"

"I'm five fucking months, Charlie. That decision's been made."

"No," Charlie said, "I meant are you gonna keep it or put it up for adoption."

"It's not an It and I don't know," Connie said, "I haven't thought about it seriously yet, I mean, to decide."

There was a change in her as she said it. Her head dropped. Charlie thought she was about to start crying again. She shook her head with her eyes closed and slapped herself on the forehead. She raised her face and stared at Charlie, her expression a curious mixture of hesitancy and what almost looked like anger. One of the things Charlie liked best about Connie was that you could watch a thought visibly cross her face.

"What?" Charlie said.

"Look," Connie said, "the only way I can do this is straight out. Here's the deal. I want to go my aunt's, in Florida. Miami Beach. I just can't be around my family right now. They're fucking me up and it's going to get worse. I gotta get out. So I want to go to Florida and have the kid there and decide.

"To do that, I got to keep my job another two months. I need the money." She explained about the Corios and what Charlie would have to do.

Charlie didn't have to think about it. "Sure," he said, "When?"

Connie sagged, the tension leaving her body. "Monday."

"Copacetic," Charlie said. He was delighted by her. "And you can do me a favor."

"You got it," Connie said.

"Tuesday night," Charlie said, "I got to go out to Toluca Lake Bob's. I'm shilling for a guy named Moon. He wants to race there, but it's hard to get it started in Toluca Lake."

"It's mostly rich kids but they're afraid of getting taken. They don't like outsiders and they really won't like Moon. He's from Pacoima, which is deep, deep Valley, and he's black.

"So he'll come out. He'll get uppity. He'll insult them. And if no one else will race him, it's up to me. I kick his ass and then usually they all sign up."

"You've done this before," Connie said.

"Yeah. Pasadena. Glendale. La Crescenta. It works."

"And why do I need to be there?"

"So I don't get bored. Plus, you're perfect cover. Who's not going to believe a gas jockey who risks his hard-earned cash with his pregnant wife watching? You can add to the drama if you want. Try to talk me out of it. Talk about saving our money for diapers."

"I'm supposed to work that night."

"Better and better. When I talk to the Corios on Monday, I tell them you have to have the night off so we can get married."

"Oh yeah," Connie said.

"And, since you'll tell Richie and Daddy and Mommy you're working, you won't have to sneak out. So you'll need to buy a ring. But you can go back to work Wednesday since we've already had our honeymoon."

"Gosh," Connie said, with an ironic flutter of eyelashes, "I wish I'd talked to you months ago. You clearly could have solved so many problems."

"Tuesday?" Charlie said.

"Monday?" Connie said.

"Deal."

"Deal."

"I've got to work until eight at Morenos," Charlie said.

"The Union Gas Station?"

"The one, my record job. I've been there nine months."

"Meet you there. Eight o'clock."

23-

Charlie raised his head just far enough to see from under his cap and watched the revolving sign at the corner of the station lot. The orange ball turned slowly, bringing its blue trademark into Charlie's view. He wondered idly, for perhaps the thousandth time since he'd come to work at Moreno's, whether the ball turned on a long shaft running through the pole, or if the motor was on top.

Cars passed randomly. In the periphery of his vision, Charlie could see the approaching lights but refused to turn his head, as though this would encourage them to pull in to the pumps. He held his breath until they were past as part of this discipline.

The traffic light at the corner turned green, and Charlie began counting aloud, "One-Mississippi, two-Mississippi...," When he reached thirty-seven, he snapped his fingers and pointed at the light with elaborate casualness. It changed to orange.

"Timing, babies, timing," Charlie said and snapped his fingers again. He thought briefly of the Ford he'd beaten away from that same light the week before.

It was nearly seven. Charlie wondered if Moon had left for Toluca Lake yet. Connie should be on the way. Things had gone well at Corios. Charlie had been suitably submissive, had promised a civil ceremony within a day, and they'd been able to escape before things got too religious. They'd actually had fun, and Connie had bought herself a ring that afternoon.

Charlie picked up a grease rag and wiped the tools that

179

were loose on the work bench before hanging them up. The rough outline of each tool was painted, white on the blue pegboard. He checked for gaps and stuffed the rag in his back pocket.

There hadn't been any customers for over an hour. Tuesdays were slow. He decided to start closing up. After cleaning the islands, he locked the outside doors and sat down in the office to empty the cash drawer into the safe.

Carrying out the trash and letting the air out of the storage tank were the last of his listed duties. Charlie dumped the contents of one trashcan into another and took it out.

While the air bled out of the compressor tank, he went over the checklist a final time and wrote his hours on the time sheet.

Taped to the wall beside the compressor was a yellowed notice. Waiting for the needle on the air gauge to sink to zero, Charlie contemplated the faded block printing. He was so used to seeing it that he hadn't read it in months.

JOB DESCRIPTION

YOUR JOB IS A SALESMAN, SELL YOUR SELF! THEN LOOK FOR THE NEED, AND SELL IT YOUR FIRST OBLIGATION IS TO THE CUSTOMER DRIVING INTO THE PUMP BLOCK, RUN TO GREET HIM YOU HAVE A POSITION OF TRUST, AND THAT IS THE SAFEGUARDING OF COMPANY FUNDS. A MIS-USE OF THIS TRUST WILL RESULT IN PROSECUTION AND OR TERMINATION IF NOT ENGAGED IN SALES OR SERVICE. YOUR RESPONSIBILITY IS TO KEEP THE STATION AND PREMISES CLEAN AND TO PREFORM PREVENTIVE MAINTENANCE. ALL RECORDS SUCH AS WORK ORDERS WILL BE PREPARED NEAT AND ACCURATELY WITH THE EMPHASIS ON DOUBLE CHECKS YOU ARE EXPECTED TO REPORT FOR WORK CLEAN SHAVEN AND ON TIME!

Scratched below on the metal siding, partially obscured by

newer paint, was a response: "Chinga tu Madre and you too Moreno."

Charlie couldn't keep from smiling. The message had been left by his predecessor on nights, Augie Galarza. Augie had come up thirty dollars short one morning, fifty the next, and Moreno had fired him. Augie had left messages all around the station. Charlie grinned again, remembering his first night shift. He'd parked his Chevy in the lube room and loaded the trunk with a new battery, two tires, and all the spark plugs, filters, fan belts, and hoses the car would ever need. He'd guessed, correctly, that any shortages would be blamed on Augie. The tank was empty. Charlie shut the bleed valve, washed his hands, and walked over to the front window. He stood with his knees bent, leaning back to catch his reflection, and absorbed himself in the intricacies of combing his hair. He heard the hollow clatter of Connie's Plymouth Valiant before he saw the car. Coming up the driveway, the engine died, and the Valiant coasted to the pumps.

Connie honked the horn and bawled toward the shadowed office, "Hey boy, let's have a little service here for a cash customer."

Charlie sauntered out. Halfway to the car, he took his hands out of his pockets and adopted the fast walk and business-like leer he identified with training-film attendants. Leaning down to Connie's window, he switched the smile on and off. "Good evening. M'am," Charlie said, "May I? Check your choda? Slash your tires? Piss in your tank? M'am?"

Connie laughed. Charlie kicked the front fender, "Fuck you then, Lady. I don't wait on wrecks."

"Neither do I," Connie said, "so you must be ready to go."

"Park it in back," Charlie said, "You should let me give you a tune-up. This thing sounded like a cannery coming down the block."

Charlie drove down Los Feliz, made a right on San Fernando Road, and started north, skirting the west side of Glendale, heading toward Burbank. Charlie punched the radio keys until he found music he liked, a downtown station that seemed to play nothing but old Olympics and Coasters records. He settled back, loose and happy. The long blocks of dark buildings and signboards slid by without registering. The first strains of *Searchin'* came out of the radio. Connie cranked it up. She popped her fingers to the music, "Gonna Find her/ Gonna Find her/ Sherlocka Holmes/ Sama Spade got nothin Chile on me..." and shimmied in place.

Near Toonerville, a barrio to the west edge of Glendale, a dangerously lowered De Soto with six riders packed in bumped across the railroad tracks, caught up, and traveled with them.

Charlie, after a glance registering the occupants as too young to worry about, outwardly ignored their presence. At a stoplight the De Soto's driver, a slight youth wearing a fuzzy red shirt buttoned to the neck, pulled up on their right and got their attention. Leaning out the window, he chucked his head, eyes half closed; it looked like he was pointing with his chin.

"Hey," the boy said. "You want to buy us some beer? We got enough for a case and a six pack for you."

Charlie and Connie looked at each other.

"Sure," Charlie told him. "If you can wait till June, 1969. Meet me right here and I'll fix you <u>right</u> up."

"What?"

"I ain't twenty-one yet. Neither's she," Charlie said, pointing to Connie.

Slowly nodding, the boy pulled reflectively at several long hairs beneath his lower lip. "That's O.K., you know, I really thought you was twenty-one. You look older."

Flattered, Charlie offered a suggestion. "Why don't you go up to the Old Mill Liquor store on Colorado. There's always some wino hanging around. Make sure you got somebody covering the back door."

The driver nodded once more and pulled his head in to confer with his passengers. To Charlie, it looked like they were arguing. The light opposite changed to orange. Charlie noticed the rear window of the De Soto was being lowered. There was a flick of light in the back seat and a firecracker sailed out, sparking, and exploded behind their bumper. Charlie got on it, fishtailing across the intersection with a squeal of rubber.

He slowed and then came to a full stop just beyond the intersection. Charlie looked in the rear view mirror, his eyes narrowing, "Fucking little punks."

"They're just kids," Connie said. "You probably would have been the one to throw the firecracker a couple years back."

"Yeah, and I got my ass kicked for it."

"The story of your poor young life."

The De Soto was still at the intersection. Charlie could see the driver, turned around and reaching to hit someone in the back seat.

A mile on they made their turn, left into Burbank, crossing over the train tracks. They traveled briefly through a residential zone of pastel apartments into an area of small factories, some still working. A tire recapping plant, a tool and die works, stutteringly illuminated by smoking yellow sheets of light from arc welders. Most of the following block was a commercial plating factory, an open-sided shed where men moved about a slatted platform over troughs that reflected a blue glow on their faces and rubber aprons.

Gradually they moved into the aircraft and defense district, plants measuring in the acres, spaced by parking lots with guard booths at the entrances. At one stop, Charlie was startled by the sight of hundreds of people streaming out of a hangar. They spread out, running through the parked cars, while Charlie craned to see flames or whatever else might be the source of panic. Then he noticed the thermoses and lunch buckets they carried and heard the buzzer that marked the end of their shift.

Traffic started to pick up. They were drifting out of the industrial district. At first there were only a few lights for each block, liquor stores, bars, a bowling alley. Further west the lights began to string together, and the signs became larger and more elaborate.

The street widened to four lanes, marking the start of a solid row of motels and restaurants, and cars began to pack up around them. Four short blocks with long stoplights condensed the traffic even more until they crossed over the freeway and joined what amounted to a parade: two solid lanes of cars backed around the corner and through two intersections.

It was a ten-minute wait before Charlie turned the corner and nosed into the curb line of cars entering the drive-in. Kids, mostly high-school age, stood in groups and sat along the curb on both sides of the street, blocking the driveways and the entrance to the coffee shop, where a harried busboy tried to keep them away from the door.

The busboy ignored a rough-looking biker who had parked his motorcycle on a grass strip beside the restaurant's trademark statue, a fat boy in checkered overalls holding a hamburger aloft.

Inside, the cashier kept a wary eye on both biker and statue. Several Halloweens ago, a wit with a chainsaw had replaced the proffered hamburger with the fat boy's head, and the statue had been subject to abuse ever since. Rumor insisted that the present fat boy had an electrified mesh of bare wires beneath his fiberglass skin. The biker nodded pleasantly to Connie and Charlie when they reached his spot. Charlie nodded back, wondering what the man was doing there. There was a lull in the line's progress, and Charlie was forced to return the man's seemingly friendly gaze for an uncomfortably long time. There were no insignia on the front of the biker's faded denim vest; as they moved past him Charlie could see the back where cleaner, darker cloth outlined the name of a former club: Galloping Gooses. The man was standing now with his arm around the statue, waving to the cars.

The noise in the narrow street was deafening. A constant rumble accompanied by horns and shouting. Any gap in the line of cars provoked a squeal of tires and exhaust roar as a car lunged forward in a thirty or forty-foot performance, ending in a flare of brake lights. The cars behind would have to chase each other's bumpers to prevent cutting in.

When the lines were stalled, a continual din of racketing challenges traveled up and down the ranks. A high-school boy ahead of them, in a stock '62 Mercury with bad mufflers, was moved to floorboard his engine momentarily, producing a flatulent rattle that changed Charlie's face to an imitation of pain. The car next to the Mercury, a clean, healthy-sounding '57 Chevy with a padlocked hood, responded with a tight winging roar. The Chevy crept forward until it was even with the Merc, and Charlie could see the driver and passenger laughing. The pair were dressed in identical puffy black buttonfront sweaters and sported the widow's peaked pompadours made popular by the Everly Brothers; the man on the passenger side was pointing to a flaking chrome scoop on the car's hood. The Merc's driver had his head down. His friends got out of the car and walked toward the coffee shop.

Charlie rolled up his window, so he wouldn't have to hear any more of the Mock-Everly's dialogue. "Punks, man, nothing but punks at this place."

Charlie had never felt comfortable at the Toluca Lake drive-in. Races originated there most nights, but a good proportion of them were between kids in their parents' cars. The crowd was too large for his taste and too varied.

At Van de Kamp's, the bulk of the clientele were racers or followers of racing. Here, the racers competed for space with surfers, who didn't seem to care what they drove, custom-car enthusiasts, whom Charlie couldn't understand at all, herds of indistinguishable high-school age kids bent on socializing, and even stray carloads of dating or married couples who apparently came to eat.

Among the racers, there were few that Charlie considered serious. The majority were representative of their area, clean-cut, comparatively wealthy, and in Charlie's experience, prone to renege on bets.

At the entrance, with hard looks, honking, and threatened small collisions, the dual line squeezed into one as cars turned into the driveway. At the head of the line a lot attendant, bulky in gloves and a vinyl coat, stopped each car to determine whether they would park and eat or just wanted to drive through.

When they reached the head of the line Charlie rolled his window down to talk to the man. "Hey Carl," Charlie had read the name stitched on the jacket, "has Moon been around tonight?"

"Who?"

"Moon. Black guy, yellow Deuce Ford."

"Not tonight. You want to eat or you just going through?"

"You hungry?" Charlie asked Connie. "We can't stop, but I could get something to go."

"It's a toss-up."

"What?"

"I'm hungry," Connie said, "but if I eat I'll toss it. Could I get a coke? That usually settles my stomach."

"We'll get it to go and head down to Forest Lawn Drive. Moon must've gone straight there." He turned to the lot attendant, "We'll just hit the take-out window."

"Go head-on," Carl said, and waved them through like he held a checkered flag.

On the way out, after a stop at the take-out window, their way was blocked by a crowd surrounding a new Candy-Apple Green Thunderbird Convertible. There were three or four carhops and nearly twenty high school girls. The two closest to the driver had handed in their autograph books to be signed.

"Aww, shit," Charlie said, "Petey Powell."

"The actor?" Connie said.

"Yeah," Charlie said, although he didn't know Petey Powell as an actor, because he refused to watch the wholesome family TV comedy that Powell had starred in for six years. The show had been cancelled only a year ago when the critical mass of a fragile cast had fractured. The actor who played the wise and kindly father had begun bringing boys to his trailer in pairs which was too much for even the avoidance-trained studio cops. Mom's polite lady drunk act became public and mean, and Sis, pretty, fragile, bulimic and hardwired on diet pills undercut with Valium, had mixed prescriptions and been confined in Camarillo.

Charlie knew Petey Powell from his days of hanging out at Martell's Speed Shop in Glendale. Petey was a regular customer there. More than a regular customer. He'd wrecked four Corvettes since turning sixteen and Martell, a 300 pound fuel-injection wizard from Vermont, was delighted to soup up each new one, since the more power he put into them, the sooner he'd get to build the next one. Petey wanted to be Martell's mascot. He loved hanging out there and driving to Glendale Bob's to buy sacks of Big Boy hamburgers for the guys at the shop, ignoring the fact that they ignored him as much as they could. Petey reminded Charlie of the only other child-actor he had known, Del Rubio. Del lived with his mother in a brick apartment in Charlie's childhood neighborhood. Del had the first set of colored contact lenses Charlie had ever seen, a frightening metallic turquoise shade, and Del's favorite thing to do was to ride round and round an oval parkway on his bicycle while Charlie and his brothers threw footballs, basketballs and volleyballs at him. Del liked the attention a lot. Petey had that same quality.

Charlie began to edge into the crowd around Powell's T-Bird, honking. As the girls scattered, and some space cleared, Petey Powell whipped around, glaring. Petey had a head shaped like a kidney bean and a ludicrous tower of hair that swept up from his huge pale forehead. He broke into a smile as Charlie came closer. "Fat Charlie," he called out, "Fatty Charlie. My old buddy, buddy, buddy." Charlie flipped him the finger and gunned for the exit.

Charlie turned left off Barham, onto Forest Lawn Drive, and swung into the parking lot of a closed down gas station on the corner. Cars, perhaps twenty in all, were spread around the lot and a small crowd was gathered under the metal canopy covering the pump islands. Charlie parked behind the station, next to the phone booth. "Would you see if either of the heads is open," Connie asked. "I have to pee so bad my eyes are turning yellow."

"Good thing we got you two Cokes."

"It settled my stomach, okay? Please."

Charlie went and rattled the doors to both restrooms. Both were closed and had been for a long time.

"Sorry," he told Connie.

"I'm going to find a bush," Connie said. "I'll catch up to you."

Walking around the building, Charlie looked inside. The floors of the office and luberoom were covered with broken glass. A sign propped on the counter read, "Lease Available," followed by two lined-out phone numbers and a current one. The new windows had whitewashed X's in the centers and warning emblems of a local security patrol taped in the corners.

Charlie tried to pick out known faces, but it was too dark under the roof. As he approached the edge of one group a cigarette was spun toward him. He dodged the glowing butt and came closer, trying to see who had flicked it. He relaxed, recognizing the face, a hanger-on from Van de Kamp's named Flynn.

"Hey, Fat Charlie," Flynn said, "what's shakin', besides you?"

Charlie ignored him and spoke to the boy on his left.

"Moon been here yet?"

"Uh, I don't think so," the boy replied. "I didn't see him anyway. But I only been here an hour."

"Moon never showed," Flynn said. "He must've chickened out."

Charlie turned toward Flynn, "Did you talk to Moon about that?"

"Naw," Flynn said, "But he didn't show, did he?"

"You want to talk to him?" Charlie said. "It can be arranged."

"Knock it off."

"What?" said Charlie.

"Don't play hardass with me, that's all."

"Hey. I thought you <u>wanted</u> to play."

"Whatever you say, hardass." Flynn moved away from the group; his friend followed. Charlie thought he heard Flynn say something more but they were far enough away to disregard it.

Overhead there was a rhythmic stamp of footsteps and a voice that sounded like a barker, "Awright, Awright, Awright, Awright."

Charlie and the rest of the crowd backed out from under the canopy and looked up. A silhouette was dancing across the roof; every few steps he came down, both feet on the enameled metal, with a ringing boom. He stopped in the middle with a final jump. "Awright, Awright, Gentlemen. Gentlemen. Time to liven up these proceedings."

The group stirred around, craning heads. Someone at the edge of the crowd switched on a spotlamp mounted on the side of a pickup and tilted it. The beam wavered up and fixed on the dancer, a lean black man wearing a Levi's jacket and pants. The man feinted away from the light and then toward it. "Put down that flashlight, officer," he said, "you might not like what you see." There was laughter and an expectant hum of voices. The light swirled around the man, then darted down, picking out faces. The owner of the spotlight walked over and turned it off.

Connie appeared at his side. "Is that the guy?" she said.

"That's the guy," Charlie said.

"He's kinda cute," Connie said.

"Shut up and learn something," Charlie told her.

"Hey Moon," Flynn yelled, "go head on."

"Awright, a fan." Moon shaded his eyes, looking in Flynn's direction. "Who might you be?"

Flynn stayed silent.

"It's Flynn," his friend called out.

"Say again?"

"Dead Flynn," Charlie yelled.

"Well that's alright too," said Moon. "Now, Gentlemen, as I was saying, it is time to liven UP these proceedings."

He turned sideways, raised a knee and an arm in exaggerated profile, "The Moon is Out tonight." He pumped his arm and shifted to the other knee, "The Moon is On tonight."

Whistling and voices floated up from the crowd.

"Out to lunch."

"On the rag."

"And that's alright too," Moon said. "Where's that man with the spotlight?" After what sounded like a shoving match near the pickup, the spotlight came on. "Now, my man, will you direct that toward the far corner there, no the street side."

The light bobbed and settled on a yellow '32 Ford with spoke mags. Moon's two partners, who had been sitting on the running board, stood up, looking uneasily at each other. They looked at the crowd and at their feet while Moon continued.

"Gentlemen, what we got here is a small, slow Deuce. And while it's not running perfectly, they's six or seven burnt valves, a little rod knock and the spark plugs haven't been changed since we bought the car two years ago at a Church Sale..."

He was interrupted by Boos and cries of 'Bullshit'. "Well, we'll let that slide," Moon said. "My partners and I coasted down from the Valley because we heard there was some fine racing here."

"Now, so far we haven't seen any. I hate to think we come all this way for nothing, so I concluded it was time to introduce ourselves and see if there's any serious racers here. That man on the left is my little brother, Willy. Next to him is my sister's mistake, my nephew, Artemus. He's older than me, and the car there has no name because she hasn't earned one. She's older than me too.

"Now, I will warn you that for the Valley this is a fairly fast car. Can't say what it would be considered here. The engine, Gentlemen, is a slightly warmed small block Chevrolet."

"Bullshit," someone yelled. A tall, angular boy next to Charlie, dressed in Baker's whites and a red satin jacket called out, "Tell us what you really got, Poormouth. Tell the truth this time."

"Well it's a 327," said Moon, "and you can look at it, if you can afford it. We don't run for fun. Alright then? Gimme a little light here."

The spotlamp swung back. Moon reached in his top jacket pocket and brought out a sheaf of bills. He fanned them and held them aloft. "Three hundred dollars, Gentlemen. Three hundred says the Ford takes anything you got, two out of three. All our lunch money."

There was silence, and then a confusion of voices. "Do I hear any offers," said Moon.

Close to Connie and Charlie, three boys wearing *Kingpins* club jackets started arguing, two against one. The stocky boy in the middle seemed unconvinced. He leaned against his car, a beefy looking red Dodge that Charlie guessed to be the one Moon was looking for.

His friends besieged him. Charlie edged over to listen. One was saying, "You can take him, Pat, I know you can. I <u>know</u> that car. It's fast but he ain't that fast."

The other boy cut in, "Look, we saw him two weeks ago out at San Fernando Raceway. He's running mid-thirteens all day, right around a hundred one, two. You got almost a second on him and ten miles an hour."

Moon yelled, "I'll take a check." Charlie backed away from the threesome, silently laughing.

Connie caught on to his arm, "What's so funny?" Charlie said, "Wait a minute," and kept walking. When they were well out of earshot, he sat down on the pavement, legs stretched in front of him, laughing again.

"We won't have to work tonight. Those guys are hooked. Moon's still got the game going."

"Do you still get paid?" Connie asked.

"Yeah, not as much as if I had to run him, but twenty if he wins. Now listen and learn something."

"I wish you'd stop saying that," Connie said.

Charlie nodded toward the yellow coupe. "First of all, that Ford isn't even street-legal. He's got his trailer parked around the corner somewhere. He takes it out every Sunday to San Fernando Raceway."

"That car is an altered roadster. If he didn't cheat that's the class he'd run. You can't tell, but the whole thing's moved back about half a foot on the frame rails. It'll run low 12's, about a hundred and twenty, any time he wants.

"What he does, he goes out every Sunday and sandbags. He runs a gas class and he never runs faster than about 13:40. Then, the rest of the week he goes around finding suckers who've seen him. But he's good, he's smooth. There's guys he beats that go home and tear their cars apart, trying to find out why they ran so slow."

The threesome in the corner had apparently reached a decision. Pat, the Dodge's owner stepped out just below the canopy, backed by his two friends. Moon was sitting, swinging his legs.

"I think you just might have a race," the boy spoke with badly feigned indifference. "Like one look under the hood."

"Coming down," Moon said. He turned around and eased over, hung by his hands and dropped lightly.

The crowd moved over to the Deuce. Flashlights were produced. Moon lifted the side cover, folded it back and stepped out of the way. The three Kingpins poked the flashlights inside and shone them around. One commented on the lack of chrome.

Charlie, squeezed in next to the door, looked back at Connie with a knowing grimace. "These guys don't know what they're looking at," he said. "All they care about is to make sure it's a small block."

The trio moved aside and others shoved in. Charlie wedged out a space and pulled Connie in so she could see.

"Notice anything special?" Charlie asked.

"I don't know what I'm looking at. It looks clean, I guess. It looks littler than I thought. Shouldn't there be more to it?"

"That's the mistake those other guys made," Charlie said. "they were looking for speed stuff and never noticed what's missing. Put your head in there and look."

"I'm not going to put my head in there!"

"Just look."

"I'm not," Connie said indignantly. "Just tell me what's missing."

"Okay," Charlie said, "you got no generator. It's a magneto setup. There's no starter. There's no horn, no windshield wiper motor, nothing to add any weight. Take a look where that paint is scratched," Charlie pointed at the firewall. "All that sheetmetal is aluminum. You could lift the whole front end of this car with one hand."

They moved away from the front of the car and looked inside. The driving compartment was stark: a single bucket seat, a fire extinguisher clipped to the floor. The dash was a small brushed aluminum oval with a tachometer, oil gauge and toggle Killswitch. The clutch and brake pedals were the size of half-dollars, the accelerator pedal, the diameter of a quarter. Charlie shook his head admiringly, "Sanitary. If you look close you can tell the car's owned by a fanatic. He probably didn't have any dinner, either."

A circle was forming where the Dodge was parked. Moon was walking around the car; he leaned down to look at the rear tires and suspension. Half the people in back of him bent over to make the same inspection. He walked up front and rapped the Dodge's hood with his knuckles, then knelt to peer in the fenderwell, "All metal isn't it? No fiberglass?" The owner nodded. "And it's a Ramcharger, right? 426?" Pat nodded again. Moon stood up, "All I need to know."

"We got a race?" Pat asked.

Moon raised a hand. "Looks good to me." The boy in the red satin jacket pushed his way to the front. His face looked angry.

He nudged his glasses, broken in the middle and wrapped with tape, up higher on his nose.

"Hey," he said, "how about popping that hood?" Pat looked at Moon. "I don't need to see it," Moon said. The boy gestured toward the crowd, "We'd like to see it, buddy. I'm thinking about a side-bet and it would help to know what I'm betting on. O.K.?"

Pat triggered the latch and raised the hood. The engine was a shoehorn fit, nearly touching the sides of the compartment. The exhaust header pipes looked like a plumber's nightmare, bends snaking over and through each other and out the fenderwells. Two massive fourbarrel carburetors, the throats as big as large coffee cans, were staggered on top of a stepped ram manifold. Everything that wasn't painted, or buffed out, was chrome.

Pat tossed the keys to one of his friends. The starter ground, straining against the tight compression, until the engine kicked, with an eerie whoosh from the carburetors, and took hold. The noise was staggering. Some of the front row moved in again, covering their ears; suction from the carburetors could be felt outside the car.

Pat dropped the hood and smiled across at Moon, "You ready?"

"I'll follow you, " Moon said.

"All night long," said Pat. His manner had changed.

The sound of the Dodge seemed to inspire him with a dreamy confidence. His friends were smiling too, looking like some trap had sprung.

Moon lowered himself into the Ford. He buckled the restraining harness across his chest, tested the quick release and waggled a hand at his partners. Willy and Artemus started pushing. When the car was rolling smoothly, picking up speed, Moon popped the clutch. The engine fired up and the car jerked forward, then slowed and settled into a smooth, rhythmic idle. Healthy sounding but not exotic, a contrast to the punchy lope of the Ramcharger.

The Dodge rolled down the driveway, followed by the coupe, and there was a scramble for cars.

The parade stopped near the entrance to the Hollywood Hills Forest Lawn Cemetery and the cars swung U-turns and parked in a line. In the dark, the cemetery looked like a golf course. Behind the huge ornamental iron fence, the rolling greens built up to a spotlighted replica of Mount Vernon, that could have been a clubhouse.

The view from the other side of the street was down to the concrete ravine of the Los Angeles River, and beyond, where lines of cars streaked by on the freeway. Watching the northbound and southbound traffic simultaneously - strings of headlights becoming taillights - gave the dizzying sense of a time exposure photograph, the image lasting for seconds after turning away.

Charlie got twenty dollars down on Moon with the boy in the red jacket and headed for the starting line. The cars were being lined up opposite the entrance gates to Forest Lawn. The end of the quarter-mile was marked by a speed limit sign: 45 MPH. Five hundred feet on was the start of a curve. Pat and Moon had agreed on the conditions of the bet, but couldn't settle on a starter. "Aren't you going to be the starter?" Connie said, "I thought you were always the starter."

"Just at Vandy's," Charlie said. "I don't want to get too well known out here."

They finally agreed on a Schaefer's ambulance driver in the crowd that neither knew. The money was handed over to him, along with a flashlight and Moon explained the starting procedure to him.

"When we're staged, you blink it twice, slow, and make sure you're pointing it at us. After that second blink, you count: one to ten. Blink it again on any number. Like, you count three or four, whatever, and turn on the light, and we go. That simple."

The ambulance driver nodded and took his place between the two cars. Charlie saw that his hand was shaking.

Just before they climbed into their cars, Moon gave Pat a

chance to back out. Pat grinned and refused. One of the Kingpins muttered, "Psych-out."

"Alright," Moon said, "but don't forget; I don't want any hard feelings."

Both cars edged forward until they touched the starter's outstretched hands. The starter looked down the course to the reflector studs shining on the speed limit sign, and beyond to the curve. He turned back with a worried look. "Y'all got good brakes? That'll be a hairy bend if y' don't." Both drivers waved at him.

He backed away from them and lifted the flashlight. The engine noise rose in stages, with each blink. After the second blink Charlie saw the starter take a deep breath, almost closing his eyes. Charlie counted with him. At seven, both drivers anticipated a start, as he knew they would, and right in rhythm the starter hit the light.

Moon's Ford came out smoothly, no slippage, no tire smoke, no squealing, not even a chirp, just gone.

The Dodge never made up for the start, chasing the Deuce all the way down the course and losing ground as they wound out.

The farther away they got, the better Moon's Ford sounded, winding tighter and tighter without seeming to peak. It sounded like it should have been airborne.

The brakelights of both cars flared up, well before the curve. Moon hit his first and from the difference, Charlie guessed he must have won by at least four or five car lengths. The cars went around the curve. They reappeared a minute later, the Dodge first, flying back and squealing to a stop at the gates. Charlie started to laugh as the Dodge braked. Strips of tape had been carefully placed inside the brakelight lenses to form letters. Connie, looking at the intials asked, "What's A M F mean?"

"Adios, Mother Fucker!" Charlie told her. "But it doesn't signify much unless you're in front."

Moon idled in behind the Dodge, swung around and

reversed, backing into the lane the Dodge had taken for the first race.

Pat and his friends were scrambling. One, with a pocket gauge, knelt at the rear wheels, dropping the air pressure in both tires, hoping for a better bite on the start. Pat and the other Kingpin conferred under the hood and finally agreed on a minute adjustment to both carburetors. Moon waited amiably.

The second race wasn't as close. Pat, trying for an edge, brought it out too hard and fried the tires, skating all over the starting line. Sullen rolls of rubber smoke hid both lanes. Charlie caught glimpses of the starter, dodging in the smoke, waving the flashlight.

Moon was gone before the smoke had formed. The Deuce came out exactly the way it did in the first race, like it was already straining, and someone cut a rope.

Pat, with rapid twists of the wheel, got the Dodge in shape and followed, rocking the car with vicious shifts. The margin stayed the same. Moon went into the curve ten car lengths in front.

It was a longer wait this time. Finally, the yellow Ford came around the corner, traveling slow, swooping across the center line and back, in lazy esses.

He stopped at the starting line. Willy and Artemus climbed in the car and Moon came over to collect his money. The two Kingpins met him on the way.

"What happened to Pat?"

"Nothing, as far as I know," said Moon. "He just kept going. When he got around the curve, he hit it again and blew on by. He's probably home by now."

Charlie went looking to collect his bet, but the boy in the red jacket had disappeared. A few people claimed they'd seen him leave after the first race. No one admitted to knowing him, or could remember what kind of car he drove.

Other races were beginning now. Two Corvairs went off, to mild jeering. A Corvette beat a '56 Chevy by less than a car length and scheduled a rematch, for money. An old Plymouth went off against a Buick hearse, with inconclusive results. The ambulance driver challenged them both and turned on his rotating red light while he waited in line to race.

Moon was sitting on the Deuce's running board, counting the money, when Charlie approached with Connie. He finished the count and looked up at Charlie. "You make any money on me?"

"I will if I can find the guy," Charlie said.

"Trust," Moon said. "Ain't it wonderful? Ain't it fleeting?" He slipped Charlie a twenty under cover of a handshake, then noticing Connie, slipped him another ten.

"Brody said I should tell you hello," Charlie said.

"Where is Brody these days? I haven't seen him ... Hansen Dam I guess was the last time. He still driving for that twisted little bastard?"

"Vaca, yeah," Charlie replied. He glanced toward Connie, at the mention of Vaca's name, but could detect no reaction. "Brody and Vaca were supposed to race the Ramcharger next week. I think you blew that for them."

"That Dodge? Shit, tell Brody to leave the fish to me. Well, I better go find my trailer. We got a drive ahead of us." Artemus and Willy took their places at the back bumper as Moon got in the car.

"You should come by Van de Kamps some night. Lots of action."

"Naw. I've got no edge there. All those guys know me. I'll talk to you in a couple weeks." He waved and his partners started pushing. When the engine caught, Moon stopped and the two clambered in and then the Deuce dwindled from view, heading south, toward Travel Town.

"Did you want to watch more of these races?" Connie said.

"These guys?" Charlie said incredulously.

"Let's go then," Connie said. "I've got the lunch shift tomorrow. You going to give me my money now?"

"What?" Charlie said. "Your money?"

"I'm part of the act, aren't I? You couldn't have done it without me, could you? It'll make up for the tips I missed."

Charlie handed her the ten.

They were in the Chevy now, heading toward Griffith Park.

"First time I ever paid for a date," Charlie said. He laughed.

"Is that what this was?" Connie said. "What about that Donna?"

"What Donna?"

"I don't know. Donna, Donna, Prima Donna. The one you thought was calling when I called. Was that the Donna from Van De Kamp's? The kind of chunky one?"

Charlie smiled. "That's an eighty-pounder's perspective if I ever heard one. Yeah, Olive Oyl. That Donna. Except now it's Sardo's. Not Van de Kamp's."

"Whose So's?"

"Sardo's. It's a nightclub in Phoenix. That's where she's living now."

"Were you guys going together?"

Charlie nodded. "Yeah. Sort of. I don't know. It might still work out." He trailed off into silence, and the silence continued. It had been a month since Donna's last letter, and when he'd called her, a man had answered the phone and Charlie had hung up.

"Things are really changing," Connie said.

"Yeah."

"Everyone's going. Everyone's growing up and leaving, or you don't see them. Or something."

"Not much left," Charlie said. He shook out a cigarette. "I don't know. I've been thinking about joining the Navy." He had never thought about it at all. But as he said it, he realized he might. It suddenly made a great deal of sense.

"The Navy?" Connie grimaced wryly. "You? In those weird little pants with the bib. No, I guess it's the shirts that have a bib, on the back? The pants have something else weird. You really going to join?"

Charlie managed to look offended. "Why not? I've already passed the exam." He picked up his pack of Lucky Strikes and turned the bottom up, exposing the letters: LS/ MFT.

"You know what that stands for?"

"Yeah," Connie said, with some sarcasm, "Everybody knows that one. That's so old. 'Loose sweaters/ Means floppy tits'."

"No! Not that one. This is real. It's the entrance exam to join in San Diego."

"What?"

"It's true. You have to know." He pointed to each letter, in turn. "Look, Sailor. Mexicans Fuck Too."

"You'll do just fine. A credit to our Armed Services. Just like Richie."

"Was he in the Navy?"

"Marines. He got thrown out, if you can believe it, for fighting."

They were back at the gas station. He helped her out of the car. She unlocked the Valiant and gave him a hard hug. "Nice night," she said and was gone.

Charlie sat back down in the Chevy and looked at himself in the mirror. "Oh, shit," Charlie said. It was the best time he'd had in months.

24-

Reinhard was back on the street. Everywhere Vaca went, he heard stories of recent races. A 427 Cobra in Redondo Beach had beaten him, but the story was that Reinhard had gotten a tank of bad gas. There was some speculation that Reinhard had sandbagged because he had come back the next night, tripled the bet and won four straight before the Cobra's owner gave up.

He'd raced Moon, mostly for kicks, giving him a five car-length head start. Moon had exploded a clutch and most of a driveline trying to beat him. Witnesses said it looked and sounded like Moon's Deuce had run over a land mine.

He had beaten the three top cars from Stan's, the blown 'Vette, the Healey - now, with a new engine, Stan's number one - and the '40 Ford, all in the same night. The following week, the owners of the fastest Roadster in Orange County had paid for Reinhard's gas, out and back from Anaheim, and paid him five hundred more for their two losing runs.

Only one car, a featherweight '55 Chevy with a pumped up 327, had come close to undeniably beating Reinhard. Charlie had seen the race and talked about it for weeks.

The Chevy's owners, a syndicate out of Watts, had taken a chance, loading their gas with a pop of nitromethane fuel. They won the first race, narrowly, but the car made funny noises toward the end and Reinhard, smelling the sweet, stinging odor of burned fuel, had according to Charlie, smiled and smiled.

On the next pass, one cylinder sucked a valve and the engine came apart. It sounded, Charlie said, like someone banging a bat in a trash can. Two rods came through the block and one of them knocked a hole in the hood. Reinhard helped them put the fire out - the extinguisher fitted nicely through the hole in the hood - and settled for half the bet.

He hadn't come around Van de Kamp's at all. Vaca and Brody swung by most nights, hoping he would show, and left messages for him with the carhops. Brody decided that Reinhard was building a stake and would let them know when he was ready.

Vaca couldn't take the waiting and they began cruising other streets, other drive-ins, looking for him. Brody tried to trace him through Paul's Machine Shop, but everyone there claimed they hadn't seen him in weeks and his tools were gone. Brody thought they knew, though, if not where he was, at least what his plans were. His questions had provoked a smug and united front, but Paul dropped a few pointed hints about a new engine.

The new engine worried Vaca, particularly after he heard from some of the drivers Reinhard had beaten. Moon was building a new engine he wouldn't even let them look at. Everyone they talked to at Stan's seemed depressed and defensive.

They raced some of the same people. It had driven Vaca crazy to drive across town and then come home without something to talk about, besides Reinhard. Usually, there wasn't much money left for bets, but the comparison seemed important.

They won all those races, but found that the people they beat didn't seem to be as impressed with the Ford as they were with Reinhard's Chevy.

Brody thought Reinhard benefitted from wishful thinking. Some of it was the normal process of group memory. It seldom took more than a week to turn a lost race to a rout or a cheat, a bypassed accident into a vividly witnessed crash and burn, but it was more than that.

The drivers he had beaten and the people who had watched

seemed to like Reinhard. They talked about him with unusual deference and the races, occurring the week or even the night before, were described with such vividness, enthusiasm and unchallenged exaggeration, that they sounded like some legendary race from years before.

On a night that they visited Henry's, in Pasadena, Brody met three habitues who each claimed to have started Reinhard's race there. Each described the scene with fervor and absolute belief. Brody, describing these encounters, told Vaca, "Shit, you'd think he was the Mayflower. They all want to get over on him."

25-

The first time he heard the new engine running, even with the timing and carburetors off, and the valves set loose enough to clatter, Reinhard knew he had something special.

Accustomed to the limits of the old engine, the first few times he raced, Reinhard never brought it to its peak. Racing a roadster in Anaheim, he finally was pushed enough to keep his foot down all the way. The tach needle crept past 8,000 rpm, where he had set the red line, but the roadster was still holding at his door and against all judgment he stayed on it and watched the needle sweep past 8-5 and peg at 9,000. The sound was unlike any engine he'd ever owned or heard.

The roadster seemed to swirl backward and Reinhard, with his ears ringing, eased through the finish, not quite believing what he'd felt. When he'd backed off, it had still felt like there was pedal left, still climbing.

In the next weeks he adjusted to the sound and the light buzzing it left in his head. He couldn't get used to the power; at times, racing top end, the car was nearly uncontrollable. The steering would grow lighter as the car lifted up and the feel of the road was lost. He had no experience driving on ice, but guessed that it must feel like that. At the end of a race he felt he was aiming the car, rather than steering it. Backing off was a relief, feeling the control return. Reinhard was used to a certain amount of squirreliness in his cars. It was unavoidable when the power generated by the engine so far exceeded the engineering of the machine it was dropped into. But this was something different. He still hadn't used up the full throttle.

If he had to push it to the limit, he wasn't sure what the car would do.

He scarcely noticed the cars racing him anymore. In the first race he would find out how hard he would have to push and after that, the remaining runs were exercises. Stopping at the end of the course after a last run, he would sit, jangled but feeling loose, watching his fingers unclench from the wheel, straighten and stretch apart until he could feel the webbing between.

Without paying much attention, his bankroll had grown. Money came to him, handed through a half-opened window nearly every night. After Paul had been paid back and he had paid his ex-wife Ginger six months ahead, he left the money in the glove compartment, counting it only when it began to spill over. When he was nearly two-thousand up, he began to consider Vaca.

Reinhard gave himself and the Chevy a break, driving around in the $75.00 Studebaker truck that he'd bought for work. He went by Van de Kamp's for the first time in months, had lunch and drove away laughing, thinking of the rumors his visit would provoke.

Several regulars had interrupted his coffee, rushing through the ritual greetings to make overly casual enquiries about the Chevy and his brief, calculatedly honest replies - that he was giving the car a break, that he was tired of driving it on the street - he knew it would convince his questioners, who couldn't imagine owning a car like that and not driving it, that he was lying and probably covering up.

By evening, he estimated, the Chevy would be - impounded by the police, stolen, have blown an engine, been lost in a pink-slip race, crashed or been vandalized - and Vaca, eager for news, would have heard it all and begun to worry.

Brody would sort it out eventually, but Vaca would be edgy and hopefully a little off-balance when negotiations began.

Still irritated by Vaca's momentary holdout the night they had raced Stan's, Reinhard planned to make him sweat, to set up conditions, provoke him, so that the loss, when it finally occurred - and he was positive by now that it wouldn't even be close - would be a lasting and talked about humiliation.

26-

The word spread out, the way it always did, moving through the parked cars at Van de Kamp's, relayed to the carhops, to the cooks and the bus boys, and back to arriving customers.

It was repeated in the circles of the parking lot, circles at gas stations ringing cars on lube racks and at pump islands. At stoplights, in restrooms, at high schools, in the garages and auto parts stores and car washes of the area.

A date had definitely been set, that was known. The cars, that black Ford, the blue '58 Chevy, were well known. In conversations among the knowledgeable, the word grew more hazy when they speculated on the size of the bet, the location, and the actual night of the race. Crowds showed, following rumors, at known racing spots every night for a week preceding the real night, Saturday.

Charlie was for once staying quiet. His restraint was involuntary, forced by Vaca.

Charlie felt cheated. He had arranged the race, going between Reinhard and Brody and Vaca, in a week of hedging and diplomacy. The price and time and site had been settled, dictated by Reinhard, picked at and worried over by Vaca. When Vaca finally agreed, Charlie could no longer maintain his effacing demeanor. Smug, filled with the news, he was anxious to depart for Van de Kamp's and take his place. It showed, and Vaca reacted with conditions.

"Just keep your mouth shut," Vaca told him. "I don't want every asshole in the world hanging out and bringing the cops down on us."

Charlie looked to Brody but got no help. "I've already told everybody I'm setting it up," Charlie said.

"So what," said Vaca. "Tell them you haven't worked it all out. Or don't say anything. What's the difference? What do you care? They're all assholes."

Charlie responded bitterly, "Yeah, and they're all witnesses too," and saw some emotion twist across Vaca's features. "You want to start or not? You want to be the starter, just shut the fuck up. There's plenty others, all you have to do is flush the handle."

Charlie wanted it. At the drive-in he suffered, but confined himself to intimations of his central role.

Vaca, brooding in his garage, leaned on his elbows and looked down at what had become an abstract collection of carburetor parts, on the low table in front of him.

The carburetor was a spare and to fill time on this Friday night, he had thought he would rebuild it. He'd stripped it, placing the parts in a metal basket, and dipped them in a small drum of acrid yellow solvent. He had washed them clean, rinsing the basket with a hose, and let them dry under a gooseneck lamp, bent so the cone of light shone directly down on the small piles of parts and the torn black sweatshirt covering the table.

Vaca pushed the smaller pieces around with a screwdriver, dividing them into groups - aluminum, brass, and steel - then again by what he thought their function was. The pervasive odor of the carburetor cleaner was on his fingers and clothes. It was strongest around the parts, rising from the heat of the lamp, making his head buzz slightly and his nostrils burn.

He pushed back from the table and wheeled out to the open garage door to sit in the breeze, and clear his head. The Ford faced him on the slope of the driveway. He stared at it.

What Charlie had said about the witnesses had nagged at him all week. Before, he had worried, but with no specificity. Now the thought of the others, the faces along the curbs that Charlie had brought forward, and their eyes upon him, provoked visions.

Neither the fresh air nor the breeze was helping. It felt like someone was lightly pressing a spatula inside his skull. The buzzing in his head seemed to shift but not lessen, and he could taste the solvent in his teeth, the way he sometimes felt the taste of metal when cleaning parts with a scraper and the scraper would dig in at a burr.

He wagged his head slowly in the thickening air. The recurring visions stopped when he opened his eyes, but he couldn't seem to keep them open. Turning his head only wobbled the gassy images.

There were two. First, the blue car, the black car, blurring at speed, seeming to flick clear at the finish, but so quickly he couldn't decide which was ahead. And the second, a crowd surrounding the car; it appeared the races were over, and as the faces pressed in he looked around but all the eyes were calm, giving no clues.

The visions had the slow, maddening quality of uncontrollable dreams, the kind that always woke him, but these couldn't be stopped and their vagueness, the uncertainty of them, forced their repetition.

He knew they were caused by the clinging vapors of the carburetor solvent, but knowing didn't help. The doubts couldn't be shaken.

Vaca blinked. He suddenly realized he had lost sense of passing time. It scared him. Straining, he lifted his head, stretching his neck, and forced his eyes open.

He nudged the right wheel of his chair, and again, until it was aimed to clear the car. The running sprinklers in the strip of grass between the sidewalk and curbside drew him. He felt as though he could hear them, a tinkling sound. He set both hands well back on the wheels and pushed off. Rolling down the slope of the driveway, his eyes picked out individual beads of water, fascinating in the sunlight.

He was surprised when the chair stopped just inside the circle of one spray, feeling no connection with the hands grasping the brake levers.

He sat for a long time in the spray; it beaded, dribbled down his face, collected on his shirtfront, soaked in, and washed down, pooling between his legs, while he breathed deeper and deeper.

When his breathing settled into a more normal rhythm, he backed away to the sidewalk, to a spot where he was hit only by the occasional drop.

Vaca felt the sun, gradually. He watched the water until it suddenly did not interest him at all. He pushed back up the slope but stayed at the edge of the garage, well away from the dully gleaming carburetor pieces on the table.

He consciously tried to think in ways that seemed practical. He would probably have to buy a carburetor kit. Without some diagram, an exploded view of the carburetor, he knew he would never get it back together. Or, probably a smarter move, buy a new carb, put his back together so it looked right from the outside and return it to the parts store as a defective unit.

Already, he could imagine the outraged tone of his voice as he wheeled up to the parts counter. A new parts store, though; the owner where he did most of his business had, Vaca suspected, begun warning his help.

27-

Reinhard knew what he had to do. He just didn't want to do it. Ginger, his ex-wife, had responded to Reinhard's prepayment of six months' alimony and child support by sending her lawyer back to court, seeking an increase in child-support payments based on Reinhard's apparent increase in salary. The summons, advising him to appear in court in three weeks, had arrived that morning.

She wanted another two hundred a month, a sum that guaranteed that Reinhard would be working full-time at Paul's Machine Shop, besides what he could make racing.

He'd make the call; he'd have to. Petey Powell had made the first offer a year ago. He'd upped it several times since. Reinhard had laughed at him, each and every time. He wasn't laughing now. He thought Petey might come up even a little higher, particularly after tonight's race, when he saw how badly the Chevy would beat Vaca's Ford.

Reinhard picked up the phone to call Petey Powell and invite him to an evening of high-class street racing and negotiation.

"Ummmm," Connie said. "That feels good." Charlie watched her swollen belly - a taut pink basketball laced with blue and green veins - rubbing against his.

It did feel good. She ground slowly on top of him while he

squeezed and massaged her ass. He wished he could see more, but only a mirror would have helped. His stomach was nearly as big as hers.

She slowed and then straightened, "I've got to stop a minute."

Connie took Charlie's hands off her ass and brought them to her breasts. She looked at him, then closed her eyes, concentrating.

"Can you feel that?" She was clenching him and letting go, a strong pulsing squeeze, then release. "Ohhhh," Charlie said. The sensation was exquisite. "Got to develop those muscles," Connie said, "I'm gonna need them." She clenched him till he groaned.

Charlie had no idea why he was being given this gift. True, she was leaving for Florida tomorrow, but she'd given no preparatory hint that Charlie recognized.

She'd simply arrived that morning and let herself in with his stolen spare key. It must've been about five. He wasn't too clear on the time, but it was only six-fifteen now. She'd undressed, slipped into bed, and he'd only woken when he felt her tongue rasping across his ribs.

He hoped it was no more complicated than a farewell between friends. When he asked her, "Why?" Connie had said, "So I know you'll write to me in Florida. This was the only way I could make sure you'd write."

Her logic, Charlie thought, was probably good; he wasn't much of a letter writer. "Neither of us can afford Long Distance," Connie said, laughing.

Another reason, which he didn't want to think about too much, was that her visit had something to do with the way they would be spending their final evening.

Reinhard was racing Vaca and Brody. Charlie had finally told her about it Friday, yesterday. He had organized the match and planned to be center stage the whole night. Connie knew he couldn't stay away. The only way she would see him, on her last night in town, was to go along.

She didn't complain and she didn't blink when Vaca's name came up, but Charlie had a niggling sense that Vaca had something to do with her early-morning warmth. He really didn't want to think it through.

With a final squeeze, Connie popped off him and scuttled to the edge of the bed, where she propped herself up on hands and knees. "Come on," she said, "I want to do it doggy-style."

Charlie bounced up and stood behind her. Her shoulders sank and her buttocks rose as she presented herself. "It might be more comfortable." She reached between her legs, grasped him, and guided him in. "I want to feel all of you," Connie said.

It was the right thing to say. Charlie plunged ahead. The bedroom mirror was perfectly positioned, but Charlie closed his eyes after a moment of watching. The swaying globular reflections in the not-very-good-mirror made him want to laugh more than persevere.

28-

Cheryl leaned back against the tiled wall beside the order window, arms crossed, hugging a tray against her front. She looked warily toward her section, where three adjacent cars were flashing lights for her attention. "This is the shits," she said. "Even for a Saturday night. There are more assholes out there than I've ever seen in one place in my life."

Rumors of the imminent race, Reinhard versus Vaca and Brody, had doubled their usual Saturday night crowd. The line to enter the drive-in was backed up more than four blocks.

Reaching across the brushed steel counter, Kenny, the night manager, spun the wheel and plucked off four new orders, placing them behind the wire on the hood over the grill.

One of the cars in her section started honking. Cheryl straightened, pushing off the wall with her head and shoulders. "Somebody turn off the lights," she said. She ambled toward the car, still holding the tray against her chest.

Kenny looked up, watching her go, and wondered briefly what she had said. He reached for more orders.

Three sweating cooks worked beside him, one at the bank of deep fryers, two in front of the grill, a ten-foot iron slab over rows of burners. The one at the deep fryer shook hot fat from wire baskets of french fries and hooked them on racks to drain. Reading orders, he put in fresh potatoes, battered shrimp and fish, set the timers, and watched the baskets descend, sputtering, into the smoking oil.

The other two cooks stretched across the grill, turning long rows of hamburger patties with bursts of smoke and flames, pressing each patty with the heels of their spatulas so they sizzled, scraping the grill as they opened up clear space, then slapping down new rows. The nearest one scanned the new orders and pushed one back to Kenny. Kenny read it and put it back on the wheel, yelling at the tired, slack faces of the carhops, a double row of them now, waiting for orders, "I told you, it's 86 on the rib-eye. Give them cheeseburgers. We're running short back here."

Kenny turned to glance at the fourth cook. The man slumped on a red plastic chair between the refrigerators, grey-faced, dull-eyed, and eating a glass full of ice. His hand rested on the hat in his lap; his arm was wrapped to the elbow in a soaked towel.

A busboy kicked the back door open and staggered through before it could swing back. He carried a trashcan filled with ice, brought from the adjacent coffee shop. Kenny helped him dump it into their laboring ice machine and began scooping ice into glasses six at a time.

Turning, Kenny noticed one of the grill cooks staring fixedly at a back row of patties, unturned and shrinking to silver-dollar size. Kenny grasped his shoulder and shook it, then handed him a glass of ice water.

The ceiling ventilators spun slowly, hardly creating a swirl in the smoky room. Kenny swung the back door open and blocked it with a milk box. Returning, he brought a dozen cellophane packages of buns to the cutting board, sliced the packs open and shoved them over. He chopped fresh trays of tomatoes, lettuce, and onions, and opened the refrigerator, studying the face of the cook in the chair for signs of revival, while he pulled out stacked slices of cheese and trays of pickles, relish, and mayonnaise. The cook avoided his eyes.

He inserted himself between two busboys at the wrapping table and deftly wrapped and sacked dozens of hamburgers and cheeseburgers until they were ahead of the cooks again.

Carhops were yelling into the order and pickup windows, complaining of late orders, wrong orders, missing items. Kenny began sorting orders and pushing the trays across the open counter. The carhops milled, finding the right trays and then taking off, running across the lot. In one corner, three or four cars began honking in unison, and other cars began honking and flashing their lights.

Kenny continued, lifting and pushing trays, noting each order to be sure it was filled. Without looking, he shoved the trays forward on the counter, making room for a second row, and began adding more trays, noting each filled order as he lifted it up with a flat, viciously intoned phrase, "Fuck 'em. Every one of 'em. Just fuck 'em all," until he was finally out of trays and could only stare, white-faced and shaking, out the slot of the order window at the ranks of cars gleaming under the lights.

29-

In the parking lot, Charlie sat in his Chevy, windows rolled up, listening to Connie's light snoring. She was curled up against the passenger door with a balled sweater for a pillow.

She'd fallen asleep during dinner. It was almost like she'd passed out, but her breathing was normal.

It was now past nine and Charlie had other worries. Earlier, he'd prolonged dinner with coffee and two desserts. When he couldn't avoid it any longer, he'd joined the crowd in the back lot. He had answered their questions warily, hedging more as eight o'clock passed and they tried to pin him down to the time that Reinhard and Vaca were expected.

Convinced by now that other arrangements had been made, Charlie had retired to his car, trying to leave the impression that Vaca and Reinhard were awaiting his phone call, that there were certain unspecified conditions to be met before he would make the call.

Waiting, Charlie watched Connie sleeping, and the crowd. More than 200 had gathered, the largest group of aficionados that he had ever seen, but there was no one there he really wanted to talk with.

He'd felt that way even before the eight o'clock deadline had approached and that had surprised him a little. In the weeks of daydreaming, prior to this night, he'd seen himself in the middle of the group, explaining how he had set up the race, how Reinhard had come to him. But when the time came, looking at the faces surrounding him, he'd seen they were waiting to be entertained and expected it of him. For the first time this had seemed a burden.

Charlie got out to use the phone. As he dialed Vaca's number, he glanced toward the lot and saw faces turning to watch him. He turned his back to them. There was no answer.

Charlie dialed again, Reinhard's number this time. He held the receiver away from his ear, trying to diminish the ringing, which seemed to grow louder the longer it remained unanswered. He thought for a moment. Charlie glanced over his shoulder, spoke into the phone, and laughed. He listened through more rings and then hung up.

He walked briskly back to the Chevy, started it and drove out the exit, weaving through the fringe of the crowd before anyone had a chance to follow him. Connie never stirred.

Charlie drove down two blocks, checking the rear view mirror. No one was following. He went two more blocks, into a darkened industrial area, before turning. He wound through rutted alleys between windowless corrugated steel buildings. The Chevy jounced, coming down half a foot at the end of the paved roadway and he drove, pitching and rocking in first gear, through a patch of small garage-shops and open storage yards that ended at a street paralleling a railroad spur.

With a wide sweep through the quiet residential streets of Atwater, he made his way to the empty parking lot of an electrical rewinding and supply company, two stoplights and an underpass away from the entrance to Van de Kamp's. He parked, leaving the engine idling, to wait for Reinhard or Vaca to show.

Reinhard showed first. Charlie recognized the grilleless elliptical front of his Chevy as it turned onto Fletcher, coming his way. Charlie screeched out of the parking lot, bouncing over the curb, and sped for the intersection as Reinhard cruised by. Connie woke, flailing. Charlie accelerated through a red light, honking as he came, and slowed, braking just in back of Reinhard's bumper. "What?" Connie said.

"Wake up," Charlie told her. "Your life is passing you by."

Together, Reinhard and Charlie made the turn at the drive-in back lot and parked side by side, a few yards past the entrance; the crowd would allow them no further. They surged between the cars, pressing so close that Charlie saw only jackets, shirts and arms.

Charlie looked at Connie. "Time to go to work," he said.

"I'm fine," Connie said. "We already talked about this. I know you are one distracted idiot. Go on."

Charlie wedged his door open and slipped out. He had to jump once, to get his bearings. Using his elbows and forearms, he made his way to Reinhard's Chevy.

Without hesitation, he opened the passenger side door and squeezed in. Reinhard, talking and laughing with the admirers closest to his window, turned and looked over, mildly startled. Charlie said, "About, as we say in the trade, fucking time." Reinhard smiled and reached to shake hands, a movement that seemed clumsy in the confines of the car but one Charlie anticipated. Reinhard repeated this curious formality at every race, even if Charlie had seen him the same afternoon. "Charlie. Good to see you," Reinhard said.

Charlie shook hands. "You assholes really left me holding the bag. It's eleven o'clock, man."

"Naw. It can't be that late."

"Well, it's ten-thirty at least."

Reinhard looked through those pressed closest to his car, reached, and turned a boy's wrist to read his watch. "10:15."

"Well horseshit," Charlie said. His voice rose. "The point is, it's not when you were supposed to be here."

Reinhard turned all the way around. Charlie held his gaze momentarily. "Well, it makes me look bad."

Reinhard rubbed his chin thoughtfully, with the back of his

hand. "I went by Vaca's house about ten times," he said, "The Ford's still in the garage. Brody's truck is parked out front."

"That weasel!" Charlie said.

Reinhard shrugged. "He's just trying to change his luck. He showed up first last time."

"No. You did."

"You sure?"

"Yeah. He's just being a punk again. I'd like to rent a wheelchair and kick his ass."

Reinhard laughed. He rolled up his window, cutting off the crowd noise. "Did Petey Powell show up?"

"That asshole? What are you doing hanging out with him?"

"He wants to buy my car."

"Yeah, right," Charlie said. "Like he could drive it."

"I don't care if he can drive it. He's offering Twenty-Five Thousand."

"Jesus," Charlie said.

"Yeah," Reinhard said. "Oh yeah. That kind of money would get me straight in a lot of ways. Buy me some time."

"You wouldn't really sell it, would you? Fastest car in L.A.?"

"It is when I'm driving. I _know_ how to build another one."

Behind them, at the entrance, there was a disturbance in the crowd, people moving and then dodging and scattering as a car backed from the street into the parking lot, the brakelights flaring repeatedly as the car edged backward up the slope of the driveway.

Charlie recognized Brody, hanging out the window and yelling as he reversed. He stopped with a lurch, hitting the brakes and killing the engine, when someone pounded on the roof. Vaca was yelling out the other window, threatening that someone was going to get their ass kicked if they touched the car again.

Reinhard looked at Charlie and reached for the doorhandle. "Here we go," Charlie said.

Brody was out of the car, leaning against the doorframe,

one hand cupped on his belly and a pained expression on his face. He shook his head as Charlie approached. "Oh man, I am hurting," Brody said, "I think I got a bad pizza."

Reinhard came up, reaching to shake his other hand, "Brody. Vaca. Good to see you." Vaca nodded at him and then kept nodding.

"Cartoon time," Reinhard said, laughing.

Brody said, "Let's get it done."

Reinhard nodded at Brody's stomach, "You think you'll be O.K.?"

Brody shrugged, "It'll be alright." He rubbed it gently and then patted it. "Riverside still?"

"Riverside," Reinhard said.

Reaching into the car, Brody lifted his jacket out the window and pulled a tan clasp envelope from the pocket, handing it to Charlie. Reinhard handed over a lunch bag, folded and held by rubber bands. Charlie looked at them questioningly. "Why don't you count it in the car," Reinhard suggested. Brody, looking at the crowd gathered in back of the cars, said, "Uh...maybe when we get there." Charlie nodded and started walking toward his Chevy.

"I'll follow you," Reinhard told Brody.

The cars came out the entrance steadily. The three in the lead, Brody and Vaca, Reinhard, then Charlie, were a little ahead, dipping down into the underpass. By the time they came up the line was unbroken, stretching back to the lot. Ahead, on both sides of Fletcher Drive, waiting carloads watched their approach, wheels cramped, ready to join at the first break in the line.

Brody kept it in third, barely touching the gas, moving at a steady 35, a pace that felt stately to him, suitable to his mood. Brody felt very sure.

Vaca watched straight ahead - the signal lights, the sparse cross traffic, the streetlamps. At the intersection of Fletcher and Gottlieb, Vaca looked into the startled face of an old Mexican man standing behind a bus bench, his mouth opening wider as the line of cars neared him; he hesitated, then took off his hat and held it against his chest. Vaca looked at the lights of the houses on the hills above Riverside. He watched Brody, noting his steadiness. He felt slack, listless, committed.

The light was with them at the corner of Fletcher and Riverside. Brody swung wide at the corner and dropped down to second. When he straightened, he got on it. The Ford shot forward with a fat bellow from the pipes and Brody's face lit, eyes bright and joyous.

Reinhard watched them disappear around the bend. He sped up a little, then backed off, coasting into the curve. The Ford was parked just behind the starting line. Brody was lifting the hood.

Petey Powell's candy-apple green T-Bird was across the street. Petey's feet were sticking out the window.

Reinhard drifted in behind the Ford, parked, and climbed out. The street looked different. He looked down the course and realized that there were no streetlights. One was still lit, where the finish line was, but the rest were out. He looked up at the nearest one and saw a jagged profile; the top of the conical lamp shield was gone.

"Hey," he yelled to Brody, "somebody shot out the lamps."

Brody stepped back from the Ford, looking up. "Gives it some atmosphere, don't you think?"

"It's fucking dark."

The glow of the adjacent freeway was magnified. The cliff on the other side of the street could barely be seen.

Other cars were pulling up now, sorting themselves out, parking on both sides. Reinhard watched. It was nearly a minute before they stopped coming around the bend. Forty cars, he guessed, maybe fifty.

In the car behind him the dome light winked on. He saw

Charlie opening the envelope. There was a girl with him. Reinhard hadn't noticed her before. As she shifted in the seat he saw her stomach. *Oh Charlie,* Reinhard thought, *welcome to the working world. Too late for that little lecture.*

Across the street, Petey Powell, yawning, was getting out of his T-Bird. Reinhard felt in his back pocket for the socket and ratchet, snapped them together, and got under the Chevy to unbolt the collector flanges.

He felt someone kicking at the soles of his shoes and Petey Powell's familiar breathless whine, "Reiney, Reiney, Reinhard. I fell asleep. Do you need any help?"

"All done," Reinhard said. He watched Petey's feet moving away, toward Charlie's Chevy. "Fatty Charlie," Petey Powell said, "Fatty, Fatty. Whattya, Whattya, Whattya doing? Oooh, money. Money, money, money."

Charlie looked at the bills laid out on the seat and ignored Petey Powell. Ten new hundred dollar bills from Vaca. Reinhard had a mixed lot of twenties and fifties. Charlie turned the radio off and recounted the money.

Satisfied, he repackaged the bills and stuffed them in the glove box. He checked the lock and looked to Connie. "You want to watch or you want to stay in the car?"

"I'm cold," Connie said, hugging herself. Charlie, who was never cold, took off his jacket and handed it to her. She turned it around and held it against her, the sleeves draped over her shoulders, the back covering her front. "I'll have to lock the doors, for the money. Just honk if anyone gets weird."

"I'll be okay," Connie said, "but get that idiot out of here." She pointed behind Charlie to Petey Powell, who had silently pressed his face against Charlie's window - eyes crossed, nose smeared, lips and tongue splayed against the glass. Charlie smacked the glass. "Is that your wifey, knifey, lifey?" Petey sang. "Can I meet her? Want to see a magic trick?"

Charlie reached to switch off the dome light, stiffening and looking up as the distant wail of a siren reached him. He switched off the light and rolled his window down. The siren grew louder. All the way down the course, headlights were snapping off. Petey sprinted for his car. In seconds, the street was dark.

The siren kept coming. Charlie reached for the ignition key. He saw a flashing light approaching the Glendale Boulevard overpass. The white paint and red cross became visible as it approached the intersection at the end of the course.

The ambulance, lit up inside and empty, ran the red light and continued up the hill, the siren dying to a moan as it approached the top, turning off for the convalescent hospital, Guthrie's Sanitarium.

The headlights stayed off, but interior lights flickered as doors opened up and down the lines of parked cars; there was a stir of movement and voices.

Charlie locked the doors and checked them. Brody and Reinhard were waiting beside the Chevy. "O.K.," Charlie said, "is it still three out of five?" Reinhard nodded. "And you got a light?" Brody asked.

"Come on," Charlie said, "you think I'd show up without a light?" Charlie switched it on and held it under his chin, illuminating his face eerily. He turned it off and put it back in his pocket. "Three blinks, you're staged," he said. "One more and you go. It'll be between a one and five count."

"Who's judging the finish?" Brody said.

"Willy Lum and Saint."

Neither Reinhard or Brody said anything more. Brody looked to Vaca. Vaca, white-faced and rigid, nodding his head. Charlie held his hands out, palms up, and moved them away from him slightly, as if to say, "So?"

"Ready when you are," Reinhard said.

Charlie walked to the center of the road as they got in their cars. He looked down the course. Everyone seemed to be grouped at the finish. "Let's roll," Charlie yelled and the crowd began drifting to the sides. Charlie aimed his flashlight at the finish and blinked. Two lights blinked back, both on the same side, and then one crossed to the freeway side, still blinking.

The starters on both cars cranked away, laboring. Brody and Reinhard had bumped the timing, making them harder to start.

The Ford caught first, the cranking slowed almost to a stop, and then the engine erupted into noise. The Chevy started, stumbling momentarily, then roaring. The cars backed out from the curb, moving slowly, clutches barely engaged, four flames dancing on the pavement from the open head pipes.

Charlie checked his position against the luminous marks on the curbs while the cars straightened in their lanes and began to creep forward. He waved them up. The noise was amazing, each car punctuating the solid roar of a high idle with tight winging revs, the flames beneath the cars ceasing at the instant the throttles opened and then shooting down even further, washing out to the sides.

They eased forward until the hoods touched Charlie's outstretched hands. Charlie backed up and lifted the flashlight. The light at the intersection had just changed to green. Brody and Vaca and Reinhard watched him carefully.

Charlie decided to go with a long start, guessing that one of them would try to beat a quick count.

He blinked once, twice, and paused. The engines raced higher with each blink. Reinhard was concentrating but looked relaxed; Brody's face looked grotesque, nearly pop-eyed, in the light of the second blink. Vaca was shaking and blinked each time the light blinked. Charlie breathed in deeply, enjoying the familiar smell of the exhaust gases and hot oil. He blinked the third time and started his count to five.

Brody jumped on three, unable to hold any longer. The Ford lunged forward, smoking the tires, and traveled ten car lengths before braking. Reinhard idled down and took his hands off the wheel.

Charlie turned to watch the Ford back up. Vaca was yelling, punching the dashboard for emphasis. Brody looked back over his shoulder, guiding the Ford into place.

Charlie lined them up again, conscious of Vaca's stare. He

decided to shake them up, going with a slow stage and a quick count. He paused for a ten count between staging blinks. Between the second and third, Vaca yelled something at Brody, advice or a warning. Whatever it was, Brody's eyes flickered toward Vaca, distracted, and he lost Charlie's rhythm.

Charlie started them on two and Reinhard read it perfectly, almost in motion as the light blinked. He was two lengths off the line before Brody recovered.

Charlie could see Brody cursing, before the car was hidden in rubber smoke. His rage affected his start. Spinning the tires, he veered to the right before regaining traction. Charlie held his ears until they were past. As they made their first shifts, Reinhard was four car lengths ahead and Charlie relaxed, knowing that Brody couldn't make it up. They wound out and at the finish Brody had closed to within two lengths, but it sounded like Reinhard had backed off. The light blinked in Reinhard's lane and kept blinking as the cars passed through the intersection. Reinhard stopped just after the light and swung into a driveway. The Ford disappeared into the darkness under the Hyperion Avenue bridge.

The Ford's headlights swept the huge slab of the bridge's main support and the shadowed areas beneath the vaulted ceiling and ribbed supports as Brody made a wide turnaround.

Vaca was yelling, "I told you. He was going with a fast count. You could see it coming. Why the fuck didn't you jump?"

Brody slammed on the brakes. "Don't ever. I mean, don't you ever yell at me again when we're staged."

"I was telling you..." Vaca shouted.

"Shut up, man."

"And I was right..."

Brody put his foot down on the gas pedal and revved the engine up until the car shook, so he couldn't hear what Vaca was saying. He kept it there until Vaca backed off, shaking his shoulder and pointing at the tachometer needle, vibrating close to the red line.

Brody let up. The echoes resounded between the pillars.

Brody rolled the window down, hawked and spat. He listened critically to the last of the echoes and tapped the throttle to hear the resonance again. "That's one," he said. "So forget about it." Brody slipped the shifter in gear and looked over. Vaca was shaking, showing the effort it took to restrain himself. "If I blow the next one you can yell." He revved again and let it die down. "If you yell before that," Brody said, with some coldness, "you can drive it yourself."

Vaca held up a cupped, shaking hand, gesturing as though he were waiting for words. Unable to find them or afraid of saying them, he finally waved in the general direction of the roadway and dropped the hand back in his lap, where it curled and flexed, curled and flexed.

Brody eased the clutch out slowly, waiting for the front wheels to drop off the curb.

Reinhard waited at the starting line. He'd switched to the freeway lane and burned out once, making sure of the traction. He had wanted to be certain that Brody's start hadn't been caused by a buildup of rubber on that side.

The Ford was crossing the intersection. Reinhard watched it come, admiring the way it looked, sitting up solid, the front end lifting a little at speed. He'd been startled at the Ford's speed. Vaca had definitely made some changes since the last race.

He hadn't been truly tested, but it felt like the Ford was closing at the end.

Charlie watched the Ford roar past and swing around, still trying to decide on a count. He wanted a fair start this time.

The Ford rolled up to Charlie's palm. Vaca was already bracing himself. Brody looked more relaxed. Charlie decided to try two again.

He staged them quickly this time. Brody seemed to pick up his rhythm, revving with each blink and peaking just before the last. He wasn't rolling but appeared to have sensed the count. Reinhard had a good start, but Brody shaded him by half a car.

With sawing bellows, rubber smoke billowing from the rear

wheel wells, they churned past Charlie, accelerating gometrically as the tires took hold.

Charlie spun to watch them. The cars lurched with the hard shift to second, seemed to shrink, rocked again going into third, and Charlie could no longer judge who was ahead.

The cars swept toward the finish line and a gathering roar from the crowd there. Charlie waited, hands twisting on the barrel of the flashlight as he went up on his toes. The crowd yelled, an explosive "ahhhhh," sounding to Charlie, a quarter mile distant, like the collective sigh of a crowd witnessing fireworks. The light blinked on the Ford's side.

In the Ford, past the finish line, heading for the green light at one hundred and twenty, Vaca was rocking, laughing and slapping the dash with his free hand as he watched Reinhard drop back, dwindling further as he hit the brakes early.

He yelled giddily as they flashed through the intersection and began to slow. Brody shifted down and down, braking for their turnaround, glancing at Vaca between shifts.

Vaca was bouncing on the seat as they stopped, looking out the windshield. "We didn't beat him that bad," Brody said. Vaca didn't reply, continuing to smile, though the smile seemed to fix.

Brody bent to check the oil pressure and temperature gauges under the dash. The oil was steady at fifty pounds; the water temperature was near two hundred ten, but dropping. Brody straightened and looked at Vaca again.

Driving slowly back toward the start, Brody continued monitoring the gauges and spoke lightly, talking about how sweet it was running, before finally coming to what was on his mind.

As they neared and passed the crowd, Brody said, "It's going to be tighter than you think. He could've won." Vaca continued to watch ahead. Brody said, "Well, fuck it, Vaca, what do you think? If he gets a good start, I think he'll beat us."

Vaca's voice was toneless, "And if you get a good start, we'll beat him. You worried about the money?"

"All's I'm saying is, it's going to be close."

"I'll cover your share of the bet."

"You know me better than that, man. Come on. What's the big deal? It's still your car if we win. Sit this one out. You and that chair make two hundred pounds. You give me that edge and it's a lock."

"No," Vaca's voice grew shrill. "Bullshit." Brody looked at him and was shamed by the naked hunger and pain in Vaca's eyes. Vaca was saying, "If we lose we lose. Everything stays the same." It was nearly a chant. "Nothing gets left out. If we lose, we lose. Everything stays the same ..." He trailed off, running out of breath.

Brody slowed, approaching a smiling Charlie, passed him and began the wide swing that would bring them back to the start. Stopping, still avoiding Vaca's eyes, Brody said, "Okay. We'll run as is."

Vaca pushed a hand through his hair, fingers spread and trembling. He brought his hand down to eye level, tensed it, trying to make it steady, but it only stopped for a moment. He watched the trembling with distaste.

In back of the starting line, Reinhard took a hard look at the Ford. He hadn't thought it was possible. Even with the jump Brody got, he should have pulled him at the end. For the first time, Reinhard realized, he would have to put the full pedal to the metal, use it all up. That concerned him. At the end of the last race, as he'd charged from behind, the steering had gotten that familiar slushy feel and then something scarier, a greasy sliding sensation, and the car drifted right. He'd had to back off to regain control. It was fine right up to around 125 miles per. He hated to think there were limits. He hated to think they applied to him.

Charlie was waving them forward. Vaca looked past his hand, following Charlie's movements. Charlie's manner was brusque. His motioning was snappy, almost flourishing. He stabbed with a forefinger to the place where he wanted Reinhard to stop, spun, and repeated the gesture for the Ford.

Without pausing to check their positions, he turned around and blinked toward the finish line.

His manner irritated Vaca. The irritation passed as he sensed what might be an advantage. Vaca told Brody, "Look at him. He thinks he's in charge."

Brody peered out, concentrating on Charlie's back.

"Go on one," Vaca said. "He thinks he can fake us out."

Charlie turned. Brody tried to catch his expression.

Charlie stood, holding the flashlight loosely, fixing the cars in turn. He rolled his shoulders and lifted the light, held it steady and blinked. Blinked again. Between the second and third blink, there was a longer pause. In the pause, Brody decided Vaca was right. The light came on, the last staging blink.

Brody applied a delicate pressure to the gas pedal, the increment raising the engine to the howling pitch that could only be sustained for seconds. As the flashlight dimmed, Brody dropped his head, counting off one, and popped the clutch.

The light blinked like it was tied to his leg. In the sweep of headlights lifting as the front end picked up, Brody caught the flash of consternation on Charlie's face. Vaca whooped exultantly and yelled, "Banzai!"

The Ford shook itself into motion, the front end picking up and up as the tires dug in - the back end settling, the light fiberglass fenders and hood flexing slightly with the torque - and they were away from the line while Reinhard's tires were just beginning to bite.

Vaca continued to whoop and yell. Brody kept his foot buried, feeling the building force of the engine in the small of his back and the hollow space beneath his breastbone. His left foot moved closer to the clutch as the tachometer needle swept over. The engine note convulsed as the left foot stabbed down and he threw the shifter back to second. The force of the torque rocked the car. Brody could hear Reinhard's shift but couldn't see the Chevy. Vaca was screaming, "You got him. You got him." From the angle Vaca was turned to, Brody guessed Reinhard was well behind.

Brody wound out in second, not even looking at the tach now, sensing the shift point by the sound and the feel. He jammed it into third; a crisp shift, letting up a hair on the gas for the longer throw. Reinhard's shift sounded mushy to him, as though he'd backed off between gears. He still couldn't sense where Reinhard was.

Brody risked a glance at Vaca and saw that his angle had altered, but he still seemed to look out the back rather than the side.

Brody made the last shift, a perfectly coordinated motion, not even putting the clutch all the way in as he slammed the shifter home.

His foot strained at the gas pedal; Brody pulled on the steering wheel, lifting himself off the seat, putting his weight on that foot, forcing it tighter to the floor. Reinhard was still winding out, pushing to the limit before making his shift.

Brody looked over his shoulder. Reinhard was gaining, but still a half-car length behind. Forced to shift, Reinhard dropped back another half car. Then, fourth gear hammered home, he surged toward them, and Vaca started to pound the dash and scream.

As soon as he hit fourth gear, Reinhard knew he had them. Hands pulling back on the wheel, foot straining against the accelerator pedal, all he had to do was hold on.

With three hundred feet left to the finish, the Chevy crept up - to the Ford's trunk, the rear wheels, the rear side window, then the door, and Vaca's contorted face. He was pulling now and sure.

Reinhard concentrated now on the tach and the speedometer: 9,200 RPM and nearing 128 miles per hour, both new marks.

He was never sure if it was at or past the finish, when the Chevy started to skate. The crowd and the finish line widened and narrowed and flashed past, and somewhere in there Reinhard drifted right and when he tried to correct, everything went very wrong very fast. The front end lifted, skimming, bounced back on its left tire, bounced right, and then the car was airborne and then rolling over. It skidded through the intersection on its back and slammed into the massive foundation pillar of the Hyperion Bridge.

To Brody, it looked like a kite catching the wind. The Chevy was perpendicular, 3,000 pounds standing straight up in front of them, and then twisted like a gust of wind had snagged it, whipping it into rollovers and the final skid. The crunching noise as it hit the concrete was shocking. Vaca was yelling incoherently, and then his mind seemed to clear. "We got him," Vaca crowed.

Brody pumped the brakes and geared down. When he'd gained some control, he locked the brakes and cramped the wheel, letting up as the Ford went into its skid, tires squealing, then pumping again as the car slewed around. He used five of six lanes, ending facing the intersection. He headed back to the bridge and bounced over the curb, sliding to a stop.

Brody ran to the Chevy. The car was canted against the pillar, upside down. Steaming green coolant from the cracked radiator was pooling beneath the car. The hood was folded back like crumpled tinfoil, and the engine and transmission were pushed into the car.

He couldn't see Reinhard. The battery had been thrown clear and there didn't seem to be any gas leaks. That was the good news.

Brody smashed the passenger-side window, rolled down what remained, and stuck his head in. Reinhard was trapped between the transmission and the collapsed seat, held in upside down. The roof had held, and Reinhard was supported by it.

Brody reached down and took Reinhard's wrist. The pulse was steady. Reinhard turned a little. There was a bruise on his forehead. His eyes were unfocused.

Brody said, "Wayne, hey Wayne, can you hear me?"

Reinhard said, "Lights... Motherfucker..." and his eyes came into focus, startled.

Reinhard blinked and raised his hands to his head. "Move slow," Brody told him. Reinhard took his hands away, holding them like he was lifting a globe over his ears.

He moved his head slowly, side to side, and then shook it. Brody pressed Reinhard's hands back against his temples, stopping the movement. "Don't man, don't," he said. "Just stay slow."

Reinhard looked at him, squinting like Brody was a light. "My ears are ringing."

Brody stripped off his jacket and wadded it under Reinhard's head. "I don't know what to do, man." He stroked Reinhard's forehead. "Somebody should be here soon."

From the start line, Charlie had seen Reinhard's Chevy drift and float and then stand straight up. The noise was worse than the sight. The noise hung in his ears, a crunch and a grating bang as the sheetmetal collapsed. Glass from the headlights showered upward, chrome trim buckled, popping free.

In the frightening silence that followed, he could hear the excited buzz of voices from the crowd at the finish line, and then Petey Powell's T-Bird, roaring to life and squealing through a U-Turn. Petey gunned the car toward Fletcher, away from the accident.

Charlie dropped his keys once, then got them in the lock and jumped in his Chevy. He shook Connie awake. "We got a problem," Charlie said.

Charlie rolled down his window, slowing as he approached the finish line. The crowd was breaking up; some were running toward their cars, others were walking toward the intersection and the accident. He heard the first siren.

Charlie called Willie Lum over. "See if you can turn those idiots around," Charlie yelled. "The cops will be here." Without waiting for a reply, he drove on through the stragglers.

He pulled over and parked close to Vaca's Ford. He could

see Vaca watching, leaning forward intently, one arm on the dashboard, his chin resting on the arm.

Connie got out of the car with him and together they pushed through the murmuring crowd around the wrecked Chevy. Brody was still leaned in, holding Reinhard's shaking hand.

Charlie pressed a hand to Brody's shoulder, "How's he doing?"

"Not too good."

The siren was growing louder.

"Split, Brody," Charlie said. "You can't be here."

The sound of another siren, coming from the south, joined the first. Charlie stood up and faced the crowd, "Get out of here, now. Anybody here when the cops get here is going to get busted."

Charlie's words and the sound of a third siren closing in provoked a panicked sprint for the cars.

Charlie turned back to Brody. "They'll bust your ass and send you back."

The sound of the siren wavered, nearing the far side of the hill behind them.

"You'll take care of Reinhard?"

Connie moved forward, "I'll take over." She knelt beside the car and reached a hand in.

Charlie said, "Yeah. Go on, make it."

"Tell him I'm sorry."

Red and white lights topped the hill. Brody started running. Charlie followed him to the fence. He could hear him, crashing down through the bottlebrush and small pines that covered the slope above the freeway. Brody fell out, bent over, arms protecting his head. He ran north on the freeway, watching the oncoming headlights, and turned at the first break in the traffic. He crossed the four southbound lanes, shaking a fist at a Buick that had blinked its highbeams at him without slowing.

On his second attempt, Brody straddled the median divider fence and eased down. In stuttering sprints, he crossed the last four lanes, dodging to the sound of horns and squealing tires.

He disappeared after swinging over the fence and appeared again near the horse path paralleling the L.A. River. Brody stopped after climbing the banked earth beyond the horse path and looked down at the concrete riverbed and the slim trail of water shining in the center gutter. Brody vanished over the mound and did not reappear.

Vaca was honking the Ford's horn steadily. Connie backed out the window and yelled to Charlie, "Get him to knock that off, will you. It's making this guy upset."

Charlie walked over and leaned in the driver's side door, open, just as Brody had left it.

"Where the fuck is Brody?" Vaca said, "And what's that bitch doing here."

"Watch your mouth, man," Charlie said. "You're talking about my wife." Charlie loved the shocked look that Vaca gave him.

"Brody split. If he gets busted again, he has to finish his sentence."

"Fuck that, what about me? If I get busted they impound the car. Get in. Here's the keys. Get me out of here."

"Reinhard's hurt bad. I've got to stay and make sure he makes it to the hospital. I'm gonna tell the cops I was driving for you."

With their sirens moaning to a stop, a Fire Department ambulance van and a fire truck were descending the hill. The truck parked at the curb. The ambulance bounced over the curb and parked on the dirt beside Reinhard. Two paramedics got out. Charlie left Vaca cursing and joined them. The driver, a young man with a buzz cut, was helping Connie up. Connie looked at his nameplate, *Cruz*, and then at the plate of the older paramedic, *Rowe*, who had taken her hand. "I'm Eugene Rowe, M'am. You can call me Corky. Is this your husband?" Cruz had already dropped to his knees and was taking Reinhard's vital signs.

"No," Connie said, "I don't know the guy. I just stopped to see if I could help." Corky looked visibly relieved. Cruz called out, "Corky, you better take a look at this."

"We thank you, M'am. We'll look after him from here." Corky dropped to his hands and knees and peered into the Chevy. He pulled a flashlight from a loop on his blue overall leg and shone it in. After a moment, he pulled out and walked around to the other side of the car, shining the light in the engine compartment. He went to talk to the waiting firemen, who had finished putting out flares and were leaning against the truck. They nodded and began opening a side compartment on the truck, pulling out several large metal trunks.

The police arrived at last, driving in without flashing lights or sirens. They parked on the far side of the street and joined the firemen inside the circle of flares. After a brief conversation, one went to look at Reinhard's Chevy and the other took a clipboard out from under his arm, checked his watch and the cross streets and began filling out a form.

Stepping through the ring of flares, Charlie called out, "Officer?"

The policeman with the clipboard turned. Charlie recognized the face before the nameplate - *Martinez* - even registered and he groaned.

Martinez advanced, smiling, "So, where did you hide Brody?"

Charlie jammed his hands in his jacket pockets as Martinez shone the light in his eyes. "He's sick tonight. I ended up driving."

Martinez walked him away from the cars, guiding him firmly by the elbow until they were out of earshot, and he let him loose. Martinez stepped back, turning for a moment to look at his partner, pacing off the skidmarks. Charlie got the feeling he was being settled down. He shook out a cigarette, lit it, and waited.

"Save all the bullshit, Charlie," Martinez said. "We were watching the whole time." Charlie looked at him questioningly.

"Hey, cops get bored too."

Charlie waited.

Martinez turned away and yelled to his partner, "Did anyone check the gas yet? Maybe our Fire-Brothers could get an extinguisher out. Something to go with the flares."

Turning back, he hooked his thumbs in his belt and shifted his weight with a creak of leather. "So. That creates a few problems, some of which are already taken care of. We were no place near here. We were having coffee over on Sunset when the call came in. That's why we got here so late."

"Here's the way it's going to go down. From a careful analysis of the skidmarks, which I'll do tomorrow when I have more light, and from other unspecified evidence called in by informed and concerned citizens, I've determined that there was Streetracing going on here tonight.

"That means one Exhibition of Speed Citation for Reinhard and one for Brody."

"That means he'll go up," Charlie said.

"He can contest it if he wants. I personally wouldn't go to court with witnesses on my side like you or Vaca. Them old ladies won't like you."

Charlie lifted his cigarette and felt his elbow gripped solidly. Martinez was standing very close.

"One small thing," Martinez said. "Just one more. There isn't going to be any more racing down here. You can spread the word - and you should, because we won't fuck around. It'll be impound time, or you can wait and let us bust you. But either way: none, nada, no more. Comprende?"

Charlie nodded until his elbow was dropped.

Reinhard was saying, "It's funny, I don't feel too bad."

Inside the Chevy, Corky Rowe was writing numbers on a form sheet. He stopped. "I won't ask you for your registration, pardner, 'cause I don't think you can reach it. But your name would help."

Reinhard studied the man's creased, ruddy face. He looked like an aged blonde surfer, blonde hair fading to brown and grey, eyes red and pouched, nose pitted and stomach paunched, but still with the hint of health and youthful beauty. The pervasive odor of crumb donuts accompanied him like an aura. Reinhard trusted him.

"Reinhard, Wayne."

"Been in the Army?"

"Something like that."

"You can call me Corky."

"What are you guys going to do."

"Well, that's a tough question, Pard. It's pretty much up to you. This here is what the Fire Department calls <u>Special Circumstance</u>. You get no sugar. I have to tell you straight."

One of the firemen shone a light in from above. "You need any help, Corky?"

Corky looked at him and the look was enough to back the fireman away. "Here's the deal," Corky said. "You're fine now. You'll be fine until we move you."

"What?" Reinhard said.

"You got no head injuries, nothing wrong with the top half of you. That's the reason you feel fine. What you also got is an engine and a transmission sitting on your lap. Your inferior vena cava artery is ruptured. You don't feel it because you have about a thousand pounds of metal acting as a tourniquet. As soon as we cut that away, you start to bleed into your abdomen. Once the pressure is relieved, you got roughly one to two minutes."

"To what?" Reinhard said.

Corky looked at him mildly. "To die."

"Jesus," Reinhard said. "I guess that's good to know."

"Now you're on company time," Corky said. "You have, as we like to say, 'a grasp of the situation.' Which means I have to ask you the two questions that the Fire Department needs to know. One, should we contact your family?"

"Divorced," Reinhard said. "Ginger will love this. One of the terms of the settlement was I had to keep up a life insurance policy for the kids."

"Any other family we could reach?"

"I'm not going to wake my brother for this. For what? What would my chances be in the Emergency Room?"

"The nearest is ten minutes away," Corky said. "If we were there now, they couldn't do diddly."

Charlie had walked the block with Connie in tow, leaned against him. The paramedic had given them the news. "Jesus," Connie said, "what kind of God we got? What'd he do?" He put her back carefully in his Chevy and went to check on Reinhard.

Vaca honked the horn as he went by. "What?" Charlie said.

"You ready to drive me home? Martinez gave me my ticket, thanks to you, asshole."

"Brody's ticket."

"My car is on there. If I get busted again, it gets impounded. Where's my money?"

"The bet?" Charlie said.

"Yeah, my money. The two thousand bucks you're holding."

Charlie understood, on every level, that he didn't give a shit. The night, Brody, Reinhard, had done him.

"That's Reinhard's," Charlie said. "He won two of three. Willy Lum and Saint said he got the last one. That's it. It's like in boxing. If there's a foul and you can't continue, whoever's ahead, wins."

"<u>Give me my money!</u>" Vaca yelled.

Charlie went to stand vigil with Reinhard.

"Number two on the big list," Corky was saying. "Do you want to talk to a minister or a priest or a rabbi or any other spiritual advisor?"

"I'm not a churchgoer," Reinhard said, "I was raised Lutheran but I stopped going in high school."

The Firemen were unpacking equipment and setting up beside the car. "What are they doing?" Reinhard asked.

"They're putting the tool together that we'll use to cut you out of here. *Jaws of Life*, it's called."

"Yeah, I know it," Reinhard said. "Hurst makes it. Same people that make my shifter. Good tool. Good hydraulics."

"Good tool," Corky said. "You want some time to yourself? To pray or whatever?"

"Can I get a drink?" Reinhard said.

"You mean water?"

"Jack Daniels," Reinhard said. "On the rocks. A splash of water."

"I can't, pardner, " Corky said. "I'd like to but I really can't."

"Cut me loose," Reinhard said.

The Firemen had started up their elaborate tool. The shears cleaved through the sheetmetal impressively but Charlie, finally, couldn't watch.

He walked to the intersection and watched Martinez and his partner, a slight, worried-looking young policeman named McManus, clean up. They swept the pavement clean with long-handled whisk brooms and made a pile of metal parts on the sidewalk.

Martinez turned on the domelight in the squad car, sat, and began writing his report. McManus kept sweeping, though there was nothing left to sweep.

The firemen had finished their cutting. Two of them twisted long pry bars and the front end separated. The engine and transmission dropped forward and away with a resounding thump and the two paramedics were pulling Reinhard onto a gurney while the car was still rocking.

Connie joined Charlie at the curb. She slumped against him as he put his arm around her. The paramedics hustled Reinhard into the ambulance. In seconds, the ambulance was turned around and with siren wailing shot over the curb and headed right toward Los Feliz, speeding toward Glendale Memorial Hospital. Connie began crying.

Behind them, Charlie heard a starter grating. He turned. The Ford's engine caught and the car lurched backward to the middle of the street and died.

Vaca cranked the wheel until it was straight, then leaned to reach the shifter and the key. The Ford moved forward in small shuddering jerks, traveling solely on the strength of the starter. The engine caught again, roared. The lights flared up and it died, coasting only a few feet. The starter began grinding again.

Martinez kicked open the door of the squad car and came running. He rapped on the Ford's window. "Hey, wild man. Hey." He pounded on the roof, "Hey. Hey, hey, hey..."

Vaca hunched over, twisting the key. The Ford jumped forward, its motion becoming eccentric as the starter wore down. Vaca stared out through the spokes of the steering wheel, keeping his hand on the key, watching the headlights dim.

Just ahead, the road began to slope toward the intersection. Vaca switched the headlights off and the starter picked up the boost. As the Ford edged forward, Martinez broke for his car.

The police car squealed away from the curb, the door

banging shut as it shot forward. Martinez swung a wide U and braked, facing the Ford. He eased up the slope, lining up to the Ford's front end, and idled forward until he braked a yard from the Ford's bumper. The Ford continued, the starter groaning as it started to bind.

It reached the bumper of the police car and stopped.

Vaca continued to turn the key until the starter crawled and smoked. It stopped. The solenoid clicked a few times, then it was quiet.

Martinez set his emergency brake and got out. Vaca slumped behind the wheel. When Martinez rapped on his window, he tried the key again. McManus approached from the other side and reached for the door handle. Vaca lunged, stretching across the seat as McManus swung the door open. McManus held the door and waited for Martinez to come around.

"Shut the damn door," Vaca yelled. "Get that car out of my way."

"Watch it, wild man," Martinez said.

Vaca pulled himself upright. "Shut the damn door."

"You planning to coast home?"

"Shut that door or I'll kick your ass."

Martinez bent in. He tipped his hat back, nudging the brim with his flashlight. "I told you once to watch it."

Vaca swung, a roundhouse right arcing from the back seat. His fist hit Martinez' temple and the policeman pitched sideways, knocked off his feet. His hand hit the doorframe and the flashlight skipped on the pavement.

McManus pulled Martinez out. Reaching around Martinez's waist, he clasped his hands and yanked. Martinez was up immediately. He pulled his club and came in, using it as a prod until Vaca was backed up enough to give him swinging room.

McManus ran to the other side. He cracked the window with his first swing and punched the glass out with the club.

Martinez was inside the car, kneeling on the seat, bringing

his club down on Vaca's upraised arms in short, chopping strokes. As McManus reached and pulled the inside doorhandle, Martinez stopped swinging and held the club out, gripping it two-handed. Vaca grabbed for it, exposing his head. McManus shoved his forearm against the back of Vaca's neck and reached around with the other arm, a chokehold. He pulled against his forearm until Vaca's hands slipped from the club. He maintained the pressure as he pulled Vaca, hands fluttering, to the door.

They each took an arm and lugged him backward, his heels dragging and his feet kicking up each time they hit a bump.

Together they grabbed his pantlegs, lifting him off the ground, and slung him into the back seat of the squad car. He rolled off onto the floor and McManus kicked the door closed.

Martinez swung the car around in reverse. Pulling forward, he rolled the window down and yelled to Charlie, pointing back at the Ford. "Park that fucker for me, will you? Leave it where the tow truck can find it."

"Sure," Charlie said.

The cruiser moved smoothly toward the intersection. A car was coming down the hill, so they waited on the red.

Charlie sat down on the curb. McManus turned, looking into the back seat. A hand reached up, the fingers probing for the gaps in the wire mesh separating the seats. McManus watched the hand finding its hold until the other came up beside it and he leveled his club like a paddle and whacked the knuckles until they stopped pulling and slipped down from the wire.

At first, Charlie thought they'd turned the siren on. Then it broke, started again and he realized Vaca was howling.

McManus was yelling, banging on the mesh. The howling grew louder. There was no pain or mourning to the sound, only rage; it was clearly defined by the stops to gather breath.

McManus stopped hitting the wire and faced forward. His shoulders raised, his head seemed to shrink between them. Vaca stopped for a longer moment, then started again this time in a higher register. Connie put Charlie's jacket over her head. Charlie looked down at his shoes and wished for the light to change.

30-

Connie adjusted her hat and sat up. She still wasn't used to the Florida sun, but she loved the humidity. Her zits, rashes, and dandruff had vanished. Her skin looked better than it had since she was in grammar school. The baby rolled over on the blanket, gurgled, and clawed at the grass. The Mail, a Cuban woman who was friendly to the baby, but sneered at Connie's California Spanish, was coming up the walk.

There were magazines and bills for her Aunt Rosalie and two letters, one from her mother for Rosalie and one from Charlie.

She tore open the pale teal-colored envelope. The stationery heading, with flourished anchors and flowing ropes, said: At Sea/ USS Minton. She knew from Charlie's earlier letters that it was an Aircraft Carrier.

Dear Connie,

I can't tell you exactly where I am or the Censors will cut the ---- out of this letter. I guess it's okay to say that I'm near that place that I thought would be like Hawaii. Believe me, that place is not at all like Hawaii.

It's a weird place. That's about all I can say. I don't guess you heard about Lamont. I wouldn't have if you hadn't got me started on this letter-writing kick. My letter to him came back marked <u>Deceased</u>, which is the Army way of saying: No

Longer at this Address. So I checked and found out from his mom that he got killed after only three days in that place that's not like Hawaii. He stepped on a land mine. Did you know Lamont? I can't remember if you did. He was a good guy but you knew he was one of those guys who was going to bite the big one over here.

Anyway, I am doing pretty well. You won't recognize me. The food is good but I have lost 40 pounds. I've been certified as an air frame mechanic and am working now for my engine certification. When this is over I think I will have a trade.

I've already started planning my next car and I hope you'll get to see it. It'll be a Chevy (Some Surprise) but I have a lot of ideas. I hope to be home soon. Two years is pretty soon.

Send me pictures of you and of the kid. Are you sure Richie is a good name for him? I know you said Richard, but hey that also means Dick, Dicky, Rick, Ricky, and Richie, and you know he'll end up Richie or his uncle will kick his ass. Probably yours too. You know what I mean. Please write soon.

Faithfully Yours in Christ,

Charlie 'Low Fat' La Monda

Connie smiled at the signature, a scrawled illiterate's X. It was an old joke between them, as was the ending, copied after a local Cardinal's autograph. It replicated Charlie's signature in her yearbook.

Connie could picture the big flat-topped ship on the ocean

and the country which looked, from the newscasts she had seen, something like South Florida. But she couldn't quite see Charlie on the ship or imagine what he might do there.

The baby grabbed at the grass too hard and snatched himself over. He looked up at Connie, baffled, undecided as to whether he should cry. Before he could decide, Connie lifted him up. "Come on, Big Boy," she said, "let's get you into the shade."

She sat him down in the sandbox, under the arbor. The baby crawled immediately to his favorite toy, a yellow Tonka Dump Truck, and whacked it happily against the side of the sandbox.

"Boys and their toys," Connie said.